# HAUSSITTER

# HAUSSITTER

BRENDAN NORTON

Cover and internal art illustrated by Adrian DKC.
Book layout and formatting by Phillip Gessert
Author photo by Sam Nagel Photography

ISBN: 979-8-9924779-1-7

www.brendannorton.com

*For Buffy, Hermione, & Winnie*

# SOMMERSONNENWENDE

S TEPPING OFF THE outbound train, he clocked the SUV purring ahead, in the parking lot of the Wynnewood Station. He checked its color against the pic on his phone, gazing over the rim of his shades.

"Brian?" she called through the open window, to which he nodded wiltingly and braced himself, slinking out into the heat.

"How's it going?" he mustered, ducking in the backseat.

"Uh-huh," she nodded, glancing through the rearview, "Doin' all right there?"

"Just melting," he whimpered, "It's so hot."

"*Yeahh,* we should all be down the shore," she said, and the wheel spun in her hand as she weaved back out to Lancaster Avenue.

"I'd rather winter," said Brian, with a cringe. He dabbed at the beads of sweat dotting his scalp.

They cruised down Penn Road to a straight rush of Montgomery Ave., then made their way back into the twisting wilds of upper Wynnewood by way of Gypsy Lane, the speed limit a flirty 30, the SUV bouncing over every hill. Three-story houses rose upon handsome ½-acre inclines. Stately shrubs guarded every mailbox. A skin-sizzling haze hung over all, dyeing the greens much too green. Brian's driver slowed to edge around a landscaping truck, its team spread out over two properties, the coveralled men riding mowers the size of chariots or else wielding hedge clippers like broadswords, showers of twigs bursting at their every swipe.

"Visiting a friend?" the driver offered, twisting a beaded braid round her finger.

"Job interview," said Brian. Through the rearview, she peeped the Muppet Babies T-shirt and jean shorts; his big black sunglasses which widened at the sides, like owl eyes.

"Casual job," she muttered, inching past the truck and raising a hand to the landscaper who sat on its hood, mopping at his face with a sleeve.

"It's a housesitting gig," said Brian, "They're rich, so the gayer I look, the more likely she is to hire me."

"I feel that," said the driver.

"Love your braids," he fibbed.

They rode in punctured silence all the way to Hemlock Way, then up its wending coil, where sunburned kids walked a panting golden retriever and a real estate agent hammered a placard into a patch of soil, wobbling on stilettos. The road crested after that to a dazzling sapphire sky, and the driver tore up the little hill so they seemed for a time to tumble out into the beyond. A cul-de-sac opened quite suddenly on their left.

"Dang, that's it!" exclaimed the driver, swinging wide across the opposing lane, "Hold up." The pickup behind them let loose a blaring honk, but managed to slow in time, avoiding the worst.

"I think—*uhh,* that one," said Brian, squinting ahead at the widest part of the block. The driver banked into a wide U-turn, pausing halfway around to stop in front of the property at the far end of the circle.

"Hope you get the job," she said, and she turned round in her seat to look at him.

"Thanks," he said, "It's a weird one."

"How do you mean?"

"...let's just say if I wind up on the news, these are the people who ate me."

"You want me to take you back?" she said, peering up at the big house, "I mean it, I won't charge."

"No, no," he laughed, and he really did find it funny, "I'm from out this way. I can handle it."

The driver reached into the console at her side.

"Mint for good luck?" she said, "Breath's prolly good, but it might help that weed cologne."

He flipped a hand out. She reached back and shook a box, depositing a blue-speckled pellet in his palm.

"Cheers," Brian gulped, then he slipped out the back. His phone buzzed as she pulled away; a notification to tip. He clocked the time and sent the screen to sleep.

The big house on the far side of Hemlock Circle sat apart from its neighbors, on a fan-shaped acreage where flowers abounded and summer veggies ripened in a gorg fenced enclosure. A stone bench crouched beside a puff of an elderberry tree. No sidewalks rounded the Circle, so the lawn stretched from road to house, cropped with just a little on top so the grass seemed to toss its hair with every ripple of summer breeze. A meandering cobblestone drive snaked through a columned *porte-cochère* and around to the wooded back. The creature looming over all was a grand Tudor in three distinct stories: her bottommost ring of busy rubblestone; a pale brick belting her middle; and a half-timbered topper for a crown, its wood nearly black to match her slate roofing, the black-lined windows. A run of wide granite steps led up to the mouth of the house, where a regiment of potted blooms stood sentry on the veranda so anyone who approached the oak-and-iron door would have to pick their way through frondescence to ring the bell. Brian nearly did, then remembered Mallory's voicemail had said to meet at the back.

Right as one started up the drive, some low stonework huddled up among hawthorns; a gold placard fixed to the stone proclaimed *DAS NEST* in stately script. Brian booped the name as he passed by, as if to say, *hey girl, you're a little fucking quirky, what's good?*

A brick footpath led up and around, past diamond-paned windows peeking in on a dining room and sprawling kitchen, before reaching the back door, at kitchen's rear. Brian slid off his owl shades and knocked thrice, then appraised the house's ample backside while he waited, stepping into the shade to escape the sun. Up under an eave on the third floor, a casement window hung wide open.

"Fuck me," he muttered, shading his eyes, "Don't say they don't have air conditioning."

Upon his complaint, a wide spray of pink came flying out the open casement; bits of gossamer thrown to the underside of the eave that then floated down into the summer light, spinning all in unison until landing by the back path, just to Brian's side. A handful of pastel petals. One touched down upon his shoulder, its white underbelly exposed.

The kitchen door swung wide. Brian plastered on a grin.

"*Hi theeeere–*" he warbled, so cheery it stung.

"*NOOO!*" screamed the woman in the house, and before Brian could properly gasp, a standard poodle in dark apricot had bounded forward and reared up to his chest, a pink polka-dotted diaper buckled round its bottom, its tail a mad blur through the opening, "BAD GIRL. THAT IS NOT HOW WE GREET GUESTS. NO! NO! NO!"

With a huff, the poodle pushed off Brian and circled round herself on the back path, tail tucked, then she crouched to all fours, sliding onto her belly, whence she crawled to her mistress' feet in the doorway. The pooch writhed under the dread finger pointing down.

Brian resurrected his grin.

"*I'm Bri–*" he tried.

"*Nooooo,*" the woman warned, at the dog's merest twitch. Poodle froze, chin to the pavement. The woman glowered down. Brian grit his teeth.

Finally, finger retracted, and the lady squatted beside the pooch, ruffling her head frizz, "*Good,* Ursula! *Good listening*!"

"Very good," Brian agreed, his face hot though he stood in the shade off the house, "Hi again. I'm–"

"You must be *Brian,*" said the woman, gazing up at him for the first time, eyes wide and cattish, "I'm Mallory Bain-Dahlhaus. Come inside." She stood and the poodle trailed her into the kitchen. Brian followed, clicking the door shut behind them.

"Lovely," he said, gesturing largely at marble and paneling, at the implements all around: espresso machine, the Le Creuset, the Miele fridge.

"It *is*," Mallory agreed, and she grabbed two cans of seltzer from the island countertop, "Pomegranate or mandarin orange?"

"Whichever you don't want," Brian demurred.

She flung the pomegranate and he just barely caught it. Presently, they came to sitting side by side at the kitchen island, on very tall bar stools. Mallory sported performance sweats in wanton cyan. A blush silk hair-tie clasped her mass of champagne blonde, streaked with gray and white, into a high and tight ponytail. He could immediately tell she'd never had a lick of work or drop of Boty, judging by crow's feet, the faintest lipstick lines. She perched on one bare foot; the other lodged itself down in the stool slats.

"You don't have hair," she began.

"I don't," said Brian, and he tapped at the tab of his can with a finger, to dispel any fizz.

"I like that," said Mallory, "So fresh. I could lick you."

"I'm competitive," he admitted, "Figured I'd shave, beat male pattern baldness to the punch."

"And you're gay," she said, gesturing vaguely at the Muppet Babies, the jorts.

"Guilty," Brian simpered, "Stone me."

He cracked his seltzer. Mallory reached across the marble and slid a hand over his.

"Gays have always been a vital ingredient to my personal growth," she intimated.

"Aw," said he, nodding sagely, "You're welcome."

"And this is *Urs-ula!*" Mallory squealed, including the good girl who sat, tail wagging, between their stools, "Ursula, *he-answered-our-ad! Yes-he-did!*"

Brian slid off the stool and bent to one knee beside the pooch.

"Hello, gorgeous," he crooned, scratching behind those velvet ears, "My goodness, what a face. *Hel-lo!*"

"She's very young," Mallory tutted, sipping her mandarin orange, "And it's high summer, so she's reeking. Hence the diaper. You should see her vulva, it's completely engorged."

Brian steadied himself on the leg of the stool. Ursula licked the back of his hand.

"We breed," Mallory clarified, as he climbed back to the counter, "Well, we're *trying* to breed her. She's bled very late, I have reservations. And several of the neighbors *also* breed, only they have unneutered males, so walks have been a nightmare. Like dangling steak."

"So she'll need–" Brian started, "I mean, the diaper's for...?"

"The discharge," said Mallory.

"Right."

"She'll be mated next week if all goes to plan, and we'll be past all this.

I don't expect you'll have to deal with any diapers yourself, but I'll leave extra in the pantry just in case."

"And that's just like changing a baby?" he said, "Or...?"

"I wouldn't know," Mallory shrugged.

Brian fiddled with the tab of his seltzer.

"There's a cat, too, right?" he said, leaning back on his stool to peek into the next room, "I adore dogs, but I think if the chips are down, I'm more of a cat man."

"You and my husband," she said, "The cat is his. You won't see him today, he doesn't like strangers. Spooks easily."

"What's his name?"

"My husband?"

"No," Brian smirked, "The cat."

"Oh, I was talking about Campbell. Shall we take a tour?"

The lounge at *DAS NEST* bathed in crisp daylight from a pair of palladian windows. Potted ferns framed a gigantic stone fireplace. The furniture was *not* to be lounged upon. Brian clutched the back of a giltwood sofa. Mallory perched upon a leather studded chaise. Ursula chewed her paw in the corner.

"You do plays," said the lady of the house.

"I do," said Brian, fishing a pack of gum from his pocket, "I did. Mostly I design costumes now? Sometimes for plays, but also for drag queens? Mostly for drag queens." He unwrapped a stick and folded it in half with his teeth before smacking away. As an afterthought, he offered one to Mallory. She wrinkled her nose.

"Max isn't allowed in here," she said, "He pisses in the bird of paradise."

"I assume Max is the cat."

"The bamboo needs watering twice a week," she pointed, "Those, once a week."

"Got it," Brian nodded.

"Let's go upstairs."

At the top of the first flight, Mallory opened a door and the second floor hall stretched before them, with portals down its length. Framed landscapes great and small filled the walls, trending to the abstract, in smudges and streaks of crimson and indigo. A teal Oriental runner underfoot led to the far end and another closed door. Ursula nudged a wet nose under Brian's hand and whined.

"Our bedroom," said Mallory, pointing to the different rooms down the hall, "His office. My office. Bathroom. Sheets and towels."

A digital thermostat on the wall read 59 degrees Fahrenheit.

"I'll pack a jacket," Brian quipped, and he nodded at its little green screen.

"We all like it cold," said Mallory. Down at the other end of the hall, the other door gave a tremble. Its knob twitched this way and that.

"Oh, is that Mr. Cat?"

Mallory snapped for the dog.

"Let's go upstairs!" she trilled.

The third floor looked just like the second, only entirely undecorated. Mallory opened the door to a long stretch of bare walls, with no Oriental runner to soften one's step. The little Brian could see of the rooms made them seem just as empty. And just like downstairs, there stood a matching door at the end of the hall, yet it opened wide to what looked like an identical set of stairs to the ones they'd just climbed. Ursula lingered behind, down by the second floor landing, ears pricked.

"So is this where..." Brian trailed off.

"There's nothing here right now," said Mallory, her gaze lost in the middle distance, then she snapped to, "Let's look at the map."

Back on the ground floor, in her spacious front hall, Mallory stood before a framed map hanging above the black teak sideboard. Ursula watched squirrels through the sidelight windows astride the massive oak-and-iron front door. Brian stood with fists stuffed in his jort pockets, studying the image on the wall.

Behind glass, the whole of *DAS NEST* spread out over an intricate cross-section, from basement to roof, like someone had sliced off the front of the property or erected a stage set. Twin staircases at the house's extreme left and right climbed from first floor to third. On the second floor, right at dead center, stood the Master Bedroom—and it was labelled accordingly, in tight, careful script, with what looked to Brian's untrained eye to be Germanesque translation beneath, in a smaller hand: *Hauptschlafzimmer*. The other rooms bore similar epithets: Front Hall / *Vorhalle*, Powder Room / *Gästetoilette,* Lounge / *Wohnzimmer*, Dining Room / *Esszimmer*, and the Kitchen / *Küche* on the ground floor; His and Her Offices / *Sein Büro und ihres* and a Master Bath / *Haupt-badezimmer* joined the Master Bedroom on the second floor; and two numbered Guest Rooms / *Gästezimmer*, and accompanying Baths / *Gästebadezimmer* occupied the third floor. The artist had colored a moonlit night to frame the cross-section, and the elderberry tree and shrubbery along the bottom, accurate to what Brian had seen walking up the drive, lay bathed in silver luminescence. The *porte-cochère* extended off the Kitchen / *Küche*, past the bounds of the artist's view. And at the very bottom, doubled in the same meticulous script: THE NEST / *DAS NEST*.

"This is my home," said Mallory.

"Right," said Brian, smacking his gum, "We just did the tour, so I'm familiar."

"Point to where you are," she said.

Brian smirked. Mallory waited.

"Oh, you're serious."

"Point," she commanded.

He stepped forward and put his forefinger to the map, at the Front Hall / *Vorhalle*.

"I'll be It," said Mallory, and she likewise brought a finger to the glass, pointing at a Guest Bath up on the third floor. Brian's gaze slid over the space between; the second floor which separated his finger from hers.

"This is the...*thing* from the ad?" he asked.

"Go get a snack," said Mallory, and there was a challenge in her vocal fry, in the lift of brow, "The kitchen, on the right."

Slowly, Brian drew his finger across the first floor, through *Esszimmer* to *Küche*, watching all the while as Mallory's finger slid just as slowly over the third floor in the opposing direction, past *Gästebadezimmer* and *Gästezimmer*, so their two fingers moved as opposites; then she stopped when he did.

"Try the stairs," she urged, and Brian chuckled breathlessly, dragging his pointer over the glass to the stairway on the right of the house; Mallory's finger trailed to the top of the stairs on the left side of the map. As his ascended, hers descended.

"That's how it works," she said, "It'll be wherever you're not."

Brian nodded like he understood, but his forehead creased to ridges. Lingering at the top of the house, he set his finger roving, faster than before, along the length of the third floor. Mallory matched his speed perfectly, zipping her pointer past *Wohnzimmer* and *Vorhalle* on the ground floor. Their arms crossed mid-air.

"It's like magnets," said Brian. He doubled back across the third floor and Mallory likewise reversed her own momentum. Their arms uncrossed, and as he flew back down to the first floor, she soared back up the other stairs to the third. Brian withdrew from the map, laying a palm over his throat, his other hand high on one hip. Mallory kept on pointing where she'd landed, on the *Gästebadezimmer* across the house from the *Vorhalle*.

"Right now, I'm Its host," said Mallory, just as casually as she'd explained the plants, "When we leave, we'll transfer that to you. Temporarily, of course. When we get home, well, it's just a simple switch back."

Brian blew a little bubble that popped right away, the whiff of peppermint bracing in his nose.

"OK—*OK*, so," he tried, and pointed to the *Vorhalle* again, eyeing her digit across the house, "Am I allowed to ask?"

"Ask away, sweets."

While wondering where to start, he took a little meander up the stairs again. Mallory immediately circled her finger round in response—only instead of going all the way up, he detoured at the second floor and began to cross. Mallory's pointer stopped short on the other side of the house.

"See?" she clucked, "We're already covering the most important rule: no second floor."

Brian's finger hovered over His Office / *Sein Büro*, just down the hall from hers.

"No second floor?"

"Well, look what happens," said Mallory, and she moseyed along towards Brian's finger until they met in the middle, at the Master Bedroom / *Hauptschlafzimmer*. Quite suddenly, she gobbled his whole hand under hers, pinning it to the glass.

"You got me," Brian chuckled, despite himself. He squirmed under her grip.

"And that's just what we *don't* want," she stressed, holding him in her gaze, pressing down on his hand, a knuckle cracking under the crunch, "No second floor, and it's a perfect loop. No second floor, and you *never* have to worry."

Brian pressed his gum to the roof of his mouth. He half-expected the glass to crack into his palm.

"Heard," he nodded, "No second floor."

"Fabulous," said Mallory, and she released him at once, "Everything you need will be on the first or the third floor, anyway. I'll pull sheets and towels before we go."

"Fab," said Brian, nursing his hand behind his back, rubbing the tendons.

"Let's have tea!"

"What flavor is this?"

"Pu'er," said Mallory, "It's fermented."

"Earthy," said Brian, and he reached for the jar of honey she'd set out, "So dog and cat and demon. Where's Uncle Joey? You got yourself a full house." Mallory choked a little on her tea. She smacked the marble countertop, trying to swallow, then tossed her head back to bray at the ceiling fan; really, too much for the joke. Ursula plopped her diapered bum on an Etruscan tile, ears cocked.

"I do!" she crowed, *"I do,* it's crazy. But what can I say, I like the bustle."

"And you want me to babysit," said Brian, wide-eyed, fighting the urge to laugh with her. He stuck his gum behind his ear and plucked a dried date from the bowl she'd set out for the tea.

"Yes, please," Mallory grinned winningly.

"I've done a lot of weird shit for money," said Brian, "But you might've opened a new door for me."

"*Ooh,* stories," she demanded.

"You show me yours," he pussyfooted, "Seems only fair. Tell me about the..."

Mallory pouted and sipped at her pu'er. One hand snaked down and grasped a clump of poodle-frizz, raking her nails over Ursula's scalp. The pooch panted in ecstasy.

"*Sein Name ist das Gegenteil,*" the lady began, her voice warm, "It just means the Opposite, nothing spooky. I caught It in 1997, in Spandau, in Germany."

"Oh, Spandau like Spandau Ballet?" said Brian, "I love them. Well, my mom does. She listens—"

"It's a borough of Berlin."

"Right on," he course-corrected, then he couldn't help himself: "You sound very Main Line to me. Is your family German, or what's the connection?"

"Oh, I'm all-American mutt," said Mallory, "Just a slouching beast, cultureless. No, Campbell's our resident kraut—well, halfway. His papa was Rainer Dahlhaus, the epicosmologist. Big man over at the university, he perfected temporal nucleic psychometry. Now Campbell's little big man. Some guys really swell after their dads shrink on the vine. All those juices."

Brian's thumb went straight through the flesh of the date he'd been gripping. He reached for a cloth napkin in the island rack to wipe away the grit.

"But I suppose *my* connection," said his hostess, "Is I wound up at our sister institution, the *Universitat Hagzissa,* for my doctorate in parapsychology. That was '91 to '97, and the big man himself flew back to teach a semester in '94. Such a delicious time to be in *Deutschland,* Bri, you'll never know. The Wall had been down just two years, and everyone was still ripe for a fucking. And then techno happened, and floor-length leather happened, and 1995 was just...MDMA and neon lipstick."

"*Yesss,*" Brian affirmed, with a half-hearted snap, "So she brought a little rave back home?"

"Sure did," Mallory beamed, "Good, old Rainer turned me on to *das Wütendes Heer* for my thesis. The Raging Host? Also not a band, but Central Europe's spectral horde of unchristened babes and unrepentant sinners. They who ride he-goat steeds on the night wind along *der Schimmelreiter*: Pale Rider, huntsman most extraordinaire!"

"Hot."

"Extremely," the lady agreed, squirming rhythmically in her seat, "The Host is part gas cloud, part paradox. They cull souls like a farmer culls a herd, reaving the sleeping masses, drawing us through little wormholes in our consciousness to their cosmic orgy. Hens lay snake eggs as the Host flies by. Milk curdles to green snot. And sometimes they'll filter down through permutations in the electromagnetic spectrum to ravage an inno- cent girl or maybe a troublemaking boy like yourself. Or they'll ride the solar winds to a bed and breakfast, demanding salt for their wounds."

"Spectral things," Brian nodded, munching his date, "So what, you caught one?"

Mallory nearly vibrated.

"My demon rode as rear guard," she buzzed, "Always trailing the slow- est imps, for It prefers to feast in the wake of the others' carnage. You know that shitty pit in your stomach when you feel the very worst has passed, and you suddenly realize it hasn't?"

Brian nodded again and again. He stuffed the rest of the date in his face.

"I should be honest," he said, through a mouthful, "I'm not sure I'm super qualified—"

"I'll tell you something, Bri," said Mallory, "Mine is a very special specimen, given many fancy, special names by human animals. *Hagerer Herumtreiber*, the Gaunt Prowler. Brother Catastrophe. The Scavenger Prince. But really, It's a friendly autodidact, like the best of us. Bookish. Crafty. Never quite satisfied with Its credentials, casting wide nets for the next degree, fuck, kill—so to speak!"

She laid her hands flat on the marble.

"It can never hurt you here in my house, Brian. I want you to know that. You have to believe it: *It can never hurt you here in the house.*"

"Got it."

"Say it."

"It's, *ah*—" he tried with a hollow chuckle, hating himself for playing along, quibbling where possible, "Yeah, so you're saying your demon can never hurt me. Here, in your house."

"*Completely harmless,*" she said, cementing it, "But oh-so-magnificent still."

Bri realized he'd been pulsing nonstop Kegels; he made himself stop squeezing. Gooch muscles ached. Mallory plucked a puckered date from the bowl. She rolled it between her thumb and fingers, squeezing the flesh near to bursting.

"I saw an etching first in an abbey, months before we met," she said, her grey-golden ponytail resting over her shoulder, "Sun streaming through stained glass. Steam rising off my coffee. You never think you'll see a nightbloom by day, but then the world just..."

Crow's feet loosened. Champagne flyaways floated from her hairline.

"I had to take my bra off, right there in front of the monk."

Ursula the poodle brought a pom-pom'd paw to Brian's lap, and he set to slowly scritching her head.

"Thin frame," Mallory relived, carving traces through the air, "Eight feet tall...*oh, Bri: Its pink horns.* Back in Its Host days, when tracking with the Dreadhounds, It donned this great-helm with ram spirals of raw tourmaline. I mean: punk before punk. Then those times It walks naked and alone, It takes what form It will, so even a mother would mistake my fiend for her child." She rubbed her lips together, twisting the ends of her prosecco pony. Split ends frizzed away with static.

"So how'd you catch it?" Bri asked, heart pounding.

Mallory's gaze flicked over.

"Sleight of puss," she purred, and when she didn't go on, he blustered aloud:

*"Immediately elaborate!"*

"I showed you mine," she said, stroking that champagne body from its scrunchy on down, "So what's the weirdest shit you've done for money?"

Brian took a bracing breath. Sweet Ursula licked her own nose again and again.

"Well, I know I won't shock your senses," said he, "But I did a little sex work after college, a little porn."

"Oh, who hasn't?" Mallory scoffed, "Campbell is Lutheran stock, the whole marriage is sex work."

*"Oof,"* Brian cringed, "Let's see. I...sold weed to an old professor?"

The lady of the house stirred her pu'er, unimpressed.

"I—*oh!* I licked a squirrel once in 5th grade for $10. Tyler Brugel held it down and I licked its back."

"You already said sex work," she zinged.

*"Touché,"* said Bri, "Yeah, I always thought Tyler was a little too into it.

Oh, also: one time, I answered this crazy lady's help wanted. She needed someone to stay at her gorgeous house and watch her demon."

"Sounds like a fucking *nut*," Mallory winked, and she reached a tanned arm to the long stretch of counter opposite the kitchen island, where an Aigner bag crouched beside a six-slice toaster, "Hope she paid well." And from the bag, she fished a Montblanc pen and a sterile sample cup and a powder blue wallet which she zipped open to a snakeskin checkbook.

"Yeah, the ad made it sound really generous," said Brian, side-eyeing the plastic cup on the counter, "But then, I don't know, we clicked. And I told her how I still owed my dentist $200 for a filling, so she threw in a little extra, for my trouble. I mean, she also had *plants*, so."

"Wow," said Mallory, impressed, "You really are a whore."

He watched her scribble out his name and tack on an extra two-hundo to the total with a satisfied smirk. In huge, barbaric swipes, she signed *M. Bain-Dahlhaus*, then ripped the check from its spine.

"We leave Friday after next, back the following Sunday," she said, holding out his pay and the little sample cup, "And I need you to pee in this, for the binding spell."

"Because it isn't real," said Brian, and he hefted his backpack to the marble counter, setting his phone on the closest stool, "Or it's the husband in a gimp suit, and I guess I'm not totally opposed."

"You're certifiable," blared the voice on speakerphone. Onscreen, the timer under *Andrew Yoon* ticked over to 38 minutes.

*"Just a widdle mutant byproduct of capitawism,"* Brian baby-voiced, and he fetched a treat for Ursula so she'd stop pawing at his chest, "Down, girl! I see a check with my name on it and my asshole uncorks."

"*O-pa!*" cried Andrew, startling the pooch.

"*O-pa!*" Brian called back, then he pouted, "Aw, I miss serving with you."

*"Wish I knew how to quit youuu,"* Andrew drawled, doing his worst Gyllenhaal, while Brian started opening cabinets, "I don't miss serving, actually. Nikos wouldn't stop calling me Drew, as in ew."

*"Drewww,"* Brian moaned, in a bad Greek accent, "Where are you? Is that Sheena Beaston?"

"Dressing room at Mindy's. Sheena's out tonight. *Lindy Hip-Hopera* is here."

"That name."

*"Gorl."*

Drag shenanigans crescendoed in the background, sending the speaker audio to staccato crackles.

"I can't find the cups," said Brian, "There's a cabinet of vases, but no cups."

"Mason jars or vases?"

"Vases, bitch, I know what a mason jar looks like."

"Guess you're drinking out of a vase, *bitch*," Andrew gruffed, butch as he could.

Brian selected a large glass pedestal jar and hefted it to the sink for a quick scrub. *Pample-mousse* dish soap waited beside the fresh sponge in the flowered dish. Late afternoon sun shone through meaty magnolia leaves just outside the kitchen windows, smoldering gold on the bruised veins of black-and-blue marble, glinting feverishly in the metallic sheen of the six-slice toaster. A magnet on the side of the fridge pinned down a Moyamensing University banner; another read *THE 105TH ANNUAL CONFERENCE OF OCCULT SCIENTISTS,* its shape an eye lined in black kohl.

"Is demon-sitting the most interesting thing about me now?" Brian mused, "Have I peaked?"

"Brother-in-*Chriiist*," Andrew whined, then he murmured something to a voice on his end; a roomful of drag queen laughter pealed out, then: "Do I need to head out there with a priest? My mom's crushing on hers, she'll send him if I ask."

"It's just a job. I pissed in a cup and everything."

*"They drug tested you!?"* Andrew screeched, the speaker fuzzing out again.

"Least the dog's out of diapers," Brian muttered, rinsing out the glass chalice.

"Friend," said Andrew, and his voice got kinder and quieter, like he'd taken Brian off speaker and cradled him close, "You are high empathy, no boundaries. So you maybe don't need this shit."

"I do, actually. Her check cleared, so cell phone is paid, rent is actually paid. Fucking gutted my landlord, he might off himself. A bitch *thirsts* for eviction."

"So take the dog for a walk, leave dinner, and *get the fuck out*. You don't have to sleep there."

"I already spent 30 bucks getting here from the city. I'm not doing that multiple times a day, Andrew."

"So stay with your mom, isn't she like 10 minutes away?"

Brian clenched his jaw. He sucked air through his nose. The silence stretched on.

"You're still not talking," Andrew sighed.

"I'm not going anywhere," Bri declared, and he angled the glass jar under the faucet filter and watched the crystal water pour in, "I'm gonna open the bottle of pinot I brought and roll a hefty joint and get absolutely shit-wrecked in this mansion with this stunning dog, and you're extremely jealous, and I don't blame you."

"K," said Andrew, "Well, my gig starts in 20, so if you start hearing voices, don't call back, because–"

*"I won't."*

*"I'll be onstage* with Benjamins in my crack, and I don't just mean money, baby. And *you're* extremely jealous, and I don't blame *you*."

"Not really," said Brian, and he took Andrew off speaker, "I've been in that crack."

"Lies," lied Andrew, "Love you, bitch."

"Love you."

Brian tossed his phone to the counter. With a grunt, he hefted the pedestal jar from the sink and took a long, grateful gulp. Twin trickles burst out the sides of his mouth before plunging over his Adam's apple and into the nadir of his V-neck. On the hardwood floor by the open portal to the dining room—*der Ésszimer*, Brian recalled, spasmodically, as he drained the vase dry—Ursula licked between her legs most diligently. The soft, insistent lap of tongue on pudenda bubbled up against the perfectly cavernous silence of the kitchen.

"All right, enough," Brian called out, to the poodle, "Pretty sure that's why they had you in diapers."

In the dream, she wore a huge blue-ribboned sunhat and the beach stretched out of sight before her, the sand blinding gold across half the horizon.

*"Mom!"* he hollered, sprinting after her, "Mom, wait! *Wait!"*

But with every stride, his feet sunk deeper in the sand. He hurled himself forward into an especially quick patch and was near instantly buried to his hips, and plunging fast.

She turned back just as his head went under. He tried to shout, to apologize, to curse her, to eat his way through the grit, but all he could do was choke and sink, the stuff under his tongue, filling his sinuses, caving in his lungs, until miles below the surface, terrible teeth found him in the sandy depths and ripped his arm clean to the bone.

*"What!?"* he cried out, waking to a cat straddling his forearm, "No, no, *get off!"*

The little night creep jumped back in surprise, but remained abed, down by his feet.

"You scared the shit out of me, dude."

Brian groped for his phone on the bedside table, swiped on the screen for the flashlight. He inspected his arm where the cat had bit him. Light red teeth marks, the stuff of play bites, lined the softest parts of his flesh. The blue-gray cat licked a paw and swiped aside an eye, quite pleased with himself.

"You could have asked. *Wake up, man.* Use your words, not your teeth."

Yellow eyes stared from the dark. Brian stared back.

"So you're Max. You're very handsome."

Ears pricked. A tail jumped.

*"Ohh,* he likes a compliment."

Paws stretched forth. A jaw yawned. A belly slid low along the comforter.

"Fine, just don't bite."

Brian clicked the flashlight off. He lay back and entered the passcode to his phone, checked the news. *More carbon. Fewer birds. This one simple test can prove if you'll live to 100.* He flicked the screen off.

"Night, kitty. I'll bite back if I have to."

He turned over on his side, pulled the comforter around his ears. His breath settled low and slow.

*DAS NEST* inhaled in tandem, filling its rooms with icy air con. On every shared exhale, rooms settled, snugger every cycle, the house compressing. Brian nearly set to rocking with the rhythm, drifting out to a dark sea, and he nodded off and awoke five times or more, a little flustered at continually waking to a strange bed.

Reviving once again, he heard the cry down the hall.

"Hello?"

He sat up in bed. The door stood open a crack, as he'd left it earlier. The cat stared at the crack.

*"Fuuuck,"* Brian breathed. He stood with a heavy sigh, adjusted his balls. He had to strain to hear the whimpers, even holding his breath and focusing, which meant it had to be from downstairs, on one of the other floors. It went on and on, *sotto voce.*

"Is this why you woke me up?"

But the cat just stared.

Bri grabbed his phone again and made for the door, then cut for the closer of the twin stairwells. Passing cars from the road out behind the house flared up now and again, sometimes drowning out the cries. He descended in darkness, shaky on the unfamiliar steps. Halfway down, he could hear well enough to know it was the dog, down on the ground floor. He continued on, somewhat surer of himself.

"Ursula, honey?" he called out, flipping on the lounge lights before moving on, his bare toes chilly on the stonework in the front hall. Rounding the corner of the dining room, he spotted her through the kitchen portal, off by the back door, curled in a circle, her whole body trembling. He rushed to her side.

The poor pood lay in a puddle of urine.

*"Ohh,* sweet baby," groaned Brian, cradling her head as she licked his wrist again and again, "It's OK, bud. No biggie, I'll clean up. Let's get you out."

He switched on the overheads and scanned the room for the key to the back door. There it lay, on the counter next to the fridge, which stood open a crack.

*"Huh,"* said Brian, stopping short of the counter.

He considered the crack. It wasn't enough to signal the internal light, he'd have hardly noticed it.

Ursula whined.

"OK, lovey, I'm comin'."

Briefly, he opened the fridge and gave its contents a once-over, then shut the door properly and gathered key and leash to lead the good girl outside, to the back walk.

"Your mom left extremely detailed instructions on bathing, so I guess we'll do the 2AM crash course," he said to the little lady, who somehow still had so much more to pee, "And then I gotta find something for the floor. Maybe a towel and then we just wash it?"

The quieter roars of the neighborhood played on undisturbed by daytime traffic, by bird or buzz of bee: leaves rustling in the breeze, cicadas chirping in the grass. The heat had cooled some in the night, but it was still too warm for Brian's liking. He shivered, body melting from the frigid air in the house.

Ursula finished. She sniffed the spot in the yard, then clipped back to Brian's side.

"*Good girl!*" he squealed, performatively excited so to cheer her up, "*Oh,* you're so good!"

She dropped to a lunge with a deep *woof,* then they ran out into the yard, circling round one another. Brian batted around her mouth, goading her on, and she play-snapped at his fingers. As he came in to pat her back, a light in a neighbor's house switched on, up on the second floor.

"Shit," he whispered to the pooch, "Come on, we're too loud."

The two of them scurried back inside.

"Anyway, I'd love to talk to Ursula," said Mallory, her face full-screen on Brian's laptop, that champagne mane unbound, spread across half the screen, "I have *big* big news."

"Sure thing," he said and stood to call Miss Ladyface to the kitchen, "Urs! Here, girl!"

The lovely bounded in, full of energy.

*"Here she is!"*

"Put your laptop on one of the stools. I have to see her."

Brian scooted the laptop to a kitchen stool, then angled the screen poochward and went to his knees off-camera, biting his lips between his teeth. Unseen, still he forced himself to grin.

*"Here she is!"*

"Ursula," said Mallory, "I have *big* big news."

Urs looked to Bri, raising an apricot paw.

"She's not looking," said Mallory, "Brian, make her look."

"Uh-huh," said Brian, and he reached out to angle her snoot to the screen.

"Little higher."

*"Uh-huh."*

Behind Mallory, a bespectacled, besweater-vested man with a tremendous salt-and-pepper beard came shuffling into frame from a darkened room, hands stuffed deep in his pockets, head tilted all the way back so he gazed up at the ceiling. Big beardo huffed and puffed, pacing to the far side of the room, then he swiveled, marching back and offscreen again.

"Ursula," Mallory tried again, "Darling. *You're gonna be a fat mommy, squishy baby!"*

The poodle licked her nose, looking at Brian. She thumped her tail on the kitchen floor.

*"Wowww,"* Brian fawned, leaning into frame, "She's so excited!"

"Well, we just had an extremely fulfilling reading, you guys," Mallory rolled on, and she brought a hand in frame, inspecting her claws, "I made the girl do it six times, starting with one card and working our way on up to a full-deck Lotus spread. She's very talented, everyone wants her. Whatever old Cassandra was, she's the opposite. I booked years ago, we spent a small fortune. Think tuition-sized. But we beheaded a python! Once in a lifetime stuff. So it's *definitely* going to be a healthy litter."

"Oh," said Bri, "Uh-huh. *So I thought* – did Urs take a doggy pregnancy test, or...?"

"That deck!" raged big beardo, pacing into frame again, "It was novelty, Mal! Klimt! *SCHEISS KLIMT!"*

"She may have a slight discharge brewing," said Mallory, waggling a talon, "I would keep an eye."

"Much too fucking *optimistisch*," ranted beardo, pacing offscreen again, "Nine of swords in gold leaf!? One wants to puke!"

"Heed a message, not the messenger," Mallory sniped, whipping around, "And Klimt was Austrian, Campbell. It's auspicious."

*"Verheissungsvoll,"* Campbell scoffed.

*"Hiii,"* cooed Brian, leaning further into view, "Is that your husband? Hi, I'm Brian!" Ursula sneezed.

"It was a *super* reading," Mallory reiterated, facing front again, "She pulled eight of wands for you, Bri."

He felt his face flush.

"What's that one?"

"Flow state," she said, brows bouncing, "Go with the flow, babe."

Campbell rushed into frame, hovering suddenly at Mallory's side. His glasses sat at the tip of his nose. He leaned his head back to peer through the oversized lenses.

"I do not sign off on this *angebliche Tarotkartenlesung,"* he chewed out, directly to camera, so he seemed to address both Brian and the dog, "The deck was not standard and was, in fact, novelty."

"Don't listen, mama-mama," cooed Mallory, to Ursula, "Daddy's never trusted tarot."

"Tremendously silly," said Campbell, to his wife, "My new TA is a tasseographer. Let me bring Julia in."

*"Tea leaves,"* Mallory stage-whispered to camera.

"I beg of you. *BEG.* Otherwise we've wasted a python, Mallory. There are heat exchanges at play. Karmic debts."

"How do you say 'karmic debts' in German?" Bri joked, third-wheeling it up, supes uncomfy in the silence between the couple. The dueling glares shifted his way.

"Anyway, honeybutt–"

"I'd rather you behead *ME,* Mallory. Augur my severed neck over fucking Klimt."

*"Anyway,* sugarpup, you got babies in your belly!" Mallory trilled, resurrecting her cheer, "So Bri, you'll properly pamper her, all right?"

*"All riiight,"* Brian sang, grin aching.

"And has It said hello yet?"

Campbell and Mallory watched the screen, teeth lightly bared.

*"Uhh,* nope!" Bri chirped, "Not yet, anyway."

"Untoward dreams?" asked Campbell.

"No," Bri lied.

"Well...you will dream," said Mallory, "You will." And she came to stare above camera, face going slack. Her hubs raked a covetous gaze over that elfin face, cervine neck, the great ridge of her clavicle. Brian and Ursula waited on their end, panting just a little.

"*So I–*" Bri tried.

"I'm done with the laptop," said Mallory, to no one, and she stood and wandered off, voice fading, "I'll be floating in the bath. Don't come in." Campbell promptly settled into the chair she'd abandoned, then set to work clicking and typing, the chat screen obviously superseded for a more important window.

"K," said Brian, sharing a side eye with Ursula, "Bye, guys! Enjoy the rest of the trip!"

He hovered the cursor over the red X to close the chat, then lingered on, playing voyeur for just another moment. Giant lenses reflected what looked like an open email.

*Lieber Katzenmeister!*

read the salutation, over Campbell's eyes.

Brian pumped faster and faster and eventually came, semen spurting in his hand, toes *en pointe*. He turned his face to the pillow, high on the alien scent of someone else's detergent.

Max yowled out in the hall. A beat later, *whump!* Cat butt slammed the bottom of the guest door.

"Can I have *JUST* a minute?" Brian hollered, dick already deflating, "You're not a part of this." He reached for the tissues on the bedside and scrubbed one over his pubes, where a few drops had landed, then balled the mess in one hand and tossed it on the bed. He stood, a little shaky and naked from the waist down.

"That was productive," he breathed, shaking out his cheeks with a shiver, "*Uhhh,* let's fuckin' eat." He paused the porn on his phone, leaving the actors' expressions pained. Upon opening the guest room door, there sprawled Maxcat, tail over ears.

"Did you do a somersault, creep?"

*Rowww,* Max moaned, then Mr. Kittybutt wrenched himself up from the carpet and stalked off along the hall, tail a-twitch, whiskers fanned wide.

"He's a male mo-del, male mo-del," chanted Brian, as he made for the stairs, *"Ka-ka-de-ka-ka-ka."*

Down the eastward stairwell they loped, did man and cat, passing the locked door to the second floor, before emerging down in the kitchen. Brian washed his hands in the sink, then flipped the switch on the electric kettle and made for the fridge. As he perused, Ursula made her way in from the dining room, wiggling her hiney.

"Good nap?"

Miss Thing rounded the marble island, blinking sleep from her amber eyes. She yawned and stretched to a lunge, tail slowly wagging. Max slinked up to her, rubbing his cheek along her apricot thigh. Brian scooted the carton of milk aside, then the yogurts behind it, then a jar of red cabbage. He bent at the waist to look in back. A white cardboard box hid in the rear corner, done up in a merlot ribbon, a black tag in its knot. He leaned closer. *Willkommen B!* read the careful script.

"Is this..." he trailed off.

Brian reached in and eased it out. The message was handwritten, in precisely carved, tiny loops. The ribbon twisted round itself in curlicue, then trussed over and under, making a thick knot at the center of every side of the cube, with an economical bow on top, bunny-ears style. Brian could just about fit a finger under the lid. He did his best to peek.

A sprig lay inside; a bloom.

He shook the box a little, tried to widen the crack. Honey and vomit reeked from within.

"Oh, *ew,*" he gagged, and tossed the box to the counter.

*Mom, help*

he texted Andrew, pronto,

*i think there's a weird lil gift for*
*me in the fridge?*
*it reeks* 😖

He set his phone on the counter beside the box. Ursula and Max had backed away, almost to the dining room portal.

"Do you smell that?" he asked, of the pets. Pooch barked thrice. Kitty sneezed twice.

*Ding!* Andrew's reply came back.

*boy if you don't stop*

*i'm not kidding!!*

Brian snapped a pic of the box, then a close-up of the tag, and sent them along, too.

*wtf is this ribbonwork*
*#marthastewart*

*what does it smell like*

*ur butt*

*bye*

*honestly, day-old puke*

*i was gonna say, hdyk it's for you?*
*but puke's perfect, you'll look gr8 in that*

*it looks like a flower*
*i can kinda peek*

In response, Andrew sent that GIF of Sasha Velour from the Season 9 *Drag Race* finale, lifting her wig to reveal a cascade of rose petals.

*do i open it?*
*it just says B*
*that could be anyone*

An ellipsis pulsed as Andrew typed a response, then it disappeared. It didn't come back.

"Ew, fuck you too," Brian huffed, meaning it a little, then he looked around for the pets. Max had fled. Ursula had retreated to the dining room, swallowing over and over, then she retched. Her tummy seized up and down, pumping.

"*Yeahhh*, let's crack the windows."

Bri set to the task, nudie butt bouncing past the countertops, weiner flapping to and fro. The white cardboard box sat where it had landed, in the shadow under the microwave.

"Move, move!" barked Mallory, and she elbowed Brian, then Ursula aside as she came barrelling through the front door, peasant skirt gathered to her knees, *I gotta pee!* She flung tote, purse, and handbag to the stone floor and took off for the powder room, bent at the waist, the poodle nipping her heels. Campbell pushed through a moment later, lugging a trio of suitcases-on-wheels, with a metallic aqua-green fanny pack clipped round his pot belly, and another two handbags slung crossbody, like external kidneys. A steady stream of sweat trickled off his nose and into the bramble of his beard.

"I know we haven't met yet," said Campbell, stopping short in the hall, glasses fogged, cheeks beet-red, "But I take serious issue with what you call watering the plants."

"Oh, I'm so sorry," Brian evaporated, "They looked fine this morning."

*"C'mere,"* said the man of the house, and he gave a perfunctory wave before turning heel and heading back out to the veranda. Brian followed, edging past the luggage, already picking at a hangnail.

The pots on the patio bunched in loose cliques spread down the entire width of the house. It took eight trips with a jumbo watering can to hit every plant, a Herculean task Brian had accomplished every second day, save the Wednesday he missed that he'd pushed onto Thursday because he got high.

"I was just out here this morning, I–"

"You've cosseted them," said Campbell, and he stood with hands high on the hips of his khaki shorts, squinting out into the sun.

"I—*no,* I really just–"

"Pampered like diaper babies," said Campbell, "You've breastfed them, man."

"Heard. Are they gonna– "

"And men can lactate, with all the same nutrients," he clarified, "Though I'm not saying you actually have done that here."

"Heard," said Bri.

"If I could lactate, I wouldn't waste it on others," Campbell decided, then and there, and he cupped one of his own tits thoughtfully, beard nestling in the open collar of his polo, "I'd hoard it all for myself, for my bones...not *muttermilch* but *vatermilch*..."

Brian wanted to interject, keep the convo light and rolling, but it proved too Hallmark a moment. Campbell came drifting back to Earth.

"Should there *be* a next time," said big beardo, and he laid a heavy, sweaty palm on Brian's shoulder, "I expect you to bereave them. You have opposable thumbs, they should fear you." And he hocked a loogie at the begonias. Bri shied away, toward the front door swinging wide. Mallory willowed out.

"Everything's *fab fab fab*, Bri," she said, screwing the lid on a sterile cup, "Ursula's glowing."

"Faboo," said Bri, gaze flicking to the container, despite himself, "She's a peachbutt."

"I'm gonna run down the basement, reset the spell," said Mallory, swishing yellow round the cup, "Hang around one more minute?"

Brian nodded extra-exuberantly, to which the lady of the house beamed. She melted back inside.

"I'm gonna grab my bag," he said to Campbell, who had gone picking his way through the pots, lifting leaves and sighing in exasperation...here and there, spitting at the buds. Bri retreated to the empty hall, where his bag lay on the checkerboard floor. He squatted to dig out his headphones, then looked up the SEPTA rail schedule back to the city. If the stars aligned, he could just make the next train and be back home, after a sub-way transfer, in probably an hour. He ordered a ride to the station, then slung the bag over his shoulder and pushed himself to standing, ambling closer to the lounge portal.

"Mallory?" he called out, loud enough to be heard through the base-ment door, "You good?"

A long beat passed, and Campbell trudged back in, nudging the oak door click-shut behind with a socked-and-sandaled foot. Heaving a wounded sigh, the galoof grabbed all three suitcases again and shuffled off through the lounge and upstairs, lifting the jumbo roller cases up to his waistline as he went, beefy arms bulging.

*"Dang,"* Bri whispered, impressed, then he cried out: "Nice to meet you, Campbell!"

*DAS NEST* settled. Ursula barked twice, somewhere upstairs. Brian watched his driver inch closer on the little onscreen map. The blue basement door under the lounge stairs remained closed.

"Thanks for waiting," said Mallory, and there she was, suddenly behind him, "Spell's all set."

"Awesome," said Bri, riding a shiver, "My ride's almost here. I think I got everything, I did a once-over. Thanks so much." He made for the door.

"We'll do it again, you," she said, and her blouse was undone to mid-chest, but she unbuttoned it still more as he went, all the way to the bottom, revealing a pale strip of flat belly, "I'll be in touch soon."

"Thanks," he said, tripping over himself to get out, *"Yup yup,* thanks again."

A maroon SUV pulled into the cul-de-sac as Brian hustled to the curb. He pried the temples of his sunglasses apart with his teeth. His head-phones dragged behind on the walkway. Greeting his driver, Bri went to load his stuff in the trunk, shooting glances back at *DAS NEST* all the while: at its stonework and timbers, its windows large and small. In the middle room on the second floor, one could see Campbell stripping off handbags and fanny pack and then a very soaked polo to reveal great whorls of chest hair on strapping man-boobs. Through leveled quarter arcs and rounded windows, one could spot Mallory, in pieces, as she scaled the stairs above the kitchen, stopping to kick her shoes off, shimmy-ing out of the peasant skirt. And as Brian small-talked the driver and they circled back out to the main road, he could just make out, through the mirroring dear windows on the opposite side of the house, the towering figure that descended from the third floor. It moved with Mallory's speed, matching her elasticity, her feral grace: bending like she would bend, slip-ping shoulders as she would shed a blouse, as if in shared orbit, like twin satellites, like electrons.

# OKTOBERFEST

D OOR TO DOOR, it came to $60 with a tip, but he'd managed to fit a
duffel, laptop case, four bags of groceries, *and* the portable sewing
machine in the trunk, so it just felt worth it? The driver lent a hand with
the food, literally, piling brown paper handles all atop one wrist, trailing a
step behind as they scaled the drive.

"Show-off," said Brian, nudging a chin at the feat of groceries.

"I'm a beefcake," said the driver, who wasn't, and they stepped gaily,
crunching over a quilt of yellow leaves, then under the *porte-cochere.*

"Told you, it's *stupid,*" said Brian, and he glanced back over the sewing
machine in his arms, "It's just the two of them and the animals."

"They need another?" said the cutie driver, "I'd be a good goldfish."

They rounded the path to the back door. Brian set his duffel down and
cradled the sewing machine.

"Close your eyes and turn around," he said, faux-shy, "Just in case you're
a murderer."

The driver smirked, but dutifully obeyed. Bri fetched the hide-a-key
from the fake pinecone and set it to the lock, but the kitchen door swung
wide before he could give it a turn.

"What the *fuck,*" unloaded Campbell Dahlhaus, leaning out the door,
"Are you moving in?"

"Campbell, *hiii*," said Brian, shoulders leveling, chest puffing up, *"I thought*—you don't have a flight?"

"Delayed, due to all the locusts," Campbell bristled, through his beard, "What is this?"

"Groceries!" Bri cheeped, gesturing back to the bags and the driver, who meekly waved from the hip, "I mean, it's 15 days, so." Campbo pursed his lips at the mass in Brian's arms, at its lavender vinyl dust cover.

"And what is *that?*"

"Sewing machine," said Brian, all porcelain cheer, and he raised a corner of the cover, "All thanks to you and Mallory." Mr. Mallory combed stubby fingers through his beard thicket, inspecting under the cover. Then, a brown bear losing interest, he heaved himself inside, flinging the door in his wake. Bri swiveled round to the driver.

"Thanks again," he said, with a see-ya wink, "Drive safe." Taking the hint, the third wheel set the groceries by the door and set off back down to his car. Brian grabbed the duffel and laptop case and lugged them inside, then went back for the other bags.

*Awoooo*, howled Miss Pooch Thing, waddling in from the dining room, a gaggle of whelps fighting for her swollen teats.

*"Puppieeeeeees!"* Brian squealed, dropping the groceries, then he practically took a running slide at the whole family. The babies swarmed, four—*no, five!* – baked potatoes in crimpled, dimpled fur suits! *Five puffy, bitey, smooshy, nippy popkins!* Three were ginger like mama, with a fourth in chocolate phantom, and the last, littlest in silver beige. They pounced and twirled and fell over on their squish faces.

Campbell appeared again, stomping down the kitchen stairs, stapled document and red marker in hand.

"Look, I know we've never met," said the house daddy, rounding the marble island, "And I should give a whistle-stop tour, but I don't have time for you. My wife wrote a *megalomaniacal* care guide for the puppies and the house and my cat and our demon, which I have now proofread and graded to a benevolent B+. Truly, it's *labyrinthisch*. I wish you luck." He scribbled a last, furious thought, circled it eight or nine times, then slapped the packet down on the marble, mightily pleased with himself.

"What are their names?" Brian asked, enduring licks, "They're *so* stinking cute."

*"Erde...Luft...Feuer,"* Campbell pointed, naming the three little red

pups, "The chocolate's *Wasser*. And we don't name runts." The eensy silver beige wagged its tail and yipped, eyes bulging.

Mama Ursula sniffed Bri's ear, then gave his neck a careful lick. Campbell moseyed over to the duffel and the brown paper bags. He bent over and eased out one of the jumbo bottles of cab sauv.

"*Ahh,* the cheap stuff," he said, holding the bottle to the light, and he shot Brian a devilish grin, "Little 15-day bender?"

"Just a bottle with dinner," said Bri, a touch flirtier than intended, "Doctor's orders."

Campbell chuckled. Nigh reverentially, he placed the jumbo wine dead center of the kitchen island. The puppies broke off from lick-attack mode one by one, sniffing out their milk. Brian leaned over to smooch Ursula atop her head poof, then he stood and made for the bags.

"So what's the—*conference* this time?" said Bri, lifting the groceries to the counter, "And where's Mallory? I thought she'd–"

Silver runt bounced at Brian's heels, pawing his ankles.

"*Ohh,* a spitfire. Little, little...you!"

The runt sat on its tail and wobbled. Campbell rummaged through one of the big sliding island drawers, only to pull out a familiar sterile cup. He slid it down the marble.

"I need your piss," he said to Brian, "Before I go."

"Pick up, *pick up,*" he whispered, the duffel bag slipping down the stairs, its strap slack in his free hand. The call rang and rang and rang. Brian's heart throbbed in his inner ear. He forced himself to swallow.

"Hello."

"Campbell, *hi–*" he began.

"You have reached the voicemail of Dr. Dahlhaus. If you are calling to schedule a private tutoring session, please email Julia Whitlock at jwhitlock@moyamensing.edu. If you are calling to book a reading, public or private, of my book, *Leerer Spiegel,* please call Arthur Lang at Hexerei House Publishing."

"*Come on*, man, *please...*"

"If you are calling in regards to the annual faculty masquerade, I am sad to inform you that I will no longer be performing my naughty duties as *der Katzenmeister*. A suitable replacement will be chosen from among department heads. All other callers, leave a concise message after the tone. *Auf wiedersehen!*"

"Campbell, *hi*, it's Brian," said Brian, sweat beading his temples, one foot two steps higher than the other, "From the house. Hey, so I know you're probably boarding, or maybe you already took off, but I just wanted to say—*to let you know* that the door is open. To the second floor. It was closed last time? And locked. And...now it's open."

Brian eyed the open door on the landing above. The strap in his hands went taut as the duffel slid almost to the bottom step, hovering there.

"So I didn't know if you—*if I* should close it again. I'm looking at it now. The way it opens—*well*, you know your own door. I'd have to reach from the top step, like, across the open doorway. And I just thought maybe you and Mallory didn't want me to see—or *be* seen. Or see any-thing, like, down the hall."

He licked his lips. One of the puppies cried from the fenced-in arena down in the front hall.

"OK, call me back," he finished rather flatly, then clicked to hang up. Out the quarter arc windows, one had a focused view of lawn and leaves and impish wind, the micro-landscape in motion, grass rustling free. Brian ran a palm over the stubble atop his head. He clicked over to his favorited numbers, skipping over *Mom* and *Amber Weed* to *Andrew Yoon*, who answered on the second ring.

"I can't talk, I'm catering a wedding."

"Straight or gay?"

"Straight."

"You can talk. Remember that house?"

*"No,"* Andrew whispered. "Sweet Caroline" blared in the background, right at the part where everyone sings along.

"The one with...*the one you hate on principle*," Brian enunciated, bat-tling Neil Diamond.

*"What happened?"*

*"THEDOOR'SOPEN,"* Brian boomed, hating how his voice carried up the stairs, and how it echoed back, "It's not supposed to be."

"The...*soap?*" Andrew repeated, lost.

*"I'LL TEXT YOU."*

He ended the call and opened his messages to see Campbell had already responded, via text.

*Hi*
*It wants doors open now*

Brian's stomach plummeted to his b-hole.
He took a screenshot and copied it into a new text to Andrew.

*2nd fl door is supposed 2b shut*
*so house is like a closed loop*
*now 2nd fl is open!*
*this^ is how homeowner responds*

He watched the messages get sent, one by one, the screenshot last, its progress bar freezing *right* at the end. It lingered. Brian's skin crept. He peeked up at the door. He made himself let go of the duffel strap, his fingers cramped and indented. The duffel slid to the ground floor with a *whump.*

*i already got written up today*

Andrew replied, after a bit,

*i can't be on my phone*
*call u later mwah*

A little warning symbol popped up beside the unsent screenshot, and just like that, the wireless network icon went blank. Brian swipe-clicked over to cell service to find only the smallest bar alive. It pulsed. It flickered.

A whine pealed out above. He pitched his head straight back, nearly pulling a muscle.

Max the cat gazed down over the edge, up on the third floor, pupils huge. Kitty chittered to himself.

*"Not helping!"* Brian seethed, then he scrolled through his contacts for Mallory's digits; gave her a try just in case.

*"Mm...you know what to do,"* moaned her voicemail, without ringing, then immediately came the *beep.*

Bri hung up. From his perspective down on the stairs, one could only see the darkened angle where wall met ceiling in the second floor hall, a patch of it beyond the open door. He rose a single step and the view enlarged; another, and he could see the tops of doors down the span. In gradations, he eased himself up the stairwell, leaning hard against the wall, craning his neck to see just that teensy bit more. The second floor came into focus. Raising his phone to eye level, he dialed 9 1 1 just in case, then hovered a finger over the call button.

Leaning out into open view, Brian could just make out the bare foot, the pale leg in the stairwell on the other side of the house, through the open door at the far end of the hall. He shrank back.

*Mrowww,* yowled Max, descending from the third floor, *mowwwww.* Mr. Catfellow came sauntering down, bumping his rump against the open hall door, running a banister slat over his cheek. He sniffed at the air, then flopped to his side on the second floor landing, gazing off down the hall.

Lowering to haunches, Bri pulled himself up by balusters, one step at a time, holding 9 1 1 at the ready in his free hand. He slid his nose past the last bar, making ghastly eye contact with the face just peeking around the balustrade on the other stairs. That uncanny eye widened as Brian felt his own go huge. Fingers fumbling, he must have clicked the call button, for it rang twice, the tone barely audible from his sweaty hand.

*"911, what is your emergency?"* said the tinny little voice, but Brian was past hearing. Horrified, he continued to rise up to the landing, just as that figure crawled out from the far stairwell: a slice of nose, bushy brows, that thick bramble of salt-and-pepper beard over a familiar, snooty grimace...

"CAMPBELL!" Brian yelped, sick with relief, and he nearly collapsed to his side, just like the cat, *"Fuck,* Campbell, *don't do that!"* He hung his head, heart racing, all the adrenaline steaming off in a hot flash.

On the landing, the cat licked a blue-gray paw again and again, then swiped it over his nose.

*"911, can you hear me?"*

"False alarm," gasped Brian, bringing the mouthpiece up to his face, "I'm so sorry. K, bye." He hung up.

Composing himself, he stood and brushed a dust bunny from his knees. He sent his phone to sleep, then climbed to the landing, glaring down at his feet, trying to find the words. He balled a fist at his side.

"Listen," he said, raising his gaze down the hall, *"I have put up with–"*

Campbell stood at the other end, completely nude, a fist balled at one hip. A great mane of chest hair plunged wild over his belly before exploding to a bush as brambly as his beard.

In the silence, Maxcat licked and licked and licked.

Brian's hand went slack at his side, and so did Campbell's.

Brian shifted to his other hip. So did Campbell.

An eensy burp bubbled up Brian's throat, and as he took a bracing gulp to send it back down, he saw Campbell's shoulders rise with the same hiccuping gulp.

"This isn't funny," said Brian,     "This isn't funny," said Campbell,

as one.

And yet one couldn't help but to kind of laugh! The same guilty smile crept over their cheeks, both fighting to suppress its rise, lips twitching.

*"Seriously."*                    *"Seriously."*

Brian's gut went sourer the more he fought the giggles. Campbell's penis jiggled from the same effort.

"STOP."                    "STOP."

They ran brisk hands over face, over beard, swiping amusement away.

"Campbell. *CAMPBELL.*"          "Campbell. *CAMPBELL.*"

Brian squeezed his eyes shut. Acid gurgled in his throat. He took a long, conscious breath, then blew it away. Quite suddenly, cat bod slinked twixt his shins, sending a jolt through his nerves, slamming his eyes open.

And there she stood, where Campbell had stood: *Mallory.*

Hair unbound, the tips of her graying champagne locks nearly but not quite covering her nipples. Belly scooped, pubis bare. The growing terror in her eyes reflecting his.

Dread certainty blossomed then. In perfect sync, Brian and *das Gegenteil* gasped in panic and dashed for the twin hallway doors, then slammed them shut with a double bang.

"Good job, lady. *Big* big walk!"

He fished for the key, eyeing the kitchen through the back windows. Ursula panted, pushed to the absolute brink, her leash taut. They'd walked all the way down Hemlock Way to a local trail, trekked its 2.5 miles, scaled the hill again, then circled the cul-de-sac eight or nine times, until neighbors started peeking through their shades, phones to their ears. The sun had hunkered down beyond the rear fencing. The backyard was a nest of shadows.

Nothing stirred in the kitchen but the blinking digital clock on the espresso machine.

Upon turning the key, puppy laments howled from the front hall in harmonic quintet. Brian stepped aside to let Ursula through. Oh so gingerly, knees almost locking up, she hefted herself over the back stone step, then dutifully turned to face him, coming to a half-squat just inside; the best she could do just then for a *sit*.

"OK, OK, biscuit for a babe," muttered Bri, and he reached an arm inside for the tin, on the counter by the door, his hand groping unseen. He raised up on tiptoes so as not to set a foot inside. Swiping blind, he of course smacked the rim, the biscuit tin then flying with an outsized clatter across the ceramic tiles.

Ursula gruffed, so over it.

One of the next door neighbors had an elevated porch in deep dark redwood with a huge umbrella spanning its width. A white-haired couple leaned on its railing with glasses of vino, watching Brian. He reached in the house to nudge Ursula's nose out of the way, then pulled the door shut and gave the neighbors a dinky, tepid wave. He made a show of taking out his phone. The older couple didn't budge, didn't stop watching. Brian came to sitting on the little iron bench under the black walnut. Onscreen, he navigated to his favorite contacts. His finger hovered over *Andrew Yoon* before slowly shifting up to *Mom.* And he really almost pressed his finger to the screen.

Butcher knife in hand, he sat on the duffel in the front hall, watching puppers snore in their pen, sneaking glances now and again at the framed map above the sideboard. Brian imagined a little sketch of himself in the *Vorhalle*—sitting on a mini duffel, watching mini puplets snooze—then he scanned to the furthest orbit of the house, that *Gästezimmer* upstairs where he was meant to sleep...where he *had already* slept, over the summer.

Thaumaturgically...thermodynamically...was It just sitting up there on an invisible duffel of Its own? When he crawled up to bed, did It slink down to sleep midair, just there, over the puppies' pen?

Miss Goody Goody Gumdrops could be heard in the kitchen, lapping away at her water bowl. Brian had had to refill it twice already. *Click-a-click!* went her nails on the dining room's hardwood, and that apricot pompadour appeared around the corner. Lady Urs licked her nose, chin soaked, a little waterfall dribbling onto the *Vorhalle's* checkerboard stone.

"Hi, you," said Brian, voice thick.

She plodded over the tiles to join at puppy-watching, giving the butcher blade in Brian's hand a careful sniff. The slow-roasted smoochburgers slept all in a row like a stupid ad or something, the nameless runt playing biggest spoon, clinging to a weightier sibling, twitching in her sleep.

Something scurried around upstairs; almost certainly Maximus Catus, but just in case...

"I don't think they should sleep down here tonight," he said to Ursula, so they emptied a wicker basket of its collection of *The New Yorker*, filled it with sleeping puppies, and hauled basket and duffel to the third floor. And where before Brian had left the door open a crack, he wedged it shut, and slid the hickory wood dresser into the knob. Ursula cocked her head at the fire hazard, but found a nice spot on the guest room rug to watch her babies. Brian stripped and leapt into bed, clutching his knees to his chest, gripping the knife in a jittery fist. He left the bedside lamp on.

"Night, peeps," he said, to the dogs.

He sucked at the glass pipe until the weed burned to its last ember, then a little more, so he got a mouthful of burnt resin as a kicker. Trying not to cough, he bent and blew the smoke out the bathroom window in spurts, for absolute ages, all those years of musical theatre having imbued him with otherworldly lung capacity. "Lovergirl" by Teena Marie played on his phone, sat in the bottom of a big glass vase, for the DIY speaker effect. Brian shook his hips to the beat and lip synced along, using the handle of the butcher knife as a mic. The water in the shower ran hot, filling the ceiling with vapor, fogging the mirror to a palliative film.

Teena's atonal recitative at the end of the song sent him spinning into a consumptive high, the tip of the knife carving inscrutable runes in the steam. Shuffle delivered some Earth, Wind, & Fire next. The vibe mellowed. Bri set his weapon on the rim of the sink and stepped daintily into the shower. His knots loosened in the heat. He leaned his forehead on the wall.

He could have stayed there all day, milking someone else's water bill, turning to absolute hot mush, but like a kick to the dick, the very loudest smoke detector Brian had ever heard set to wailing out in the hall. That hell screech was so much worse in the bathroom, too, with its echo, and he immediately ran stumbling out of the shower, knocking his shin on the rim of the tub, spraying droplets everywhere. He wrenched open the guest bath door and had to cover his ears. All that steam poured directly out the top of the doorway, pooling around the detector in the ceiling.

*"Fuck fuck fuck!"* he raved, and he groped behind the door for his towel. For long minutes, he stood naked in the hall, a growing puddle at his feet, snapping the towel again and again at the vapor, to dissipate it, chin sunk to chest. With nothing to cover his ears, he soon had a monstrous headache.

Finally, *finally,* the shrieking beeps shut the fuck up. Brian stood there, dazed. After a bit, he realized he'd left his knife on the sink. Heart in his throat, he went backing into the bathroom again, peering left and right down the hall at the empty stairwells until he could snatch it up again.

The brief catastrophe had turned the bathroom to a swamp. Water trickled down the walls, collected where the floor dipped under the sink. Out the bathroom window, faraway sirens grew a little louder. Brian clocked the racket, then did a tortoise-like double-take. He opened the screen window and stuck his head out into an overcast morning.

The sirens barrelled ever closer, probably reaching the bottom of the hill.

He held his breath, praying, pleading with an unforgiving cosmos, but then a Lower Merion fire truck came careening into the cul-de-sac, and another behind it, with a police cruiser on their heels. They circled round and came to a stop in front of the house.

*"FUCK!"* Brian barked, pulling back inside, and he rubbed at his scalp

till it burned. Throwing the towel round his waist, he paced out in the hall until he heard the doorbell ring out below, followed by a flurry of knocks, then puppy yowls from the kitchen. He bit his lip and tasted burnt weed.

The slap of his own wet feet on the stairs, the quake he wrought with his furious sprint reverberated back from the far side of the house, as *das Gegenteil* pounded back up to the third floor.

Right as he came skidding around the corner to the *Vorhalle,* Brian remembered the knife in his fist. He looked around for a hiding spot, then stabbed it soilward, into the closest potted plant. He took a breath to calm himself, sucked in his belly, and unlocked the front door with the key from the sideboard.

"I am *so so so* sorry," he blabbed, straightaway, "I had the shower too–"

A trio of firemen stood there among the dead flowers on the veranda. They ranged in age from FratBro.biz to Harder, Daddy™. They crested six feet. One rested the butt of an axe on his shoulder. Another hauled a three-story ladder.

*"Fucking hot,"* Bri finished.

"Sir, we're responding to a sensor alert on the third floor."

*"Yeah, it's*—I had the water too warm. Steam set off the—*we're all good here."*

Bri's nips went hard in the autumn air, or from the ripe collection of civil servicemen. He kept a hand on the fold of his towel so it didn't drop. The cop out in the patrol car opened his driver side door and stood, leaning on the roof. He had a butt chin; Clark Kent hair. He looked out over the property.

"You're saying there's no emergency?" said the ladderman, "No fire?"

"No fire. Just a very humid shower. I'd offer to show you, but it's way up on the third floor."

"Are you sure, sir?" said the hunk with the axe, "You're a little hype for 7AM."

All around the cul-de-sac, neighbors had stepped out of their houses, sipping coffee, pulling robes tight. The cop closed his door and made his way around the patrol car. At a blast from his radio, he turned his head to his shoulder-mounted receiver and gave a quick reply, squinting up at *DAS NEST.*

*"No*—yes," Brian said, shivering a bit, "You just surprised me. And I got the alarm to stop, so I don't–"

"The homeowner set it up so the station gets an alert," said the third, eldest fireman, "We come no matter what. Are *you* the homeowner, sir?"

"I am," Brian lied, regretting it at once.

"And can you verify your name and secret code so we know it's you?"

"*Of course* I can," he fibbed again, then he took a half-step back in the doorway. The cop meandered up the walk, one hand by his holster. The neighbors stared.

*Woof,* greeted Miss Pooch Smooch, and she came nuzzling up to Brian, wiggling that apricot hiney.

"This is Ursula!" he pivoted, "Ursula, meet the fire boys!"

"She don't come when the doorbell rings?" asked the axeman, and he shared a look with his buddies, "That's weird, 'specially for a hunter type."

"She's a new mom," said Brian, "Very concerned with her puppies. They're in the kitchen. You want to meet 'em? I could bring 'em out."

"Name," said the eldest of the three, "And secret code."

The cop had almost joined them on the veranda.

"Campbell," said Brian, "Campbell Dahlhaus. D-A-H-L-H...A-U-S."

The dadbods waited. The one twirled his axe.

"*The code...*" he mused, "*Gosh,* I think my wife might've..."

Eyebrows raised. He had never felt gayer.

"All good?" asked Officer Buttchin, stepping up to join them.

"*Das Gegenteil,*" Brian blurted, having never spoken the words aloud, "Is that it?"

The older fireman pulled his phone from his jacket pocket. He unlocked the screen.

"*Dahlhaus...*" he muttered, skimming aloud, "Geh-ghen-teal."

"Ghee-ghen-tile," Brian corrected.

"All good, Danny," said the firedaddy to the approaching cop, who threw Brian a friendly wave and traipsed back down the way he came.

"Sorry for the trouble, sir," said the one with the axe.

"Watch that hot water," said the eldest.

"I'd take a look at those puppies," said the ladderman.

After the tiny munches had settled from all the attention, after he'd waved goodbye to the first responders, after he mopped up the puddles in the guest bath and threw on some clothes and fed the cat and made a PB&J and smoked another bowl, Brian thought to check on It.

Slow and steady, he scaled the stairs to the second floor landing and its door. He took the handle in hand, then froze a little beat, psyching himself up, shoulders rising and falling. With his other knuckles, he rapped pretty lightly, and could just make out the other knocks, muffled but in time.

Opening the hallway revealed a new skin: that driver from the other day, the one who'd carried the groceries. Chest sunken, leg hair growing wild up to a hairless torso, so he seemed to wear fur stockings. Kinda weasely mouth. Mole under his right eye. It stood in the other portal, holding the door exactly as open as Brian did. Warm afternoon light lit It from behind.

| | |
|---|---|
| "Sorry–" Brian started. | "Sorry–" *das Gegenteil* started. |

They cleared their throats.

| | |
|---|---|
| "S-sorry for all the excitement earlier." | "S-sorry for all the excitement earlier." |

The thing stared at him, eyes wide. They each took a single step forward.

| | |
|---|---|
| *"Did you...*need anything?" | *"Did you...*need anything?" |

The rooms down the length of the hall remained closed. The digital thermostat read 52 degrees. If there was a light switch, Brian couldn't remember where to find it. His throat went dry.

| | |
|---|---|
| "OK, sweet," he rasped, backing away. | "OK, sweet," It rasped, backing away. |

They reached for their doors. Brian very nearly closed his, then he shared a last look with the driver-skin; his own trepidation, his own searching gaze reflected back, so guileless. He withdrew his hand. Back downstairs he went, so back up It went, and there the doors stood, ajar.

In the dream, her house was ablaze. He wore the leaden legs of nightmares, and no matter how hard he pushed himself, he could only manage the stairs one step at a time, vision swaying. Reaching the landing, he waved black smoke away to reveal a door he didn't recognize, next to her bedroom; but since he knew in his gut he was dreaming, he didn't take the bait. He faced the door he wanted and tried the knob: locked tight.

"*Mmmmooom!*" he fought to scream, through mouth-molasses, "*Fffffire!*"

Yet her door would not budge. Brian threw a shoulder into it, summoning all his strength, but the solid wood threw him right back. He bent over with a hack, a spitting wretch, then recalled the unfamiliar door; the dream bait. He groped for its knob, which loomed larger than the others in the house, made entirely of cut glass. He throttled the thing, throwing the door back.

A sea of fresh oxygen lay beyond. A boundless hall. 10,000 doors. Brian stumbled in; sucked at the cool air. He leaned heavily upon his own knees. The fire raged behind, in the house, which soon would be lost, yet the flames came no further than the threshold. He shivered off the heat of it.

A shape emerged from one of the manifold doors. A face too familiar.

"Bri," she said, stepping into the warm glow off the blaze, "*Puppy.*"

She wore one of her old nightgowns. Raising its hem to her shins, she took quite a purposeful step forward, and he felt his spine stiffen in response. His mirroring leg jerked, knee hinging, then when that foot planted, the other followed. Something beyond his own motor control propelled him forward, mother-bound.

"I think you need help," she said.     "I think I need help," she made
                                                                    him say.

Flickers of others faces — of Mallory, of himself — superimposed onto hers, so she was as a looking glass, reflecting. She...*they* upped their pace: first striding, then cantering, then out-and-out sprinting at one another. The doors whizzed by. They spread their arms wide in anticipation of embrace. Brian fought every involuntary step. He braced for impact. She wore a crown of blue fire.

"*I'M RIGHT HERE!*"          "*I'M RIGHT HERE!*"

All quiet in *DAS NEST*. The cat slept at his feet. The puppies snored in their wicker basket. Only Ursula reacted as Brian turned over in bed, raising her head slightly from the rug. She gazed at him, out of it.

*"Go back to sleep,"* he whispered, and she did, with a last lick of her nose.

He tried to follow her lead. He tossed and turned. Max stirred from the shifting, then arose with a yawn and leapt to the floor. Brian caught a glimpse of his blue tail disappearing through the crack in the door. He lay awake a while; counting sheep, reliving mistakes. Eventually, he gave in and got up too, creeping out the door without waking a single pup. He tiptoed to the closest stairs and started down.

Just above the landing, he dithered a hot sec, eyeing the wide open door, then he trudged onward and down. He threw *das Gegenteil* a wave in passing, barely glancing at that housemate down the hall.

In the kitchen, Brian found a tin of spiced hot chocolate and a small, hardy vase of red clay, still having yet to track down any mugs or glasses. He filled a saucepan with the milk he'd brought and set it to a low boil on the stove, stirring off and on so it didn't burn. Maxcat jumped up on the counter to observe with the doped, unblinking stare of a night stalker.

They opened a window while the cocoa cooled. Music drifted on the wind outside...some nighttime electronica, probably from a parked car the street over. Teenagers, necking. Brian leaned close to the screen and took a heady whiff of October. Max lay on the sill, jumpy at any hint of movement through the screen.

Once brewed, the chocolate tasted of peppercorn and campfire and smooth red clay. It ran in rivulets down his throat and burned in his gut, rolling the sweetest shivers up his spine.

He left the window cracked for the cat; set the stoppers so it couldn't be opened further.

"Night, cat."

He ruffled pointed ears, then turned off the hanging lights and scaled the stairs back to the landing, where he raised his mug to *das Gegenteil*, who didn't have a mug of Its own, but who raised a fist regardless. Brian nearly continued on, then he turned back for a closer look.

The youngest fireman, the ladderman, stood there in the shadows. His quads bulged. Those obliques lay scalloped, distinct from one another. A tribal tattoo encircled his bicep.

As the ladderman sipped the air, Brian sipped his cocoa. Spice and clay thickened in his blood. He set the red vase to the floor and *das Gegenteil* bent to mime the same. They unbent together and Brian got an absolute eyeful. Thighs for days. Braggable genitalia. Ken doll muscles stretching from pointy hip points. Hungry eyes drank Brian in like he was nude, though he wasn't.

He fixed that lickety-split, shucking his drawers.

They straddled the very heart of *DAS NEST* that night, from their own shadowy ends of the hall. Puppet obeyed puppeteer, so it really wasn't voyeurism at all—or exhibitionism, for that matter—but rather an extension of self-love, of imagination. Or that's how Brian justified it.

When he finally came, *das Gegenteil* shivered all over. The ladderman's pretty cheeks flushed. Nothing shot out, but still he held his hand flat after, like Brian did, trying not to drip on the floor.

The moment passed, but the mood didn't outright die, for that sheepish grin mirrored his own.

"Night,"                                    "Night,"

they said.

He had to finish the garment by Thursday so Andrew had it for his Friday gig. It was a basic evening gown in electric violet, and he'd already done the tracing, cutting, pinning, and first seams. Elastic was needed next along the bust. Lugging the portable to the lounge, he set up on an antique desk where the light streamed brightest from the palladian windows. He spun the tension to a 4, on a zigzag stitch, then upped the dial to a 7 upon hitting a tight spot. The puppies yapped in the kitchen, and he had to pause until they stopped.

He cracked his neck to each side.

Outside, a school bus pulled into the cul-de-sac. Two girls got off and skipped up one of the neighbor drives. The trees had shed half their leaves. Bare branches reached through balding circlets of burnt orange, of ochre.

The yellow bus turned back out on the main road. A woman waited in an open door for the girls, a glass of wine in hand.

Maxcat appeared, hopping up on the desk. Brian had to nudge him away when he tried to sniff directly at the needle, at the bobbin holder.

"Careful," said Brian, flicking at his blue tail, "It's not for panther people."

He started in again on the bustline and, having slightly changed his grip to scold the cat, the sewing needle took a plunge straight through his right pointer finger, at the top center of his bitten-down nail, punching a hole through keratin, through meat, to emerge out the other side. As the needle retracted, it brought his hand with it. Reflexively, he raised his foot off the pedal at once so the motor stopped. He stared at the skewer through his flesh, his hand still jerking up and down as the machinery slowed. Maxcat stared, too. He sniffed at the scene.

Brian drew a humongous, shaky breath, then yowled. Max fled, scurrying up the lounge stairs.

Cherry-red blood dribbled down upon the throat plate, the fabric, staining Andrew's poor violet magenta. The little cleaning kit that came with the machine leaned against the far leg of the desk, on Brian's right side. He tried reaching his left hand under his right arm to grasp for the handle, but came up about a foot short. He raised himself off the desk chair to try to swivel around, but could only go so far with his hand anchored. And he needed the tool from the kit to loosen the *goddamn* screw! His finger visibly throbbed with every quickening heartbeat, smarting on every pulse.

Gritting his teeth, Brian wrapped his free arm around the machine and put his shoulder to one end, scraping it down the finished surface of the desk. He didn't dare check for scratches as he went, because what fucking choice had he? After a few shoves, he had scooted close enough to bend and fetch the stupid case. With trembling fingers, he unlatched it and fetched the screw in question. Then, as gently as possible, he loosened the needle and cut the thread. He brought the butchery to eye level, inspecting it. He went a little woozy.

Ursula appeared around the corner. She sniffed at the air, drooling.

Brian fished his phone from his right pocket with his good left hand, then opened a rideshare app and found a driver 7 minutes away. He eyed the antique desk, which thankfully bore no scratches, but did have a thin trail of blood streaming over its lacquer. The sewing machine might have been shot; any blood that hadn't streamed off the plate had poured down the bobbin holder to the inner workings. Head reeling, Bri somehow managed to get his shoes on, fill his pocket with keys and wallet, and grab paper towels from the kitchen to mop up the mess. When he rounded the corner of the lounge, he discovered Ursula licking at a puddle of gore on the floorboards under the desk.

"No!" he yelped, grabbing her by the collar, "Leave it!"

He had to yank her back with all his might, she loved the blood so. He hadn't known poodles could be such hulks. Her paws scrambled at the hardwood. For safety's sake, he dragged Ms. Daintycakes to the downstairs powder room and shut her inside.

"I'm sorry, ma'am," he said, "I can't carry you upstairs right now. And you can't vampire here."

She barked her head off, but he had to leave her. The puppies were safe in their pen in the kitchen. He jogged upstairs, looking for the cat, and found him in the second floor hall, by the door to the master bedroom. Officer Buttchin cradled his own hand at the far end, one trembling finger outstretched, his pecs like a plate of armor. No needle pierced that strange flesh, but a trickle of xanthic pus bubbled from an identical wound.

"Is *your* finger OK?" asked Brian.     "Is *your* finger OK?" asked *das Gegenteil.*

The cat looked back and forth between them. Brian eased down the hall, estimating that he could reach Max before the center line, before forbidden contact, but then Señor Snooshtoosh got up and sauntered a bit further along, so he was closer to the naked cop-skin. Brian and the demon drew to a halt.

"OK,"                              "OK,"

they said, to Max,

"Have it your way."                    "Have it your way."

And they retreated, shutting the cat in the hall from both ends.

As Brian galumphed back downstairs, he could hear the car honking outside. He ran to the door, unbolted it, then stuck out an unimpaled pointer: *1 minute!*

The very briefest of mops in no way did the job, but he got the blood off the desk as best he could, then the floorboards below, kind of. Unable to lift the machine, he had to leave it, praying no further leak would spill forth. Locking up, he dashed to the waiting car and its very squeamish driver, and was already pulling up video tutorials on treating bloodstained wood as they swerved out of the cul-de-sac and onto Hemlock Way.

Sun had just about set by the time he arrived back at *DAS NEST*, with finger wrapped and bandaged, and an errant rusty stain or two on his polo. It had been a messy affair involving wire cutters and several shots, for numbing and for tetanus. X-rays determined the needle had just grazed the tip of the bone, so it hadn't taken much to convince the attending that his pain had far exceeded sober limits. Waterworks got him a second oxy when the first 10mg didn't kick like it should have. A little blitzed, he lurched his way up the walk to the veranda, hips loosey-goosey. The driver gave a two-honk goodbye.

He could hear Ursula's sobs as he scraped the key to its hole. Through the sidelight windows, he could see the powder room door shake from frantic paws.

*"I'mmacomin'mama,"* he slurred, "Hold those horsies."

He turned the knob, then kicked the door open, leaning in the frame.

*"Daddy's home, babies!"* Brian announced, in a showman's growl, which made him fucking lose it. He bent over with witch's cackle as the dog screamed. When he finally got around to freeing her, she bolted past and out the open front door, where she promptly pissed on the patio, whining throughout. The puppies were soon crying, too, from their kitchen pen, though even through the oxy fog, Brian recalled they had pee-pee pads, and so let himself off the hook on that one.

Miss Bladder 2025 squatted for ages. He did his best to be patient. He wriggled from the pills, antsy in his pantsy.

"I should've found you a better *spoooot,"* he groaned, scanning the powder room floor in case she'd had an accident, "I'm so sorry, muffinhead."

Ursula finished with a huff, kicking a back leg over the veranda tile, then she marched back inside and past without saying hello, cantering back to her pups. Brian shut and locked the door. All the lights were off, since he'd left during the day. He fumbled around for the switches, lighting up the rooms one by one, approaching every darkened chamber with the trust of a child; of the very high. He passed his pipe where he'd left it, on the dining room table, and almost took a hit, then just managed to pace himself. He nestled it with its lighter at the base of the peacock plant and forgot it at once.

When he made his way around to the lounge and flicked on the stained glass desk lamp, his eyes took a sec to adjust to the speckled light and the spotless sewing machine on stainfree lacquer. He bumbled back a step, ears burning hot, and bent at the knees like a broken doll, upper half swaying. He scanned the floorboards, but could find no trace of the blemishes left behind. All plans of baking powder and vinegar, of steel wool and panic, turned to simple-minded relief. On the way back out, he circled round the leather studded chaise to try the blue basement door under the stairs, just as a matter of course. As ever, it remained locked.

Plodding up to bed, he almost forgot to free the cat, and had to turn back for the second floor landing, gripping the handrail for much-needed support. He let the second floor door swing wide. Maxcat lay on the runner, apparently disturbed from a lovely rest. The little grey-blue dude blinked at the interruption. At the far end of the hall, *das Gegenteil* wore the attending doc's skin, with no bandage on Its flawless finger. Tight ginger curls matched the body hair, the pubes.

"Carpet, drapes,"          "Carpet, drapes,"

they muttered, pointing at the other,

"Yeah, I was wondering."      "Yeah, I was wondering."

And Max seemed fine, so Brian waved goodnight to the naked doctor and crawled up to bed.

The demon crawled down.

Sometimes he forgot to check on the animals. They had taken to closing the hallway doors behind them, settling on the dining room chairs he'd set up so they could jerk off in relative comfort. Hours would pass, small eternities of sexual fascination broken only by desperate yelps, by cat butt somersaulting against the wood. Rage overtook Brian more than once. He had flung open doors to shriek at the interlopers. Once, Max cried at the far door and he purposefully stalked to the nearer one, wrenched it back, and lunged at the space where the cat would be, so *das Gegenteil* got to be bad cop.

Brian luxuriated in choosing, in closing his eyes and rifling through men. That TV actor with the widow's peak. The porn star with the brown eyes. The prick who called him a faggot at Wawa. He played music, made them a playlist. Alanis. Seal. He got fixated on Paula Abdul's "Opposites Attract." Together, they lip synced all the MC Skat Kat parts, for Brian knew those lines best.

They danced a split tango. Howled like rabid wolves.

Bri brought the wine in; the weed. He drank them both to hiccups, then smoked it all away. More than once, he found himself staring at himself down the hall: bald and flaccid and slouched, tits over belly, against the far door.

On Halloween, trick-or-treaters rang twice, though every room in the house was dark.

"Hello?" Campbell called from the front hall.

"Hi, Campbell!" Brian called back. He closed his laptop and stood at the kitchen island. His bags sat by the back door, along the sewing machine in its cover. Mr. Homeowner wandered in, trailed by Ursula sniffing at his big hands.

"You moved my puppies," said Campbell, clocking the pen by the kitchen stairs.

"I did," said Brian, packing up his laptop, "They were cold by the front door. Welcome back."

"Thanks, *stranger in my home*," Campbell jeered, and he squatted down to inspect the bitty snoot-crumbles, "This one looks stout." He grimaced at the silver beige, who'd put on a little weight over the 15 days.

"Her name's *Äther*," said Brian, slinging the bag over his shoulder, "German for aether, I looked it up. Y'know, in keeping with your whole elements thing."

Campbell's brows drew together. His beard-bush dropped to a fright-ful frown.

"Listen, Mr. Elements*sss*," Mr. Man sibilated, all a-bluster, "I know we've never *met–*"

"We've met, Campbell," Brian snapped, "This is the fifth fucking time we've met." He couldn't help but to picture the doof naked. He hid a smirk in his shoulder as he draped his laptop bag atop his duffel. The puppies lined up inside their pen, up on hinders, tails swishing in unison. Campbell bent and ruffled all but the runt. Brian ordered a car, then fetched a sample cup from the big island drawer and slid it down the counter.

"OK," he said, "My car's here in a few, so if you need to pee for the spell...*chop-chop.*"

Campbell's tongue probed his bottom lip, perhaps to ready a vicious reply, but if so, he swallowed it. He palmed the cup and made for the downstairs powder room.

"*6 minutes,*" Bri called after him, watching the car icon scoot closer on his phone screen.

With 2 minutes to go, Campbell reappeared, sans cup. He wore a mask of contrition. He held one arm behind his back.

"It says you left your gift behind," he said, and quite elegantly, he produced a withered boutonnière, its blooms having long since dried out. With great care, Brian took hold of the stems across the kitchen island. He gave the thing a whiff: a mild, almost dear suggestion of honey and vomit lingered. A long black pin topped with a tiny bloodstone ran through the double stem. One flower was anemic violet, the other nearly cocoa brown, but he could see it had once been speckled white.

"The box," Brian breathed, "From summer."

"It's a gardener," said Campbell, "Whatever else my wife may call It, whatever armor or scenthounds It used in ages past, It's a gardener first."

"What are these?"

"Henbane," Campbell noted, "The demon would call it *Bilsenkraut.* Reeks of day-old puke. And deadly belladonna; *die Tollkirsche.* Flawless smell-a-like for the inside of your favorite vagina."

"I don't have one of those," said Brian.

"You should see Its greenhouse next time, in my office. It doesn't grow nightshades for just anyone."

Bri's face flushed. He pinned the boutonnière there and then, stabbing it through the heart of his nice puff jacket.

"I'm honored," he said, and he meant it.

"So long," said Campbell, then he wandered off upstairs, "Whatever your name is."

The puppies rassled in their pen; even little Äther joined in. Brian considered dawdling, making one last vase of tea, in the hopes Campbell might head up to the third floor and send It down his way, but the car arrived and his nerves got the better of him. He grabbed bags and sewing machine and snuck out by the back door, peering through the kitchen, the dining room windows as he went, turning bodily so he stepped backwards down the cobbled drive.

# WINTERSCHLAF

H IS KNEES ACTUALLY buckled when Mallory handed him the check.

"We made it an even $10,000," said she, applying mascara in the *Vorhalle* mirror, "You may have to shovel snow. The power can be finicky. *Y'know?* You just never know."

"Wow," said Brian, "Thank you. This is too generous."

"Oh, it's all embezzled from the endowment. And there's no one else we trust," she said, and her reflection winked at him, "Not for a whole month."

*"MALLORY, WE ARE GOING TO BE SO FUCKING LATE,"* barked Campbell, stomping down the lounge stairs in dress shirt and tighty-whities.

*"We..."* Mallory trailed off, switching eyes, "...are going to be *magnificent.*" She towered on nude pumps. Trunks and totes, beach bags and briefcases piled mountainously upon the checkerboard tiles.

"Burnt olive or puce?" Campbell inquired, holding up two equally foul neckties to his face-bush, which had brambled well beyond his collarbone. Brian cringed.

"What's the occasion?"

"Xmas with our exes," said Campbell, "Everything's very deliberate and awful and *erotisch*."

"OK. So...neither?"

*"Ooh,"* cooed Mallory, "Unbutton yourself, darling. Give the world a hairy gorilla show."

"Puce it is," said Campbell, and he made for the stairs again, briefs showing off those professor cheeks.

"I don't know why you ask!" Mal called after him, then she swiveled round to Brian, "I don't know why he asks, he knows exactly how he likes to groom. My Linebacker Princess."

"Are you excited?" Brian asked.

"Achingly," she said, and she opened the coat closet to disappear entirely in its depths, only to reemerge with a knee-length spotted fur, which she twirled about her shoulders so it soared into place, "I think we all crave being airborne. I know I do."

"That isn't real."

*"Sure iiis,"* Mallory purred, "Big mama lynx. I shot her myself from a helicopter, for the vernal equinox. We made an amulet of her heart. One of our best trips."

"Where do they even let you do that?"

"Eastern Europe," she said, then she turned her head to the stairs, *"CAMPBELL DAHLHAUS, WE ARE ABSOLUTELY GOING TO BE SO VERY, VERY LATE."* Ursula poked her head around the corner at the shout. Her hair had gotten scraggly. Ungroomed frizz fell over her eyes like chunky bangs.

"I wanted to say..." Brian started, shuffling his feet like a kid, "Well, thanks a lot. I know I said that already, but I'm finally gonna get braces? For my crowding on the bottom here." He pointed to his bottom row of teeth, the front of which wasn't so much a line as a group hug.

Mallory rested a hand to her heart, dead-eyed.

"Aw," she simpered, "I'll miss your snaggles."

"Well, I'll owe my smile to you guys."

"Is that why you stopped acting?" she asked, giving herself a once-over in the mirror, "Because of your fucked-up teeth?" Brian took a sharp breath, but kept on grinning.

"Maybe," he said, for she may have been right.

*"CAMPBELL RAINER DAHLHAUS, I WILL STUFF YOU BOD-ILY IN MY WOMB AND BIRTH YOU A BETTER MAN."*

Ursula cocked her head in the dining room, that flump of frizz flopping over.

"Oh!" Mallory realized, "And we can't do urine this time. Trip's too long."

"Sorry?"

"For the spell," she clarified, and he followed her into the lounge, where she dug around in the antique desk drawers, "A tinkle's great for a short bind, but it loses potency." And she withdrew a black leather case, zipping it open to reveal a custom phlebotomy kit. All the elements lay in fresh, unopened packaging: tubes, needles, gloves, vials. Ursula butted in, poking her head between their hips, sniffing at the bloodworks.

*"Um,"* said Brian.

"Which arm has the better tap?"

"I think my left?" he said, backing away, "Are you trained for this?"

"Bri," the lady of the house drolled, "I had a pulse in the '90s, I *think* I know how to find a vein."

He butted into the studded chaise. Ursula gazed up from under her fringe with eyes most doleful.

"Or we can cancel our very special trip," Mallory went on, donning an outsized pout, "And I can take back my check and send you home and spend the next month shrieking hexes in the bath." She mimed weeping, twisting two ringed fists under her eyes. From high in her throat, she produced a sharp, keening whine. Ursula responded to the show, snapping in worried little barks, spinning in frantic circles.

"I...I guess," said Brian, disarmed by sheer silliness.

The lady's show of grief turned sly. She rummaged through the kit.

"Shit," she said, "Elastic. I think...*guest room*. Wait here."

"I could just pee, I have to go. And what about the flight, Mallory?"

"Oh, it's private," she scoffed, "Everyone'll have another drink." And she took off upstairs, quite adept in heels.

Brian fondled the corner of Mallory's check through his front pocket, then his mouth twisted to a nub. He stripped off his pullover and lay it over the arm of the sofa, then squeezed his left fist over and over so his vasculars popped. Ursula scratched herself behind an ear, zoned out; then the poodle perked. Sniffing the air, she turned tail and raced behind the armchair by the hearth, cowering there. Moments later, a bare-skinned old woman tiptoed in through the dining room from the kitchen. She had to have been 90; older. Gnarled feet arched precipitously, like she wore very tall nude pumps. Her breasts drifted apart upon the swell of her belly. Chapped labia hung inert from a white nest of pubic hair. She went reaching about the room, opening invisible drawers, rifling through ethereal closets. Then, having apparently alighted upon the object of her search, she closed her fist around empty air and swanked back out of the room, flat bottom swaying from side to side.

Brian hadn't breathed, and still didn't when Mallory *click-clack'd* her way downstairs, an orange elastic gripped in her fist.

"Sit," she commanded.

"Sit," he commanded, and the dogs all sat.

The puppies had nearly grown into their paws. Äther in particular seemed possessed of a certain pep, despite being dwarfed still by her siblings. Her silver beige coat glistened under the hanging lamps. *Frau Ursula* crouched at one end of the pooch line, and it was to her Brian gave the first biscuit. She held it between her teeth until all her pups had gotten theirs, and only then did she crunch.

With hounds sated, groceries unpacked, and duffel waiting by the stairs, Brian enjoyed a well-earned sit of his own at the marble island. He took out his phone and chose a playlist, scratching at the pit of his elbow, at the vivid indigo blotch where Mallory had stuck him. The bruise seemed to creep in real time down his arm, its advance a bilious green. He rubbed spit on the angry pinprick. All the treats he'd brought for the stay crowded one end of the island. The ounce of Jack Herer snuggled up between the bottle of poppers and little twist-bag of Xannies. Two handles of vodka towered alongside the brand-new bong, crystal water straight from the fridge in its tower, and ice cubes in its catcher, and a fresh pack in its bowl. He reached for the big mama, and the blue lighter at her side, wilting to a languorous stretch down the marble, then lit up, sucking down frozen smoke. He filled the ceiling with it.

Half a Dido album later, Brian broke the seal on one of the vodkas.

Using its cap for a mini shot glass, he knocked back half a dozen in quick succession. The puppies whined in their pen. Ursula had wandered afar.

Bri stood; found his sea legs.

"Solid," he declared, *"Solid."*

Clambering over his duffel, he scaled the kitchen stairs to the landing. The hall door stood half-cracked. Brian gripped the knob.

"You decent?"          "You decent?"

they called to one another.

And the voice that echoed his sounded deep and dulcet, so Brian eased his door open. He appraised the body on offer, swiveled his own from side to side so he could check the butt. He smiled extra wide to assess the skin's teeth. He made a muscle and eyed the muscle made.

"Sure," he said,          "Sure," It said,

boners rousing,

"We can start there."      "We can start there."

He had the plates shipped direct to *DAS NEST,* where he unpacked and washed the first two-week model with great anticipation, then fit it, with a suck of the thermoplastic, atop his bottom teeth. If he stood back apace from the mirror and didn't smile too wide, the aligner was barely noticeable. He probed at it with his tongue, appreciating the squeeze on his pearly off-whites, the gentle ache.

He jogged to the second floor hall.

"Look!"          "Look!"

they bragged, sporting underbite grins,

"Living makeover."      "Living makeover."

It wore his 10th grade French teacher. Brian's phone vibrated in his front pocket. Mr. Davidson reached a hand down his naked thigh, then brought it to his ear like a mime.

"Hello?"                              "Hello?"

*"Avon calling,"* Andrew sang, "Am I speaking to the mother of the house?"

"This is she," said Brian.          "This is she," said *das Gegenteil*.

"Hi, dumb baby."

"Hi, mean mommy."                  "Hi, mean mommy."

*"Wait,* where are you? What's going on? Who is that?" Andrew rapid-fired, and the camp fled the conversation, "Did I call while you were with a *gentleman?"*

"Nooo," Brian laughed,            "Nooo," *das Gegenteil* laughed,

and they closed their respective doors,

"It's just the TV."

*"Okaaay,"* said Andrew, clearly not convinced, "Hope the TV's on PrEP."

"Are you still *visiting meee?"* Brian asked, all chippery-doo. He danced from foot to foot, descending the stairs one hippy-hop at a time.

"Well, babe, that's why I wanted to call..." Andrew trailed off.

*"Nooooo,"* Brian groaned, and he slapped the railing, "You always do this."

"I do *not* always."

"When I'm out here you do. You said you'd come last time, in October, and you never did."

"OK, so A. You're right, I did say that."

"I know I'm right, I'm always right, unless I'm wrong."

"B," said Andrew, "I very much don't want to meet the fucking ghost or the goblin or whatever."

"Demon," Brian corrected, and the little lie just rolled off his tongue: "And I told you, It isn't real."

"And C, legit they're saying it might snow."

"So pack your ice boots, Elsa," Brian steamrolled, and he swung round the kitchen island, gripping the marble corners, propelling himself, "And I'll bear hug the poor prince if he gets too cold."

"Stop, you know I like to feel petite."

"Andrew," Brian said, in an intimate voice. He leaned his full weight on the marble counter, crossing his feet behind, lifting them all the way up to his ass.

"What."

"Their fireplace is bigger than your apartment."

Outbound trains arrived in Wynnewood at 5:28 on Fridays, assuming no weather delay, so Brian timed the potatoes to come out of the oven at 5:45. The tuna steaks needed a few minutes on each side in the cast-iron, and the salad he'd toss with blush vinaigrette once he knew Andrew met a driver and got on the road.

Maxwell Cat Cattington eyed the tuna from atop the fridge, moving not a muscle.

"Don't even think about it," said Brian, keeping Max in his periphery, "I will serve *you* for dinner."

From the kitchen cabinets to the dining room table, he ferried plates and silverware, and four mismatched vases, to be wine and water cups. Of the selection he'd brought for the trip, no bottle quite fit the bill, so he wound up stealing a nice syrah from the rack by the toaster. An old Indigo Girls album ended, the last lesbian notes swelling the kitchen with good vibes, then another Indigo Girls album began. The puppies dozed in their pen, flopped in a pile.

"Fuck, weed," Brian realized, and he looked around the room, to no avail.

He covered the uncooked tuna with a pot lid.

"Keeping you honest," he said, to the tuna-stalker.

Trudging up the kitchen stairs, Brian made sure to close the door to the second floor, so *das Gegenteil* would do the same on Its side. Then, after sneaking a peek in the good mirror on the landing, he scurried up to his room, where the bong perched on the windowsill. He clutched it with both hands, then made sure to cradle it in the crook of his arm so he could shut the third floor hall behind him on the way back down.

Returning to the marble island, he packed the bong's bowl and took a hit for good luck.

"I never made tuna steaks before," he confessed to the cat, through the smoke.

*Ding!* Andrew texted to say he was one stop away, with a car waiting. Brian sent back party hat emojis.

He uncovered the tuna steaks, brushed them with oil, then seared them on the stove. He pulled lemon potatoes from the oven; tossed the salad and sliced the pumpernickel; sang along to the chorus.

"It's not like that," he cautioned Maxcat, "He's just a friend."

Another text shot through from Andrew, and without reading it, Brian bolted to the front window, only to see a likely hatchback ease into the cul-de-sac, carving fresh tracks in the falling snow. Quick as a flash, he plated the food and dropped it at the dining table.

"*Urs*-ula! Here, girl!"

Dame Mushroom Frizz cantered in from the lounge.

"Right...here," said Brian, positioning her so she sat one click off-center of the checkerboard tiles, then he unlocked the great oak-and-iron door. As the doorbell rang, he took his position beside the pooch: nose angled high, one wrist limp at his side, the other glued to his high ribs.

Andrew rang again.

"*Enter!*"

The door creaked inward. Andrew took in the scene, overnight bag at his elbow. He'd pulled his hair up to a loose bun under his fur-lined hood. His jaw dropped.

"*This is my hooome,*" intoned Brian Bain-Dahlhaus, "And *this* is my lesbian life partner."

He peered sidelong at Ursula, who lifted a paw to the newcomer.

"*Well,* I'm actually with the homeowner's association," said Andrew, creeping in, already going to his knees for dog kisses, "And we don't tolerate homosexuality in this neighborhood. Sorry: *homobeastiality.*"

The poodle licked all over his face.

"And yet here you are kissing my wife."

Andrew stood. He and Brian smirked at one another. The moment lingered, neither budging, then it became too much and they had to hold each other tight. They squeezed too hard.

"Love the beard," said Andrew, "You look like a gay Mennonite."

"It's like three weeks old, it's not *that* long," said Brian, "And Mennonites don't have moustaches. When did you get so tall?"

"Stop, I'm 5'2".""

"You're taller than I am."

They flipped back-to-back, flat hands touching where their heads stopped, then they turned under their arms. Andrew's fingers hovered right on top of Brian's.

"Well, I'm 6-foot," said Brian, "So you're officially a skyscraper."

"I don't know what you're talking about, I'm 4'11"."

"Of course you are."

Ursula got up on her hind legs, trying to get between them. She barked, which set off puppy yips from the kitchen.

"So dinner's ready," said Brian, "Unless you want the tour first."

"*Oh,* definitely the tour," said Andrew, and he dropped his bag by the sideboard, "And I want puppies."

"Duh," said the lady of the house, then he gestured about, leading the way, "You'll notice we're standing in our *spacious* front hall. You could play chess on these tiles. Through here is the dining room, with our bold mahogany dining table and the first of our fireplaces, already roaring for the gods. And look at that stunner view of the snowy cul-de-sac."

"Why are the chairbacks so sharp?"

"To draw the eye," Brian batted back, "Also notice the busy place settings, with idiosyncratic drinking vases, which are all the rage here."

Andrew nodded, impressed. He lifted one of the wine vessels and ogled it, then took a dainty sip.

"Through here..." the evening's guide continued, and Andrew toted his wine along to the kitchen, "We find the newest additions to our growing family." Ursula rounded in front, reaching the puppies first. She gave a proud bark, wagging the poof on her tail.

"*Get the fuck outta here,*" said Andrew, as pooplets lined up along the pen fencing, yapping their little heads off, "Can I get in there with them?"

"*Uh-huh,*" Brian grinned, then he held Andrew's vase so he could enter puppyland. Ursula sniffed at the fencing. The pups swarmed the trespasser with most vicious licks.

"How do you tell these three apart?" said Andrew, after catching his breath, "They're all gingey babies."

"Yeah, I don't, really," said Bri, and he pointed at the chocolate, "That one's Wasser; German for Water. The little smidgy one is Äther. I named her since they wouldn't."

"What, was she gonna die or something?"

"I don't think so. They're just...sadistic, I guess."

Andrew picked Äther up and stared her down. She wriggled from excitement.

*"Ohmygod,"* he said, with a genuine gasp, "You know who they are, Brian!?"

"Who?"

"Geri, Mel B., Mel C.," he said, pointing to the gingers, then at the chocolate smooch, "This one is Victoria, obviously."

Brian gasped, too, undone at the accuracy. He pointed at the runt.

"So she's–"

*"BABY,"* they squealed together.

*"Awww, Emma Bun'onnn!"* Andrew whined, in a questionable Londoner accent, "I'm stealing her."

He stepped out of the pen, Äther snugged quite happily in the crook of his arm. He took back his wine.

"Well, you can take her on the tour," said Bri.

They retraced their steps to the lounge next, Ursula clipping at their heels.

"Oh, cute," said Andrew, turning to the framed map as they passed through the front hall again.

"Yeah, it's..." said Brian, losing the real estate voice, "It's the house."

*"Huh,"* said Andrew, and he leaned in to gaze at the *DAS NEST* cross-section, to read the room tags.

"Anyway, this is the lounge."

Brian circled the furniture as Andrew lingered, still stuck on the map.

"Come see the hearth."

Eventually, Andrew meandered in.

"Wow," he said, stroking Äther, "That really is bigger than my apartment."

"I thought we could set up a blanket fort," said Brian, "You braid my beard, I braid your back hair."

"Yikes."

"We could practice necking to get ready for prom."

"I don't know how to neck with another *girl,*" Andrew pouted, "You might have to teach me."

"Let's go upstairs!" Bri trilled to Ursula, who snuffed and climbed up on the chaise instead.

Andrew let little Äther sniff his wine. He sized up every painting.

"The next wing is closed," said Brian, scaling the loungeside stairs, gesturing up to the second floor hall, "For light renovations."

"So that's where they keep the bodies?" Andrew asked, milking every step, toasting invisible party-goers.

"Just the summer bodies," said Bri, his voice echoing up the stairwell, "Y'know, waterlogged drownings. Struck-by-lightnings. Winter bodies we keep in cedar, for the moths."

He was halfway to the third floor when Andrew got to the first landing.

"*Oh,* this mirror is correct," said Ms. Yoon, modeling with the pup, sucking in her cheeks.

"If you'll follow me, miss," said Brian, then upon cresting the top floor, he came to a dead stop, for there stood *das Gegenteil* facing the far door, the one to the kitchenside stairs Brian had closed that had always been open, for loop's sake. Fucking *whyyy* had he closed it!? Absolutely dandelion-brained, he could find no better answer than broken reflexes; a tic born of altered states and unfamiliar territory. He ventured up a step and It walked Itself facefirst into the door.

The skin It wore had asymmetrical love handles. A trail of fine black hair grew along Its spine. The demon stood in a growing puddle of Its own runoff, the whole sodden body speckled with dirt and wood chips and running with trickles of filthy water.

Grasping at once that he'd closed considerable distance round the loop, Brian climbed not a step further. His hand groped for the railing. Synchronously, *das Gegenteil* leaned on air, steadying Itself.

"Babe," Andrew called. Brian swiveled his head down at the call, then he caught a glimpse of the skin's swollen face swiveling away as he instinctively checked Its naked rear again.

"Do you think I could borrow her for a show?" Andrew went on, still voguing with the noodle, "I have a charity ball in January. I think she's lighter than my purse!"

"Sure."                     "Sure," the skin gurgled, facing the door.

He could not identify the body, not from behind. It bore fans of blushing stretch marks on its thighs. A menagerie of shapeless moles littered Its back, among the dirt and debris.

Ursula barked down in the front hall.

With considerable effort, Brian turned his back on the demon, knowing it turned Its front on him.

*"Hey, so guess what?"*　　　　　*"Hey, so guess what?"*

they stage-whispered,
Brian down to Andrew,
*das Gegenteil* down the hall,
and Its wet sibilance tickled his inner ear,

*"I actually gotta eat first."*　　　*"I actually gotta eat first."*

Andrew tore himself away from the magic in the mirror. He looked up, then couldn't hide the glare.

"You're drunk. Already."

*"No, that's not–"*　　　　　*"No, that's not–"*

they tried,
and it was so much harder to speak with It at his back,
like when two people pick up the phone in the same room,

*"I took ibuprofen on an empty*　　*"I took ibuprofen on an empty*
*stomach."*　　　　　*stomach."*

"So why are we whispering?" Andrew whispered.

*"...because it's sexy."*　　　*"...because it's sexy."*

One last minute switcheroo and Andrew took the seat at the foot of the dining table, with his back to the front hall and quite the imposing view of the humongous woodcut print above the mantel: an expressionist view of a young girl floating horizontally, her hair stretched into an exact replica of herself. Brian fussed over the music, scrolling endless playlists, heart like a burr in his throat. Eensy Äther sat in Andrew's lap, her chin on the handle of his spoon.

"So are they Nazis?"

Brian gave a look.

"I probably have to leave if they're Nazis," said Andrew.

"They're not Nazis."

"OK, but everything's in German, though," Andrew pressed, "That creepy sign outside. *The map.* Plus there's the very weird story of what they hired you to do, which I'm not bringing up, because I'm not gonna give energy to that, not after I convinced myself to come all the way out here."

"I told you, It's not..." Brian broke off, unable to finish the lie, "It would be very convenient, not to mention xenophobic, probably, for us to call them Nazis just because they're—I mean, there are *other* stereotypes. The engineering and, y'know, no sense of humor. And *she's* not even German."

"Did you look them up at least?"

"Yes, back in summer. He's a professor, she's his wife."

Andrew whipped out his phone.

"What's his name?"

"Dahlhaus," Brian sighed, "But spell it like it's a monthly sex party, not like D-O-L-L. Campbell Dahlhaus. He teaches at Moyamensing."

Detective Yoon clicked away.

"Oh, Alan went to Moya," he said, "I should ask if he knows him."

"Alan *who* Alan?"

"Jess' Alan," said Andrew, "The *not* brother-in-law."

Brian lowered to a squat over his phone by the fire. He wondered where the demon squatted; if It felt the flames on Its face. He typed *'80s '90s chill sexy* in the search bar.

"If you put on '90s soft rock, I'm calling the FBI," muttered Andrew, lost in his screen.

"I'm not!"

Brian cleared the search bar. So super casually, he pushed himself to standing and wandered out to the hall, then beelined his butt to the sideboard. Lighting its lamp, he went up on tiptoes before the framed map and leaned close to the glass, scanning the path he'd taken since spotting It, eyeing the distance down the third floor hall from the top of the loungeside stairs. He placed two fingers on the scene, one for himself, one for the demon, then traced his way down the stairs and through *Vorhalle* to *Esszimmer,* where Andrew sat unawares.

Most probably, had It kept Its new distance, It stood just then near the top of the stairs, where his trailing finger had stopped, or maybe a bit further downstream—the map being only an artistic approximation, after all. He peeked over at the lounge stairs where they rose beyond the lamplight and into the ceiling; the haunt between the slats where a face might have stared, a hand reached. Only empty stairs peeked back.

Clicking over from music to texts, Brian scrolled down to his last messages with Mallory and Campbell, then selected the former.

*Hey Mallory!!*

he drafted,

*Hope the trip is great! I just wanted to check in about your other guest and the loop you guys set up haha. It seems like the "spell" might have gotten messed up somehow?* 💀 *Can you chat for a bit?*

He bit down on his lip, reading it back, then deleted the quotes around *spell*, because what the fuck else was it? Ursula wandered into the hall. Bri's thumb hovered over the send button, wavering, then he tasted blood, having bitten too hard. With a lick of copper, he abruptly deleted the whole text and slid his phone back in his pocket. Ursula's snout angled over to the stairs and where they disappeared into the ceiling. She stared unblinking.

"OK," called Andrew, "I found the faculty page."

"Yeah?" said Brian. He strained his ears for Its echo, but couldn't quite catch it.

"He's the *Dean of Esoterica.*"

"...that's almost a drag name," Brian said, "The Erica part."

He started shifting back to the dining room, eyes on the lounge stairs. Socked toes felt for each checkerboard square behind him, melting to ball and heel. Ursula *woof'd* under her breath. Her nails did a tippy-tap on the tiles. The dark at the top of the stairs loomed.

"OK, *not* looking ideal on the Nazi front," Andrew called, then his voice changed, like he'd turned in his seat, "Are you checking yourself out or something? I thought you had to eat."

Brian slid in backwards.

"What'd you find?" he said.

"*Germania Obscura*," Andrew read aloud, *"An occult perspective on the land, rivers, and sky between the Vistula and Rhine.* His undergrad class last year."

"So?"

"On a scale of Maria von Trapp to Hitler, that's at least...an Indiana Jones villain. He also has–"

Andrew clicked through to another page. Brian eyed the lounge from the foot of the table.

"– a forum for grad students called *The Hedonisticum?* It's very...so I guess it's like a special program they apply for? But it's part of the Greek life, too? I don't know, fucking look."

Andrew held up his phone. A group of perhaps 50 robed students stood in front of an imposing stone archway, everyone wearing oversized papier-mâché dog heads, save for the familiar barrel-chested figure at center, who wore a big cat head instead. Only three breeds were represented among the student pooches: rottweiler, poodle, and schnauzer.

"Maybe it's a drama club?" Brian offered, then before Andrew could rebut, *"OK,* it's clearly fucked."

"Yes. Even for a drama club, which it clearly isn't."

Bri slid two fingers down the grain as he backed to the head of the table. Out in the hall, Ursula gave a deeper *woof* and lowered to her chest, rump wriggling high. She growled up at the loungeside stairs.

"Is she OK?" said Andrew, and he started to look back. Little Äther howled.

"It's the snow," Brian said, keeping his voice low, "It bugs her out. Keep reading."

"Well, he's an alum," Andrew scrolled, stroking the pup-baby, "So was his dad—or maybe that's granddad? *'Proud to be the original Moya Moths.'* Wait, what's *her* name?"

"Mallory," Brian murmured, almost back to his seat, "Mallory Dahlhaus." He reached behind for a last foothold, just as a bloated leg appeared from the dark of the second floor landing, Its dripping foot hovering backward into space. Ursula dropped her belly to the checkerboard tiles with a whimper.

"That's such a mean girl name."

"...*right?*"

Andrew glanced up. His nostrils flared.

"Oh my god, can you sit?" he said, like he'd scold a rowdy bachelorette party, mid-number, "You're making me nervous."

Brian nodded and gripped the table, staring to the middle distance to keep *das Gegenteil* in his periphery as It, too, lowered to a squat on the third step down, with cracked heels overhanging the bullnoses, and tumid thighs impossibly suspended over the drop of stairs below. Its wide ass hung midair like an indoor moon, torso cut off at the shoulders, Its head still a floor above. Bri's butt hit the seat.

"*Thank* you," said Andrew, then he raised his wine vase, brows drawn tight, "OK, cheers so you can eat and be normal, please." He took a hefty gulp, then speared a bite of tuna steak, eyes drifting back to his phone. Äther watched the fish fly past, drooling.

Brian cheers'd but didn't drink. He grabbed fork and knife with shaky hands. The room spun. He tried bending his head to the lemon potatoes on his fork, to see if he could spot the demon's face doing the same, then the tines scraped along the dental aligner he'd forgotten to take out. He pawed around to loosen it. *Das Gegenteil* lifted an arm to Its unseen head, two rooms away. Its hand retracted as Brian's did, pulling with it thick strands of mucus, the bubbles catching a glint off the lounge lamplight.

Brian dropped the braces beside his plate.

"*Holy shit!*" Andrew shrieked, at his phone, "Brian, she's Mass Extinction Mallory!"

He flipped his screen around, then stood in his seat when Brian squinted over at it, letting the puppy jump down, leaning his torso way out across the mahogany grain. The video playing showed a crowd of lookie-loos gathering around some spectacle at a familiar park, the fashion skewing summery.

"Is that Rittenhouse?"

"Here," said Andrew, and though Brian and the demon half-stood, he beat them to it, rounding the foot of the table, shepherding the phone to Brian's seat. He leaned over to share the screen, his body only slightly angled away from the hall, and the lounge and its stairs and demon just beyond.

In the clip, the cameraperson broke through the throng, and there sat Mallory behind a folding table topped in gingham cloth, her champagne mass in a tidy bun. She sported cat-eye glasses and diamond earrings and a bit of pink chiffon tied round her throat, and not much else, for she sat there topless in a nylon camping chair. A flowery banner flapping under the table read *RSVP for Mass Extinction* in inviting script.

"She's bonkers, you have to watch," said Andrew, "I'm obsessed."

"*Next cutie, please!*" chirped Mallory, and a young woman stepped up to the table.

"*Hi, I'm Beth,*" said the newest devotee, "*I love your glasses. And your tits.*"

"*Thanks, Beth,*" Mallory said, scribbling with a feather quill upon a parchment scroll bound in blackwood finials, "*What misery can I put you down for?*"

"*Um, heat stroke?*" said Beth, a little sheepish, "*But also, could I sign my ex up, too? I hate her so much.*"

"*Babe,*" Mallory tutted, and her glasses slid down her nose, "*Of course. What's her name, she's a goner.*"

"*Allison,*" Beth exalted.

"She was all over the city last summer," Andrew chipped in, "Nicki and I tried to find her one weekend but we got there too late."

"*Beth & Allison,*" sang Mallory, swishing her quill across the scroll, "*I have you down for next summer. It'll be agony, sweets.*"

Andrew took his phone back. He scrolled the video with his finger.

"Sometimes she gives out flowers or hash lollipops. She switches up the hair and mug, but it's girls out, always."

Brian stuffed his face. The demon fed itself air.

"This explains so much," Andrew went on, and his face lit up at the screen, scrubbing through, "They're *performance artists*, Brian! *Very* drag-adjacent. Everything's a grift under the glitter."

"Campbell's a professor, though," Bri garbled, through tuna and potatoes.

"Yeah, but Moyamensing's just Trump University for fantasy dorks," Andrew ragged, "My *not*-brother-in-law thinks he's a druid necromancer or some shit because he took on $100k in student loans. *Oh, this part!*" He flipped the phone back around so Brian could watch.

"*I hope you're signing yourself up, too!*" spat an older gal in cycling gear, as she passed the Mass Extinction table. The crowd broke into jeers.

"*What's that, gorgeous?*" Mallory called out, vocal fry frizzing through the boos.

"*I said you're Sodom and Gomorrah on the streets of Philadelphia,*" said the older lady, with her whole chest, and she stabbed a bony finger at all assembled, "*Shame on you all. What if a child saw this?*"

"*They'd see the naked truth, hun!*" Mallory cried, rocks glinting at her ears, areolas wobbling with every breath of fresh air, and the crowd quieted as a monstrous grin overtook her features, "*Children are doomed, too!*"

The old gal reared back and spat on the sidewalk.

"*Not mine,*" declared the cyclist, "*Not my grandchildren.*"

"*Then may they live,*" said Mallory, shedding all trace of delight in an instant, and she leaned way forward so her body disappeared behind her clawing fingers, the jut of her chin, "*May they live longer than anyone alive, and may they witness all that is to come.*"

Cycling Granny shuddered. She held Mallory's gaze too long, stuck, lip quivering, then finally she broke off and backed away from the crowd.

"*Whore,*" she whispered, then she was gone.

"*Love your helmet!*" came Mallory's zinger, then a chorus of cheers as Andrew took his phone back.

"Honestly, she's a Philly climate activist legend," he said, sliding his phone in his pocket, "And public nudity is legal, so unless she's being lewd and lascivious, cops can't do anything. She has a whole subreddit, Bri, how have you not heard of her?"

Brian shrugged. *Das Gegenteil's* back fat slid past its shoulder blades. Out the front windows, snow fell over all.

"I wonder if you're *part* of something," Andrew mulled, and he really studied Brian, and the mantel backdrop, searching for some connection in the interior design, the centerpiece painting, "Maybe it's a social experiment."

"*It—it's just—dogsitting,*" Brian whisper-sputtered, playing up having a mouth too full of tuna, "*Slash catsitting.*"

"Hm," said Andrew, unconvinced, and his gaze started to run down the table, "Where's Baby Spice?"

"Hey!" said Brian, a little loud.     "Hey!" gurgled *das Gegenteil*, a little loud.

"What was that?" said Andrew, and thank fuck, his head swiveled first toward the kitchen portal. Brian dove across the table and caught him by the hand. Miss Thing flinched, but she didn't pull away.

*"Wine,"* Bri rasped, barely audible, *"Grab it from the fridge? I gotta pee."*

Andrew nodded, taken aback. The skin on the stairs stood as Brian did, then he just managed to get It up past the second floor landing by the time Ms. Stankface turned to watch him go.

"Riesling for dessert," Brian announced, and he leaned way back on his stool to reach the fridge door, nearly toppling, held aloft only by the edge of the marble island.

"I shouldn't encourage you," Andrew groaned, his shoulders slooped from wine and weed, yet he clapped with excitement when the new bottle appeared.

"Cookie dough or mint chocky chip?" Brian inquired, leaning even further back to grasp the freezer drawer, "We gots options here."

"Cookie, obviously," said Andrew, with a yawn.

*"NO FUCKING YAWNING!"* Brian roared, and he managed a trembling crunch to rise back up with the ice cream, blood rushing from his head, "We got *miiiles* to go before we sleep."

"I fucking *travelled* miles, on a train, in a *snowstorm*, to come see you," said Andrew, his jaw dropping at the very thought, "That's how much I fucking love you."

Brian gave a bitty pornographic moan in thanks. He fetched two spoons and they flipped the lids on their respective pints.

"What were you doing upstairs earlier?" Andrew asked, after a few bites, "You took forever."

Brian swallowed.

"Leaving a trail of roses and condoms to our bed," he said, "I'm so pumped to lose my virginity to you."

"Seriously," said Andrew, cookie dough on his tongue, "You sounded like you were running laps."

"Just poopin," Bri lied, with a big shrug. He flipped the spoon in his mouth so he could lick inside the curve. Little Äther whined in the puppy pen, jumping over her siblings to launch herself at the fencing, fixated on Andrew. Maxcat licked himself on the kitchen stairs, occasionally looking up to the floors above.

Outside, wind picked up with a rattling screech, shaking the black walnut to shivers under the security lights, its branches naked out there in the torrent of snow. For half a second, the *DAS NEST* lights dimmed; almost flickered. Brian's pulse spiked and cooled.

"I can't anymore," Andrew gurgled, his face sour, but still he packed cookie dough in his cheeks, choking it down, "I'm gonna be sick."

"Pussy," said Brian, a half-pint down already.

"And we shouldn't open that." Andrew stuck his chin at the bottle of Riesling.

"K, we'll save it for breakfast."

They dropped their ice creams back in the freezer, spoons and all, then Andrew yoinked a hopping Äther from the pen. And since Brian had already taken a mad *toilette* to drive the distended skin upstairs and into a course-reversing loop of the second and third floors, he just crossed fingers that It crested the kitchen stairs ahead of them, and would be partway down the loungeside stairs by the time Andrew followed him up.

After taking turns in the guest bath, to pee and brush their teeth, they retired to Brian's room. And even though they had seen each nudie before, they still went back to back to strip to undies. Äther ran back and forth between them, sneezing from excitement. Andrew climbed under the blankets first, then Brian threw the puppy on the comforter, scooting in after her. The guys piled their feet together, toes positively icy.

"Don't fall asleep."

"I won't," Andrew fibbed, then he wormed an arm under, his head at Brian's shoulder, their silver-beige baby in the crevice between them. The wind whipped at the house again and again, but *DAS NEST* was stalwart in the storm. For long moments, Brian forgot about the gig, and the whole world was just the cocoon under the covers. Their feet thawed.

"Thanks for coming all the way out here," Brian said, more sincerely than he meant to.

"Duh."

"I don't even know how I wound up—I mean, I know *how*, but."

"Life works in mysterious ways," Andrew muttered, "Well, yours does. You don't really fail *upwards,* but more..." He screwed up his face, one eye closing. Brian turned so he could get him in knee lock, their legs intertwining.

*"What?"*

"...4th-dimensionally."

"Fuck off."

"Really, though," Andrew persisted, "You're such a glutton for it. Remember those first dresses you made? Wildly, deeply offensive to anyone who understands hems or even basic proportions. I still can't forgive myself for wearing the orange tie-dye...empire...frock...catastrophe. But you have just no dignity, so you kept sketching them, and I kept letting you humiliate me in public–"

"Wow, say how you really feel."

"And when you birthed the *single* stupidest garment of all time–"

"Surely you can't mean dungarees ball gown."

"–and I wore that nuclear garbage like it was McQueen, all your bad dresses turned retroactively fierce. And you still don't know anything about fashion, but suddenly, all these drag queens think you're partly hot shit. And I have to claim you like you're something I can't afford to lose. *No offense.*"

"No," said Brian, giant grin unfolding, "None taken. I like drunk Yoon."

"Your failure time travels, bitch," Andrew hyped, getting on a roll, "It bangs its own grandfather and births itself, and somehow doesn't even fuck up the time-space continuum...thing. In all times, in all places, there you are, being a disaster and getting lollipops for it."

"This is so mean, I'm obsessed."

"Most broke-ass person I know, all cozy in a fucking mansion. I mean, you're the only person I know ever talked his way out of a psych ward."

The wind moaned.

"Sorry," said Andrew, and he reached over Äther to put a hand to Brian's chest, "I'm drunk, that was–"

"No."

*"Really, I–"*

*"It's fine!"* Brian squealed, higher than intended, "I'm just...pissed about the 35 hours it took to do it. Four meals. One sleep. I could've done a lot with those 35 hours."

"...solved world hunger?"

"Yeah," Brian chuckled, face frozen, "Learned a viral dance, I probably could've learned a viral dance."

"Done your taxes."

"Maybe," he said, "Maybe I could've."

Andrew drew two fingers through Brian's beard.

"You really are getting good at making my dresses," he said, eyes shining in the lamplight, "So you can't kill yourself till I have a full closet."

"Deal."

They dozed off watching the puppy.

He woke to a heavy blanket of silence.

Snow piled so high on the window, he wondered for a sec if the whole house had been buried under a drift, up to the third floor. Dawn had yet to break. A hypnotic, spruce-blue light turned the furniture, the lamp, Brian's own two hands to featureless silhouettes. He spread fingers wide, searching his palms for creases, his thumb pads for prints. Little Äther must have hopped down in the night for a pee; he detected an ammonia tang in the room. Then, unable to jump back up on the bed, she had apparently persevered in scaling the rocking chair in the corner. Her tiny outline swelled and shrunk on its cushioned seat.

Andrew slept facing Brian. The quick bun he'd gathered the night before remained bound in its band. His breath came low and hot against Brian's shoulder. Their legs hadn't untwined. That face stirred.

"Hi," he whispered.

"Hi," Brian whispered back.

Andrew lifted his head a little to look out the window.

"Did we get buried?"

"I thought the same thing."

"That was maybe the best sleep of my life," Andrew whispered, "Not the bed. It's the air or something."

"I know."

"I feel like we climbed a mountain. Alpine air."

Brian giggled.

"OK, Heidi," he said.

"Where's Emma Bunton?" Andrew looked under the blanket.

"She's over there," Brian whispered, grabbing his friend's hand so he could point it puppyward in the blue dark, "I think she peed in the corner." He didn't let go. Andrew dropped his arm to Brian's chest, then he wormed a little closer.

"I forgot how much I like sleeping with you," he said, "You're a pizza oven."

"Stop, I'm already hungry."

"Pizza oven on a snow day," Andrew whispered, and his lips were at Brian's neck, "Don't get up."

The kiss had all but happened, though it had not quite happened. Andrew waited, eyes closed. His hips scooped in and out. Brian turned to face him, knowing as he did, the demon down the hall turned to Its own unseen bedmate.

"Andrew," he tried, even as they ground their bulges together, *"You should probably*...I don't want to ruin it."

"You won't," Andrew whispered, "We never have before."

Brian quit humping and took his bud's face in hands. A sudden haze refracted through the frosted double-pane so the room blushed to the darkest of pinks, like sun shining through the meat of an earlobe. Andrew gazed at him, defenseless.

"I'm a nightshade," Brian said, meaning it.

Andrew pulled him even closer; rubbed all over his back.

"So?" he said, "Tomatoes are nightshades. And eggplants."

Before long, they'd kicked their undies to the floor.

They showered with the lights off, still on a cozy high, so Brian didn't realize until he opened the guest bath door and went to flip the switch in the hall.

"Oh," he said, "The power's out."

Andrew looked through the mirror, brushing his tongue. His hair hung past his shoulders, still dripping.

"Balls," he said, "Do you think the trains are running?"

"*Uhh,* maybe?" Brian came to leaning in the doorway. He toweled off, one eye on the stairs.

"You look good a little heavier," said Andrew, "You carry it well."

"Aw, thanks for the bulimia."

Andrew spat, then reached for the mouthwash. The case for the new dental aligners sat empty on the sink counter, beside Bri's electric clippers.

"Where are your braces, buster!?" Andrew snapped, like an angry mom, "You're supposed to sleep in them, aren't you?"

"I took them out to kiss a boy," Brian whined, "It was one night."

Andrew swished and gargled, one brow arched. Little Äther tottered out from the guest room, stretching her back legs behind. She sniffed Brian's foot, then went scenting down the hall, to the top of the lounge stairs. There she sat, right at the edge, cocking her head at what she saw below.

"I have a gig tonight," said Andrew, after another spit, "I can't stay all day."

"What are you wearing?"

"This, like, iridescent cinch number."

Brian nodded.

"Not the new one?" he ventured.

"I'm playing a pearl necklace," Andrew said, "It's for a skit."

"Like cum or like oysters?"

"The joke works both ways."

"Right."

"Relax," said Andrew, flipping around to pull him into a naked hug, "We can still have breakfast."

They kissed, quick and close-mouthed, then Andrew slapped him on the ass and scooted past to the towel rack, where he gathered his hair into a fresh and fluffy wrap.

"I would have made you something pearly," said Bri.

"I know," said Andrew, twisting the towel to a turban, "Come on, let's see how much it snowed."

Only Ursula's apricot poofs could be seen cresting the field of white out back, as she tunneled across the back patio. They had let her out off-leash, because where the hell was she gonna go? The snow came up past the guys' knees, tall as they were. Äther panted in Andrew's arms from the sensory overload. Brian stepped out with a couple of Rieslings in fresh vases, his puff jacket zipped high.

"You weren't here for '96," he said, "Right?"

"Naw, we were still in Vancouver."

"That was over two feet," said Brian, "I made an ice lair for my action figures. Blasted Celine on the boombox."

"Werk, baby Bri," said Andrew, and he let Äther sniff the wine, "Oh, look at her *corsaaage.*" Brian looked down, to where Andrew pointed out the withered boutonnière pinned at his breast. The belladonna still circled a berry, long since pruned. The henbane had taken on a moldy, blue-copper sheen. A bit of down feather poked out of his jacket where the bloodstone pin stabbed through.

"You like my medal of honor?" he said.

"Yeah. Baldest Under 40?"

"Worst Seamstress," Brian grinned, "It's just a bronze, but I'm gonna ruin your career, so cross fingers for gold."

"Did you look up trains?"

"No," said Brian, "Lemme do it now."

The SEPTA site took forever on the scant cell service at *DAS NEST.* An official weather statement on the front page cut off midtext as those little bars faded in and out.

*Due to inclement weather, all Regional Rail trains will operate on a SUNDAY schedule, today,*

Brian read, "Then today's date,"

*Please note that ongoing operation may be affected by wind gusts and snow on the tracks. Shuttle service–*

"Then it cuts off. My reception isn't–"

*"Do you see that?"*

Andrew had swiveled round at the hips. He squinted through the window set in the kitchen door, unable to shade his eyes from morning glare with his hands full of puppy and drink. Brian turned to look through the big window behind him. He raised a hand over his eyes.

Inside, another Andrew rounded the marble island, the backs of Its bare thighs dimpling under each biteable butt cheek, Its hair unbound but knotted up in matted snarls. Breaking off towards the dining room portal, Its pupils scanned without purchase in a gaze unreachable. One hand snatched at the door frame to rocket Itself around the corner and out of sight.

"I thought –" Andrew started, leaning over to the door, having lost sight from his angle, "It's so bright."

"Are...*uhh, yeah,*" Brian managed, for his mouth had gone dry in an instant, "Are you sure it wasn't your reflection?" Andrew floundered for words, then looked behind him, as if Brian was right and what he'd glimpsed inside lurked outdoors instead.

"That was *so* weird," he declared, over mirthless chuckles, "I thought – *Brian,* it looked like..."

"Gimme that," Brian said, and not unkindly, he snatched Andrew's vase, to pour some wine into his own, "I'm the lush, I should be the one seeing things. Stay here, I gotta make a phone call."

"Are you *outside* the house?" asked Mallory, and Brian shot a quick wave down the walk to Andrew and the pup. Äther stood before the sheer wall that had formed by the grill, biting at the snow for all she was worth.

"Yup!" Bri grinned, playing up an ease he didn't feel. He couldn't help but pace from end to end of the *porte-cochere*, in the covered bare gully splitting the drive to snowbanks, phone glued to his ear.

"Well, It's not going to just stay frozen wherever you *left* It, Bri," Mallory chided, and he could make out gulls screaming, the roar of surf behind her vocal frizz, "My demon is at least six centuries old, It won't be cooped up like a sick parrot."

"*S-so* you're saying we're all good," he pepped, shivering all over, "And everything'll just be normal again when we–when I go inside? Because I *k-kinda* got off-loop a little, maybe, so I was wondering if you thought–"

"Brian."

"Uh-huh."

"When I drew your blood and invoked the binding spell, I gave you dominion over our property."

"Right."

"So if you don't feel comfy enough...if our home isn't up to your standards, why don't you light a match and burn the whole place to the ground?"

*"Mallory–"*

"I mean it. Put the puppies in their pen and make sure you shut Ursula and Max in a guest room so no one can hear her barking out on the street. And then just get the hell out of there, Brian. Don't worry about the paintings or Campbell's baby blanket or my research. Here's what you do: there's paint thinner in the garage, so just grab one of the nice green hand towels and soak it through, then lay it out on the dining room table."

"No, Mallory, I'm–"

"And there's some of those long fireplace matches in the credenza. But keep your distance, because when I tell you paint thinner is extremely flammable, Brian: *woah*. It will go up *fast*."

"I'm not gonna–"

"And the neighbors will be watching, they always are. Sloane and Rusty, they're on the left if you're facing the cul-de-sac. They keep their greenhouse windows unlocked. He has cancer, it won't be much of a fight, but you'll have to catch her by surprise, she's wiry. Why don't you take Campbell's Yanagiba? It's the long skinning knife on the wall. And there are gardening gloves in the drawer by the pantry."

"I'm not burning down the house, Mallory."

Andrew perked up down the walk. He squatted beside the puppy and rubbed snow from her cheeks, watching Brian all the while.

"Oh, you *won't?*" came her voice, too genuine to be sincere, "You mean you'll *stay?*"

"Yes, of course," Brian said, through his teeth.

"Even though you have to do poops and mail and deter burglars with your general fucking presence?"

"Yes."

*"Wow,* Bri," said Mallory, "You sure are a lifesaver."

*Click.*

"Everything OK?" Andrew asked, after Brian had jumped the drift to the back walk. Äther shook off a tinkle. Ursula panted, dog-grinning, absolutely plastered in snow.

"Good news," said Bri, "She said we can use the fireplace."

The logs lived in a hatch just to the side of *DAS NEST,* if one followed the lounge windows, so Brian was able to haul in a good dozen and still keep an eye on Andrew inside as he constructed their pillow fort. The morning sun had quickly given way to a bone gray phalanx of clouds from the west which foretold some precipitation yet to fall. Restless winds sent whorls spinning out over the cul-de-sac, which had accumulated so much snow already, no visible border stood between grass and asphalt, across the whole, wide Circle. Brian could barely feel his nose by the time he fetched the last log and deadbolted the great oak-and-iron door. He dropped his load on the woodpile by the hearth, then sat heavily to unlace his boots.

"Did she say we can use *that?*" Andrew asked, and he pointed at the swivel crane to the side of the firebox, "We could hang a kettle."

"Sure," said Brian, out of breath, "We can make hot toddies."

"And where does *that* go?" Andrew nodded to the blue door under the lounge stairs.

"The basement. It's always locked."

"Try the lights again."

"They won't be on."

"Just try, please."

Brian sighed. He kicked off his boots, then reached for the lamp on the end table. He clicked it over four times.

"See?"

"I can't miss this gig," Andrew fretted, as he gabled the fort roof with throw pillows, "Miss Monica's supposed to tape my number for me."

"I don't know what to tell you. You knew it was gonna snow."

Andrew stared him down; Brian broke first.

"I'll get the kettle," said Bri.

Maxcat proved the most difficult to dress, even in just a pillowcase sarong. He bit and clawed and kicked with his back legs, but never bolted from the love nest by the fire, his blue rump swaying high, pupils huge. The puppers rolled about, chewing at their couture: rubber bands and pot holders, socks and armrest covers.

Andrew had Wasser on his hind legs for the crowd.

"From the Haus of Puppy Apocalypse," he emcee'd, shimmying the snooch from side to side. Wasser's high-back aluminum foil collar glinted scandalously in the firelight.

"Beyond *Beyond Thunderdome*," Brian golf-clapped. He reached for his hot toddy and washed down the Xanny he'd palmed, when he went to pee.

"She's a housepet by day, alien hooker by night."

"But is she *funny?*"

They waited for Wasser to contribute; to land a joke.

"Pageant queens," Andrew cringed.

Ursula snored, curled up in a ball, closest to the flames. They'd balanced a periwinkle beret from the hall closet atop her flop o' frizz. Logs crackled. Outside, that deadbolt sky emitted a near-constant flurry, the winds having let up some. Everything beyond the fire fort seemed rather frigid by comparison; gloomy, even. A break in the pillows by Brian's head showed a slit view of the hall and the dining room beyond, all of it untouched by hearth's glow. He checked the vista periodically for shadows, for skins.

"Next, the Haus of It's-Real-Human-Hair!" Andrew announced, holding Äther almost to his cheek, with a pinch of his own locks seeming to spill from her head, so she was a raven-haired Rapunzel.

"Stop, where's my phone," said Brian. He pawed through the booze and cheese and crackers until finding it right in his hoodie pocket. He snapped a pic while Äther squirmed, then she made a great escape.

"Isn't she luscious?" Andrew said, stroking out his mane, "I just want to whip everything."

"My jealousy *seriously* knows no bounds."

"Shut up," Andrew laughed, "Your beard is a moment. Very fat Thor."

"Cunt," Brian tsked, then he wrinkled his nose, "I look like my dad."

"You always say you don't really remember him," said Andrew, brushing hair behind his ear.

"Well, from pictures."

Andrew crawled into the fort. He plopped at Bri's side.

"If it makes you feel better," he said, "I have my mom's resting disappointed face."

"Do you not look like your dad at all?"

"Maybe...if I wore '90s short-shorts and got one of his kitchen counter buzzcuts. He could never with all this." Andrew flipped his part like a shampoo commercial.

"Well, to dead dads!" Brian cheers'd, raising the last bit of toddy, "May they never haunt us when we're homosexually indisposed."

"Or shoplifting underwear."

"That, too."

Old school Carly Rae blared from phone speakers, amplified in the bottom of a pedestal jar. They'd stacked their plates by the fire poker. Brian sucked at the bong. The puppy party snoozed in the back of the fort. Andrew spooned with Ursula on the warm bricks, his face lit up in neon pinks and greens off his phone. With a huff, he sent the screen to sleep.

"No luck?"

"Rides are still over $80 to the city," said Andrew, batting poodle hair out of his mouth, "No trains. And I'm at 14%."

"Maybe call the club?" Brian offered, through smoke, "Bet everyone else is snowed in, too."

"I already texted," said Ms. Exasperation, "They know I'm trying to get there."

"Maybe Jess can help? Does she have all-wheel on the minivan?"

Andrew just lay there.

"She could pile the kids in, make a trip of it."

"I'm not burdening my sister," Andrew sighed.

The Jepsen tunes cut out for a call from *Littledick Prickfuckington.*

"You need to take that?"

"Landlord, it'll go to voicemail," said Brian, sliding the bong over, "It's by your head. I gotta pee."

No discernible sunset had taken place, and the logs burned low, so upon standing, Brian could make out next to nothing in the dark house.

Out front, a distant flutter of flakes in the lone streetlamp on Hemlock Way made for the only true north. He groped along the edge of the fort, sending its walls to a wobble, before trekking out into the black beyond. His eyes failed to adjust at a speed to inspire confidence.

"Take your phone," Andrew called after him, "For the light."

"Yeah, but it's playing DJ," Brian husked, "I'll be fine. Put another couple logs on."

He stumbled past the floor-to-ceiling carved pillars where the lounge ended and the hall began. Once his feet stood upon checkerboard stone, he found he could picture the path ahead a bit better. He went ahead with arms outstretched, a little faster, then slowed again once he'd shuffled over the hardwood lip of the dining room. Two steps in, and he bashed straight into an unforeseen obstacle, nearly toppling at the waist over a dining room chairback. Its legs squealed on the floor as he righted himself.

"You OK?" Andrew called.

"Yeah," he called back, "I walked into a chair."

He reached for the mahogany table and found it was further than expected. He had to lean over to grip the edge; further inspection revealed the chair had been moved from the spot beside the head. A seat not filled at dinner, nor in the hours since. Suppressing shivers, Brian pushed it back under the table, then struck out for what he hoped was the kitchen portal. Hugging the wall within, he trailed one hand along cabinet and counter until he'd traced his way around to the stairs.

"Hey," he whispered up the well, "You up there?"

He waited a moment for It to answer, for Andrew to overhear. Nothing.

"I'm coming up."

He went crawling up to the landing, where he reached, fumbling, for the doorknob, his eyes having resolved somewhat to nightvision. An outline swung open before him to reveal the murky passage beyond, and the faintest frame of a closed door at its end, with no demon to be found in the umbra therein.

"I know you're there," he hissed, then he took a step back to look up to the third floor, "Stop hiding."

Nothing stirred; not even the cat.

Brian waited another tick, then he gripped the wall and bent to all fours again, to crawl up to the next landing. He stopped just before the top, poking his head up enough to catch a view of the empty third floor.

"This isn't fair," he said, "Answer me."

He had just turned round to his bottom and hoisted himself up by the baluster when

"Hey," It answered,

in a voice too deep,
too familiar,
from the bottom of the stairs he'd just climbed,

"You up there?"

A reflexive crunch hardened to a cramp deep in Brian's gut, almost to his groin, so he froze there on the steps, head thrust clean over the railing. He shook from the sudden flex. His lips trembled in the dark.

And for a brief and hopeful moment, he really thought he might've imagined it.

"I'm coming up."

He'd never opened his eyes so wide, staring down to where the stairs did a 180° past the second floor landing. And yes—*no, God, no!*—out from the depths crawled the newest skin, Its balding head craned to look up the stairwell, neck fat folding in back, Its beard trimmed and straight like Brian's, but fully white, Its body aging but strong. Clear blue eyes he had not seen since boyhood stared unblinking up, up, up.

He could not give voice to Its name.

"*D–*" he choked, sinuses clogged at once, tears falling down the well-hole, "*D–Da–*"

"I know you're there,"

the big guy seethed,

"Stop hiding."

Brian bolted, limbs noodly. Palms too sweaty to grab the railing, heels slipping two steps at a time...yet somehow his caveman brain took over, and from the panic he rose, upright and scrambling. Up on the third floor, he bounced between the walls, jelly-legged. Careening past the first guest room, his ankles crossed and he face-planted by the bathroom.

"This isn't fair,"

came the unbearable voice,
too triggering,
too nice,
too mean,

"Answer me."

Without looking down, Brian knew he'd skinned a knee, straight through his PJ pants. A throbbing set in, and a trickle rolled down his shin as he stood, that leg already shaking too hard to put his full weight on it. Backing down the hall, Brian waved a hand behind for the railing he knew would be on his right, atop the loungeside stairs. He turned to limp down the first few steps, then squinted back down the hall.

Dad stood atop the far stairs, the whites of Its eyes burning in the dark, Its form like Brian's but older; long-gone.

*"Hi, Bri."*

A guttural moan ruptured from deep in Brian's chest. He went pounding down, down, down.

*"Nooo,* you scared the dogs!" Andrew cried, as Brian appeared back in the lounge, almost tripping again at the final stretch. The sound of puppy nails receded in the distance, as they scampered off to the hall and beyond. Ursula seized at the racket, pulled from her big snooze by the fire. Her snoot swung wildly round the room, pumped for danger, and from the depths of her chest a bestial *woof* burst again and again. She pushed herself to standing, assuming guard stance, legs splayed, each booming bark starting down below her ribs, rising in pitch and frequency.

Andrew and Brian clapped hands over ears. Someone went backing into a sofa cushion, sending the fort into a slow topple, its sweet gabled roof last to fall. Something—likely the vodka, hopefully not the bong—smacked the hardwood with a glass jangle. And perhaps fed by the chaos, a searing, undulating plume of flame erupted in the fireplace, reaching suddenly into the room, then the witchfire disappeared in a flash. A downdraft from the flue followed, blasting Andrew's hair from his face, Ursula's floomp to one side. The fire sputtered. Smoke streamed into the room.

"Jesus *Christ!*" Andrew squawked, spitting soot, "What do we *do?*"

*"Andrew,"* Brian sobbed, "Andrew, we have to...*um,* we have to –"

Yet before he could finish the thought: *click.* Every light in *DAS NEST* flicked on at once. Shadows scattered. Smoke from the fire still streamed forth, but collected above the fireplace, dissipating quickly along the ceiling. The flames steadied. The boys panted. Brian wiped tears from his nose, his beard.

"Well, hallelujah," said Andrew, then he really took Brian in, "Babe, *what happened?"*

Brian crumpled. Andrew rushed to his side.

"I scared myself!" Bri bawled, "I just scared myself. *He* – I think it was the cat, he—*he – I'm fine!"*

The puppies crept back in from the hall, giving sniff-overs as they drew near, all hyped from the histrionics. Mama Pood swept her gaze from the lounge stairs to the hall, and back again, still expecting threats from any which way.

"You should charge your phone," Brian snuffed, *"An-and* check the trains."

"I'm not going *now*, dummy."

Andrew rubbed his back. Brian shrugged him off.

"I'm just wasted," he laughed, through the tears, "Fuck, how do you stand me?"

He crawled to the remains of the pillow fort and dug out the bong, which rather miraculously had not toppled. Fishing the lighter from his hoodie pocket, he knelt there in the wreckage and held the flame to the bowl, but it cashed through, the ash befouling the clear water below.

"I'll pack another."

"I'm good," said Andrew.

"I didn't want to tell you like this."

*"When?"*

"They want me to start in May," said Andrew, and he reached for his vase of water on the nightstand, "To get ready for summer drag brunch."

*"When did they ask,"* Brian clarified, his voice hoarse. He sat at the foot of the bed, in peacock-print boxer briefs, doubled over so his nipples rested atop his belly, elbows on knees. He already had a migraine brewing,

and he gripped himself along the wide circumference of his skull as though hefting an unwieldy water balloon.

"September."

*"Right.* And I had those dresses to make, so."

"No."

"Well," said Bri, "You got your dresses."

"I still want you to make my dresses," said Andrew, arms crossed over the giant Rue McClanahan on his sleeping shirt, "Why can't you do it in San Francisco?"

*"Because I*...you don't get to move across the country and then tug on my leash."

Andrew kicked him; not too hard, but still.

"Bitch, it's California. It's an energy makeover. Are you really trying to stay in Philly forever?"

"If I do, that's my decision," said Brian, "Not yours."

Andrew chugged his water, then set the vase back on the table. He scrubbed at his face.

"Fine," he said, and he had never looked so tired, not after all-nighters in heels, "You're right. I should have told you. *I love you.* And you have an open invitation, so I hope you come, if only to visit."

"I'd really love that," said Brian, and if he didn't mean it—if Andrew didn't believe him—he didn't fucking care. He climbed over his friend's legs and crawled under the comforter. His stomach roiled.

Outside, the snow had finally stopped. A perfect sickle hung in the clear black sky.

"Is that all we want to say about it?" Andrew asked, after clicking the lamp off.

"Don't let them bill you as a K-pop Kween, with a K-W. You'll never live it down."

They fell asleep on their own sides of the bed.

"Brian," Andrew whispered, "Do you want water?"

*"Huh."*

"Do you want water?" Andrew said again, louder, "You're burning up."

"Yeah," Bri rasped, and he cracked an eye to see Andrew sneak out the guest door, both water vases in hand. The hem of his oversized tee fell almost to his knees. The thought arose that Brian, too, should get up; that he should be a shepherd in the night. Then he recalled San Francisco, and the phrase "energy makeover," and the pull of rage kept him vacillating until he'd drifted off again.

In the dream, he'd cornered the lamb in Mallory's kitchen, at the inner angle of counter where the dishwasher cozied up to the drawers of hand towels. The little sweetling pressed itself to the cherrywood, absolutely petrified. It tried to leap to the marble above, but fell back, clumsy-hoofed. Brian spread his arms wide, bending at the knees in a show of trust; of quiet dominance. The iron hand-shears dangled from his fingers, the tips of their twin blades swinging gently from side to side.

Little lamby snorted, gasping for air, but as he approached, its breath slowed and its eyes softened. It lowered itself to its belly, bent at the forelegs, tail tucked.

"*My son,*" Brian crooned, advancing with the shears, "My champion boy."

Haltingly, he reached for its pulsating nose, then slid the backs of his fingers up its snout and along its cranium, down to the curls of its neck and back. Then, cupping a palm under its chin, he raised its eyes to meet his own.

"Stay still for Daddy."

With a merciless hand, he flipped the stripling beneath him, then pinned its hip under his knee so he could throw his other foot over its legs. Working the shears under the wool, he started snipping at its chest, unzipping the long coat, freeing the wool so it peeled off in a long strip.

"You're gonna be a quarterback," Brian exalted, "You're gonna give me so many grandbabies."

*Snip-snip* went the shears, revealing the pale skin beneath, that form unencumbered. And if a dotted line of blood welled up along the shearing path, *well,* only the very closest shave would do.

"*Baaaaaaa,*" cried the lambling.

"No one'll pick on you anymore," said Brian, "When those other boys see you coming, they'll run."

*"Braaaaaa."*

He carved down its belly, then sliced along the lamb's hip, freeing the coat along its ribs. Then, raising his knee, he swung its leg back apace and pinned its skull between his thighs before it could run off. Brian started in again down near the tail.

"Hold still," he grunted, squeezing his knees together, "Let's get this part in one go."

He tried to wriggle in time with the beast to keep the line straight, but still his hand wavered back and forth so a serpentine rip ran up its back, over the knot at the base of its neck, and through the thick ringlets atop its crown. A score of nicks and gashes sprang red in his wake, soaking into the fleece.

*"Briaaaaa."*

"You're gonna be more than I ever was," said Brian, who did not feel like himself, "Better than I ever could be." He clamped a hand round the lamb's snout, pinioning its jaw together. It twisted under the vise.

*"Briaaaan,"* cried a voice that was not the lamb's, *"Briaaaan!"*

Brian snipped the shears together—*chop-chop!* – right next to the beast's eyes, just to scare it still.

*"You..."* he muttered, as he slashed up the side of its neck, under its ear, over its eye, *"...are my every dream...come to life..."* Unbending with a satisfied, falsetto *whooo!,* he gave a swivel left and right for his cramping back, then gazed down at his handiwork. The shears dripped a puddle.

*"BRIAAAAN,"* Andrew bellowed.

Brian gasped. He stood in the dark house, on the dark stairs, by the round window, with only the sickle moon through the mullions for light. In one fist, he gripped his own electric clippers from the guest bath. He turned to track its cord back up the stairs behind him, where it followed the bend up to the third floor. He held out both arms; flipped his hands over and back as if expecting to see a different set; unfamiliar skin. Suddenly let loose, the clippers dropped with a clatter down to the landing below, and Bri jumped from the dissonance.

*"BRIAAAAN!"*

"*A-Andrew?*" gasped Brian, throat scratchy, and before he knew it, he was leaping down the stairs two steps at a time, "*ANDREW!*"

"*BRIAN!*"

He vaulted down the last half-flight, landing in the lounge with a room-shaking thud, then slapped the switch on the wall, flooding the overhead lights. The rubble of the once-great fort littered the lounge, their plates still stacked by the fire. Brian raced behind the furniture and across the hall.

In the dining room, he slapped the wall again and the lights revealed all six dogs huddled in the far corner. Ursula shielded the puppies, pressing them to the wall. She raised a trembling paw at Brian, and swallowed, trying to bay, but no *woof* resounded, for the sweets was too terrified to speak.

Brian rounded through the portal into the kitchen. He flicked on the oven light.

"*HE'S UPSTAIRS!*" Andrew hollered, from somewhere behind the marble island, "*HE WENT UPSTAIRS!*"

Brian grabbed the counter to work his way around the corner, pulling himself along, feet numb.

Half the Rue McClanahan sleeping shirt lay rent upon the kitchen tiles, the other half on its owner, collar still intact. Andrew sat backed into the corner where the dishwasher met the hand towel drawers, a weeping slice down the middle of his belly, to say nothing of the hundred scratches and bloody grazes on his side and the little Brian could see of his back. Worst, most of his hair had been shorn down to raw scalp, not counting the dozen patches between the bald where she still grew, long and luscious, and sometimes only a few strands wide. A whole eyebrow was missing, and the same trajectory of its trim pointed to a much deeper gash under Andrew's ear, one that cleaved that lobe off his cheek. The flesh dangled.

Brian scrambled for a nice green hand towel.

"Hold this to your ear," he said, "I'm gonna get my phone."

"*NO!*" Andrew shrieked, and he went clinging for Brian, practically drive-tackling him to the floor, "*Don't leave me!*"

"I have to call 911."

"*It was my father!*"

Brian wiped a drop of blood before it went in Andrew's eye.

*"What?"* he said.

"My—daddy," Andrew repeated, and despite it all, his gaze was steady and his speech lucid, if stilted, *"He...said all the...things he...used to say. He gave me a buzz cut."*

"That wasn't your dad," said Brian, and he pulled Andrew close, "You hear me? That wasn't him."

"Yeah, it was," said Andrew, his body growing colder by the second, "He didn't have...*any*...and his hands weren't...*hands,* they were..."

Brian got an arm under Andrew's butt; got his own legs beneath him. Adrenaline pushed him to standing. He hefted Andrew to the counter.

"I'm just getting the phone," he said, "Right here, on the wall."

They held hands while Brian dialed on the landline, and the operator had an ambulance on its way within moments. Brian led Andrew to the hall so they could wait by the door. He fetched the nice taupe cashmere throw to wrap around his friend's shoulders, then got one of Campbell's puff vests from the hall closet for himself, since he was shaking too. He switched on the hall lamp and opened the front door so they could see out to the street.

"They're almost here," he said, to ears a little past hearing, "A couple more minutes."

The snowfall had deafened the whole world. Andrew muttered something.

"What's up, babe?"

"...you *knew.*"

Brian swallowed. His chest heaved up and down.

"No."

*"Didn't you.* You knew that thing was here."

"Andrew."

"You knew. And you still told me to come here. You knew last night. This morning, when we...*when...*"

"I thought—"

The jab came out of nowhere. Brian saw stars.

*"OK,"* he said, covering the eye that couldn't open, "OK, I knew."

Andrew really did tackle him then. The hand towel and cashmere throw went flying. Brian's coccyx hit the checkerboard tile with a gnarly crack. He barely had time to cry out in pain before Andrew's knee drove again and again into his ribs. He blocked it with his hands and Andrew immediately followed up with a hook across the jaw. The dogs sobbed.

B saw red. He couldn't get Andrew off, he'd been pinned too well, but he grabbed an arm and bit down as hard as he could. Some sloppy slaps batted around his head, but eventually Andrew pulled back just to get away from those teeth; from the crowded, jagged mess that still had yet to be dragged into place. In the lull, Bri did a quick one-two at Andrew's bleeding stomach, right on the big slice. His friend doubled over. They panted, heads side by side like a good snug.

"I'm sorry," Brian gasped, "I can explain."

"Fuck you," said Andrew.

He raised himself up again, and Brian really thought he might stand and call it a draw, or even offer a hand, but at another trickle dripping off his chin, Andrew raised two fingers to that earlobe flapping free. Wincing, his finger traced up from where the lobe ought to be, then back over to where it was. Realization spread over his face. His breath quickened. Lip curled. He wrapped both hands around Brian's throat.

*"You are...the worst fucking person..."* Andrew fumed, squeezing, *"I...have...ever known..."*

Before the world went black, the EMTs tackled Ms. Murderess to the ground.

"She's giving him some ketamine," said the one with the tattoo sleeve, all birds-of-paradise, "We call this excited delirium."

*"Uh-huh.* OK."

"Let me see."

Brian lifted the cold pack from his eye.

"That's gonna be a shiner. Does it hurt?"

"Where are you taking him?"

"Lankenau," said the EMT.

"Take him to Bryn Mawr," said Brian, "My mom knows people there."

"Lankenau's closer. "

The other one wandered back in. She bent to pet Maxcat, who flopped at her feet.

"He's flyin high now," she said, in Delco patois, "No pain. Ear's cool for now. C'I ask you some questions?"

"Sure," said Brian.

"'Member, we're not the cops," said the lady EMT, "Mmkay? You take any drugs this evenin?"

"Just weed," he said, "And a Xanax, maybe two."

"That a prescription?"

"Nope."

"Doin some drinkin tonight?" she followed up.

"Yeah."

"He ever act like this before?" said the bro with the birdy tats, "You two ever fight?"

"We're not—*no*, he…"

"You just meet tonight, hon?" the other one tried, gingerly, scratching at her neck.

"No," he scoffed, *"We're* – I've known him for years. Over a decade."

"So…we have to contact the police when there's assault," she said.

"I don't want to press charges," Brian said, and he stood, despite the pain in his rear, "I don't want that. He didn't do anything."

"Well…when we came up the walk, we saw in the house–" the one with the tats started to say.

*"You didn't fucking see anything,"* Brian thundered, then he pointed to his eye: "This was an accident. He *acci-dentally* elbowed me when I was trying to…trying to get him to…"

"To stop hurtin himself?" the lady EMT suggested.

"…yes."

The professionals shared a look.

"So in that case, hon," she said, "Hospital's defin'ly gonna recommend additional care, prolly an in-patient facility."

Brian burst into tears.

"I'm sorry," she said, "When the people we love hurt themselves, this is the best choice we got."

After they gathered their supplies, the one with the tats handed Brian a pamphlet for domestic abuse.

"Just in case," he said.

"You can ride with us," said the other one, and she let the puppies lick her hand as they came shaking into the hall, "There's a spot in back for you."

"I have to clean up," said Brian, eyeing the trail of blood from the kitchen, the stains all over Campbell's vest, the ruined hand towel and cashmere throw, "*Um,* let me give you his sister's number."

It stood at the far end of the second floor hall, like usual, like they'd reset to summer; to fall.

And It wore Andrew, as he'd been hours before.

"No," said Brian,                 "No," said *das Gegenteil,*

pointing at each other like the double Spider-Man meme,

"Take that off right now."       "Take that off right now."

It didn't. Brian shut his eyes, counted to three, opened again. Still Andrew.

"I cannot *BELIEVE* you did that,"    "I cannot *BELIEVE* you did that,"

they barked,
like scolding a cat for clawing the couch,
or the puppy for squatting in a neighbor's yard,

"Just outrageous behavior!"        "Just outrageous behavior!"

The glint; the wrinkle in Andrew's cheek belied the rage that should have been precisely mirrored.

"You love this, don't you?"         "You love this, don't you?"

Brian swallowed a mouthful of spit. He willed himself not to puke.

"I am not doing this with you anymore," he fumed, "And for the record, I always knew you were faking."

The demon gazed down the hall with Andrew's eyes.

"So it's pick and choose now? Mirror, no mirror? Loop, no loop?"

Brian took out his phone.

"What if I call Mallory and tell her what you did?"

"What if I call Mallory," It said.

Vomit bubbled up. Brian gulped it back down.
"He didn't do anything to you," he said.

"He didn't do anything to you,"

It said, and It stepped down the hall,
and Brian felt a pull to advance at the same speed,
to match the swing of Its arm.

"You humiliated yourself," Bri spat, rocking back on his heels, "Moping around all day, throwing tantrums."

"You humiliated *your*self."

"No, I didn't."

"Moping around all day–"

*"Shut up."*

"–throwing tantrums."

The slow, familiar clink of Ursula's nails on the wooden stairs approached, climbing up. Brian glanced back over his shoulder. Ms. Unwed Mother stretched her neck out, sniffing as close as she could to Brian's foot. She blinked heavily, as if to say, *remember me? I'm a friend, friend.*

"Stay on your own side of the house," Brian demanded, facing the demon again, only to find the lion's share of Andrew's hair had vanished in the moment's interim, save for those wisps holding on like weeds. Its right earlobe waggled loose. A slice on Its belly oozed.

"Love the beard," said Andrew,

spitting blood,

"You look like a gay Mennonite."

"Stop wearing Andrew. *Stop* wearing my dad."

"You look good a little heavier."

"Stop fucking with me."

"You carry it well."

"He didn't say it like that."

The fever came on in waves. Brian felt an aura building, the haze clos-ing in around his peripheral vision so every room looked like a traffic tunnel, or a hallway without end. The subsequent migraine knocked him on his ass. He alternated between hot compress and cold. He couldn't stand up for the vertigo that followed, all spinning kaleidoscope views of kitchen and stairwell and puppy and cat. He dry heaved in front of the guest toilet. Around noon Tuesday, he crawled into bed and slept till Wednesday night. Upon waking, an immediate wave of dreadful malady engulfed him totally. His brain throbbed. He had never been so dehy-drated in his life, not after all-nighters on ecstasy. He could barely open his eyes for the agony.

The dogs had pissed and shat all over the house while he'd been zonked. All five of the puppies regarded Brian with unease, loath to approach, little hackles raised when he tried. Someone had turned over the food storage bin and chewed their way through the plastic cover. The kibble eruption affected the kitchen most locally—its wreckage in every crease between the tiles, or lining the toe kick gutters beneath the base cabinets—but it spewed out to the dining room, too. After chugging three vases of water, Brian righted the bin. Only the last bit of feed remained, enough for a few days, max. The cat jumped up on top of the refrigerator and yowled.

*"I'm trying,"* Brian croaked, wincing at the kitty pitch.

He picked his way through dry poopies in the dining room, then nar-rowly avoided another mess in the hall. Enduring a wrack of chills, Brian barely made it to the fainting couch. He lay in the lounge with his head upon the leather studded armrest. Ursula followed him up. She curled beside him, resting her head on his lap.

"I'm sorry, baby," he blubbed, stroking her downy ear.

Maybe he dozed. When he opened his eyes again, Urs stood in the hall, growling at him.

"What's up," he said, looking at her sideways.

She barked. Brian followed her gaze down to the Ursula on his hip.

"Get the fuck off me," he panicked, kicking the good girl away. She leapt off, poofed tail hung low.

The second Ursula growled, and both dogs squared off, teeth bared. The room throbbed with light, with heat.

"*NO!*" Brian lost it, hurling a pillow at them, "*BAD!*" The Ursulas broke apart, one dashing off to the kitchen, the other tearing up the lounge stairs.

After that, the animals steered clear.

He slept in snatches, taken over by a pyretic mania. By the weekend, he'd cleaned the whole of *DAS NEST*, shedding layers as he sweat buckets of sick, eventually scrubbing the floors butt-naked, steam rising from his back, his calves. Daily, he burned too hot for too long, his body temperature then plummeting in response come evening. Goosefleshed, he bundled in furs from the *Vorhalle* closet. He crawled under the thick weave of the lounge carpet, curled up like a pillbug. Twice more, he set off the fire alarm with steam from a scalding shower, but no firemen ever came to check in; he wound up knocking its batteries out with the end of a broom.

Bri woke Sunday morning with an erection that ached, that would not wane with a cold shower or even upon tensing large muscle groups to try to draw the blood away. He set his mind to chores; to de-smellifying the house of pot and poop and the iron stench of blood that seemed to reek from the walls and floor vents. He stalked the house in briefs, a growing swamp soaking his Y-fronts.

Up on the third floor, he opened all the windows to let a cross-breeze in. Out in Hemlock Circle, all the snow had melted to scummy road-bumps of mud and ice. In the yards, brown grass poked through the slush. A dead fish sky hung low. Trees trembled. Upon withdrawing wayward weiner from the window, Bri turned to set eyes upon the hair that dragged along the floorboards out in the hall, split ends tugging out of sight.

He stomped after it round the corner, nostrils flaring.

A train of black tresses snaked along the hall and down the kitchenside stairs.

Brian went the other way out of spite, down to the lounge, but a bend of the same locks made a little cul-de-sac in the front hall, black weaves doubling back towards the kitchen. He cracked all the lounge windows, locking their stoppers, then stepped over the hair to do the same in the dining room, looping around to open the house up, letting the drafts in, dick raging to be freed. In the kitchen, the black mop widened where it climbed the stairs, and two of the ginger puppies snapped at the glissade up near the landing, nuzzling their noses under the mane. One had gotten a leg tangled in it. Brian climbed up to unsnarl the moop, then nudged both babes back downstairs. One tried to bite him. He followed the hair back up to the third floor, where he came finally to the split ends again somehow, the rest of the tendril having completed the house loop. The hair writhed. Brian rubbed his palms over his scalp. His glutes clenched, hips humping the air.

Hands shaking, he fetched his phone from the guest room, then opened the nearest cruising app.

The grid of headless skins sickened; beckoned.

A message shot through, the instant notification like the crack of a whip. Brian adjusted himself.

said bigd!ckslurper, 2 miles away,

*u hung?? submissive bttm here, love 2 suck n snallow*
*\*snallow*
*\*swallow lol*

Bigd!ckslurper's torso was nice, as headless torsos went, so Brian took a quick dick pic and loaded it into a message. Right before sending it, though, his thumb hovered. The hair out in the hall wriggled along the floor so he could not tell if it slithered left or right. It twisted itself to braids. He deleted the pic, then sent his location instead.

*come find out*

he wrote.

*u parTy?*

came bigd!ckslurper's immediate reply.

*nah*

*u mind if i do?*

*nah*
*just come suck this dick*

He let the guy smoke a little meth by the kitchen door, wrinkling his nose at the sweet chemical funk, then made him leave the bulbed pipe under the grill. Brian scanned for neighbors, but he hadn't seen anyone all day. The guy wore his hair combed straight back, the gelled twists like hedgehog spikes. He ran a hand through it again and again so his hand came away shinier every time.

"Yeah," said the dude, "Wow. Check this place out. All yours?"

"Nope," said Brian.

"Family?" said dude, "Rich friends?"

"I broke in, I've been squatting" Bri lied, and the guy didn't buy it, by the tweaked-out screw-smile, "It's fine, they're probably Nazis. Come on." Brian grabbed him by the shirt and led him inside and around the edge of the marble island, straight up the kitchen stairs. The dogs barked from the room he'd shut them in. High guy couldn't keep his tongue in his mouth. It dangled and waggled, coated in a thin film.

"I like your black eye," said the guy.

They stopped on the landing by the open door to the second floor hall. The landscapes rippled all around, like their arrival had been a stone thrown in a paint pond. Down the length of the hall, doors bulged, wood tumescent. High guy dropped to his knees there in the portal and undid Brian's belt with his teeth. *Das Gegenteil* rolled up at the far end of the hall, wearing Campbell.

"Hi," said high guy, Brian's zipper in his mouth.

Brian and the demon locked eyes.

"Hi,"                                        "Hi,"

they said.

"He your partner?" asked the dude.

"Nope."                                  "Nope."

"I'll suck his dick, too," said the guy, then he generously included Campbell, "I'll suck your dick, too." With graceless aplomb, he set back to the task, stuffing his face in Brian's crotch, worming around to get a bite of underwear, lips folded over choppers.

"Do it,"                                  "Do it,"

said Brian and the demon,

"Crawl down the hall."            "Crawl down the hall."

High guy grinned. He chomped at the band of Brian's briefs, growling, then sat back on his rump. He turned to face Campbell at the far end. He took in the barrel chest, the explosion of pubes. The bristly bramble beneath the empty gaze. The guy dug his thumb into the corner of his eye, snorting hard, then he started a slow crawl down the teal runner.

"You like my ass?" he shot back to Brian, "You can fuck it."

"This is what you want, right?"      "This is what you want, right?"

Brian asked the Campbell skin,
and It asked right back.

"Woah," the guy said, then he stopped for a sec, wobbly at the elbows, "You guys're...ventriloquists."

"Keep going."                          "Keep going."

High guy chuckled, but no smile reached his cracked lips. He came to a stop halfway down the hall, looking back and forth between Brian and *das Gegenteil,* then slowly he focused back on the former. Turning onto his hip, he studied Bri with a twitching eye. The flush drained from his face. He recoiled.

"What is that," he whispered, then he swung his head around to Campbell, "Is that real?"

"What do you mean?"            "What do you mean?"

*"Is that a real person,"* the dude demanded, losing it a little.

"Yeah, I'm real."                      "Yeah, I'm real."

*"Th-the fuck!?"* high guy sputtered, kicking himself down the runner, away from Brian, "Stop that. *Why's it doing that?* Make it stop doing that, man."

"I'm not – *listen, dude–"*          "I'm not – *listen, dude–"*

they tried.

*"Is that a lizard person!?"* high guy cried, and he leapt to his feet, "I don't fuck with lizard people. They stole my grandma's identity."

"I'm not—*stop it!"*                    "I'm not—*stop it!"*

Brian and *das Gegenteil* barked at one another.

"Yo, tell your lizard to stop, bro," the guy begged of Campbell, arms flailing, "I swear to God!"

What must have been all five dogs set to barking from their cell up on the third floor. Brian and the demon flinched in response, shoulders hiking to their ears. High guy assumed a martial stance, fists up to either end of the long hall.

*"I REBUKE YOU!"* he shouted at Brian, at the Campbell skin, at all the lizards out there, *"I REBUKE ALL LP'S IN THE NAME OF YAH-WEH."* And with chin set, he went running headlong into the closed door to Campbell's office, bouncing off at once, stumbling back into the opposite wall.

"Wait, dude!" Bri cried, "It's locked!"

But the dude would not be deterred. The Campbell skin squared its shoulders, driving down the hall; seeing this, high guy wheeled back and gave it another go, kicking once, twice, then three times a lady, right next to the knob. The door flew open with a bang, its lock stile cracked inward. Brian gripped himself round the skull. The skin stomped down the hall, reaching for the guy, but just missed him as the dude tore into the office. The demon followed. A crash sounded, followed by several jangly smashes, then *whooosh!* and finally, a dreadful thud. Brian held his breath, and though he really didn't want to, he crept down the hall to see.

His Office/*Sein Büro* held some 40 or 50 plants along its bookshelves and desk space, in its corners and upon its twin windowsills, one of which had been slammed open all the way to reveal the backyard. A Mallory skin stood gazing out, leaning upon the sash, one foot forward, one cheek clenched. A rough path had been torn through the room, with displaced plants and soil strewn in its wake. Decorative ceramic beer steins towered beside a pot of curling bamboo. An academic stole in the Moyamensing colors hung upon a peg, nearly engulfed by the monstera lurking in the corner; the date above the tassels read: *EST. 1894.* Brian nearly gagged on the heady musk as he stepped through, to a roomful of honeyed precipitation a good 20° warmer than the rest of the house. He picked his way through reeking perennials to join *das Gegenteil* at the window.

Down in the yard, the dude lay flat on the dead grass.

"Did he jump?" Brian asked. The demon nodded.

High guy stirred. He pushed himself to all fours.

"You OK?" Brian called down.

The guy looked back up at the window; at the naked lady beside Brian. With a groan, he made it to his feet, then took off limping down the driveway, right after doubling back for his pipe under the grill.

"You forgot your shoes!" Brian called, leaning out, but the dude had gone. Bri pulled back inside.

The Mallory skin picked up the pieces in the office. With great care, It swept earth bare-handed back into toppled pots, then righted them again.

"Yeah, Campbell said," said Bri, unsure if he should help, "You're a gardener. Have you been watering all these?"

*Das Gegenteil* reburied twisted roots. It brushed petals and fat berries free of dirt.

Brian wound around past stacked boxes of what, upon further snooping, turned out to be dozens of copies of Campbell's book, *Leerer Spiegel* (*"A wriggling, squirming exploration of fathers and sons, husbands and wives, but mostly Man as Maker; vernal but rarely puerile."*—Dr. Pieter Faber; *"Dahlhaus drags us through the proverbial mud by our throats until we, too, have gone from pissant to Übermensch."*—Senator Grant McKenzie). A photograph on the desk caught B's eye. He reached for its heavy gold frame, lifted it to the light off the window. In the photo, Campbell and Mallory posed in the *Vorhalle* upon its checkerboard tiles, surrounded by a panoply of the same glistening blooms from the office. A younger Ursula sat like a good girl by Mallory's knee, and Maxcat's kitty rump snugged in the crook of Campbell's arm, and an eight-foot figure stood between the Dahlhauses, in armour incarnadine, Its plating like reddened snake scales upon pauldron and gauntlet, the too-wide cuirass containing whatever lived inside a demon's chest. From Its great-helm spiraled a pair of asymmetrical gemstone ram horns in dusky rose, with seams of unhewn rock criss-crossing all the way to the sharpened tips. It hugged Its keepers round their shoulders, like they were just a regular, old family; like they could have splashed *Happy Ho-Ho-Holidays from Ours to Yours!* across the bottom.

Brian knew the answer, but still he flipped the photo round to ask: "Is this you?"

*Das Gegenteil* nodded.

"All that fancy armour," he mused, tracing a gemstone horn, "You almost look like a good guy."

The demon stood, a waxy bloom in Its Mallory hands.

"You too,"

It reflected.

"Well, I'm *not* happy," said Mallory, "It's a porcelain farmhouse sink, it's meant to be lustrous."

"We should have Jules come take a look at it," said Campbell, bent over the counter with his head in the basin, "She's quite savvy with stains."

"*Um,* I can get it out," said Brian, "Do you have any baking soda?"

"It's not just the *stain,* Brian."

"Fascinating circumference," Campbell concluded, popping up from the sink, his tie wet, "It might *not* be a death omen, but then again, the universe being paradoxical: *mightn't it?* I'd like to get some shutterbugs in here, see what we pick up on the negatives. And Julia's really better to spearhead this sort of thing."

"So call Julia, Campbell," Mallory sighed, balancing on one clog boot to unzip the other, "We've been home 30 seconds, I'd say you've earned it."

Dr. Flat Butt took off scampering around the marble island, all giddy giggles under his breath.

"I swear, I didn't know porcelain stained so easily. It's just –"

"*Wait!*" Campbell cried, wheeling around to Brian from the kitchen stairs, "You there. What was it from? Julia will need to know if it was a vessel of your own blood—or perhaps the blood of an enemy? Ox? Rooster?"

"It was just tea," said Brian, hands raised, "I-I just left my tea in the sink."

"Uh-huh," said Campbell, clearly crestfallen, "Well, that's substantially less *provokativ*." And he huffed on upstairs. Mallory pried her boots off, losing a few inches in the process. She took a stalk round the kitchen, wafting the air, hands churning, really going for it, just hoovering up the atmosphere, nostrils gaping wide.

"Are you getting that?" she asked, swallowing again and again, "It's like a...like a..."

"I don't—*uhh*," Brian sniffed, "I did scramble some eggs?"

"No, there's a redolent sort of...buoyancy," she said, licking at the corner of her lip, "An esprit de corps. Did you bring a public school teacher here?"

"I did not."

"Be honest with me."

"I swear, Mallory," he said.

"Were acts of chivalry performed? Were you *gallant?*"

"I absolutely, 100% was not," he said, and he'd never meant anything more. Just beyond the dining room portal, the pups huddled together, whining under their breath.

"I don't know," she bemoaned, "I just don't know. I really thought we understood each other, Brian. And now my house smells like brotherly fucking love."

Brian spread his hands wide upon the black-and-blue marble.

"Maybe this is jetlag talking," he offered, "And after a cozy night's sleep, everything'll–"

"And see, you're very glib," Mallory interjected, circling the countertop, "Which I always liked, but now that you're not saying things that are funny, it's like you're 100 feet tall and screaming." They stood at opposite corners of the island, the marmoreal veining crackling out between their hands, its surface cool.

"*MAAAL,*" Campbell bellowed, from upstairs, "*JULES'LL BE HERE IN 10. WILL YOU LET HER IN IF I'M STILL IN THE SHOWER?*" Neither Brian nor Mallory flinched. One of the ginger squishes ventured a few steps into the kitchen, but changed its mind once it got closer. The pupper turned tail and fled.

"Well, I'm *really* glad you're home safe and sound," grit Bri, breaking first, "Your house is still here, and so are all your pets." A muted shriek of water raced through the pipes along the kitchen wall to Campbell's shower. The lady of the house brooded. She pressed herself into the hard corner of the island, grinding her teeth to an underbite.

"I should frisk you," she grunted, "Before I let you go."

"You're not gonna frisk me, Mallory."

"I should have my demon pin you to the wall while I turn out your pockets."

"The only thing I stole was a bottle of wine," said Brian, and he picked up his bags, "I'll get you another, babe." He turned his back to her then, taking his leave through the dining room. The pups scattered.

"You know what I'll do then, Bri?" Mallory snipped, clipping along at his heels, "I'll make a flyer on my laptop, that's exactly what I'm gonna do. I don't need a spell or a pain transference. I will go through your social medias–"

"Just say media."

"And I will find your most unflattering photo–"

"Joke's on you, I *only* take bad photos."

"And I will send them to Campbell's office because they let me print for free. And these flyers will say *DO NOT HIRE THIS TREACH-EROUS WHORE*. And I will leave them absolutely everywhere, Brian. Cashiers will slip them in your groceries. Your mother's gonna find them in her mail slot."

Brian wheeled around. If he hadn't been holding his bags, he might have shoved her.

"And maybe I'll burn your house down for real," he snarled, "Maybe I copied your key and I'll be *back* some night." The grin that overtook Mallory's face almost ripped her cheeks apart.

*"Get the fuck out,"* she whimpered, trunk gyrating in spasms shooting up from her hips.

"Gladly, girl."

At the last second, Ursula snuck in from the lounge to try to steal a head-pat, one paw lifted, all puppy eyes under her head-floomp, but Brian angled past her on the *Vorhalle* tiles. He dropped his laptop bag to crack the great iron-and-oak door. His eyes brimmed over with tears.

"I'll send you that wine," he managed, nudging the door open with a foot.

*"You can't afford it,"* Mallory clapped back, and as soon as Brian was over the threshold, she hefted the big door shut. He planted there on the veranda long enough to order a ride to the station, then trudged down the walk to wait by the road. On the way past the property's decorative stonework, its overhang dripping with January icicles, he took a kick at the gold lettering proclaiming *DAS NEST* so the *D* went flying off.

"And I'll get you another fucking *S*," he huffed aloud, to the empty cul-de-sac, *"ASS NEST."*

# IV
# IN VOLLER BLÜTE

CARS LINED HEMLOCK Circle from tip to taint, all along its inside curve. The models skewed luxury, from cocksure mid-sizes to indecent coupes, with a svelte catering van parked closest to the house, its baby pink lettering in frilly swoops and swiggles: *Spoil Your Appetite!* 5 and 10-minute sprinkles all afternoon had covered the scene in billions of dewdrops, all refracting the same strawberry bubblegum sunset. In that lusty lighting, spring zephyrs danced a fantasia, lifting fallen petals to brief *ballons*, spreading pollen from the ornamental pear trees so the whole cul-de-sac reeked of fresh cum.

Out by the main road, Brian took a last drag off a little one-hitter, sucking until he was just pulling butane from the lighter. A smoke so thick it was almost grease wafted out the sides of his mouth, his nostrils. His feet ached from the hike. He took off his cap to run a hand through the swamp atop his scalp, then glanced back down the hill; the twisting corkscrew of Hemlock Way that climbed on past the entrance to the Circle, off and up into the vernal overgrowth of Gladwyne. He snorted and spat brown.

*DAS NEST* waited in its dead end.

B hefted his backpack high and tight so he couldn't help but to press onward, its nylon digging into his neck, the carabiner slipping under his collar. Just as soon as he started to cross the asphalt, Mallory charged right out from the house, the big door flung wide in her wake. She leapt in place on the veranda, maniacally waving, then pulled her cardigan close over a form-fitting orchid party dress and jogged down the walk, bare feet slapping the stone.

"Don't come out," Brian called, waving her back, "You don't have shoes on."

*"Bri! Bri!"* she yipped, like a dog whose owner is finally home, "Oh, Brian!" They collided by the hood of the catering van, where Mallory hurled herself bodily, flinging willowy arms round his neck, melting so she hung there, her breath hot between his polo buttons.

*"Steady,"* he choked, having nearly inhaled a champagne lock, "OK. *OK, lady.*"

"Thank fuck you're here," she said, gazing up so he got a mouthful of boozy breath, laced in licorice spice, "We have no idea where It is."

"Yeah, you said in your message."

He set Ms. Lady to her feet again, righting her as best he could, then took three giant steps back. Immediately, she trailed two steps closer, yanking at her sleeves so they overhung her hands, nibbling at the wool.

"So, *um,*" he said, one hand up to stop her coming closer, "We should talk. Before I head in."

"Yes, of course!" she agreed, *"Of course* we can talk. How are you? Let's see the teeth."

"No, Jesus Christ. That's not–" he said, stepping back again, "I mean let's...be clear. About my pay."

"Anything," said Mallory, "I'll write you a check for $5,000 right now if you come inside. *When* you come inside. My checkbook's in my purse."

"Go get it," said Brian, and to this, her face contorted, and for an uncanny instant, he could see the girl she had likely been in youth: delighted by the eensienst sliver of fun, bewildered by the same measure of obligation. Mallory's chin rose higher and higher. She toyed with her split ends.

"You're serious?" she clarified, when he didn't budge, "Even though you know I'm good for it?"

Brian nodded.

"I'm hurt you don't trust me, Bri," Mal sighed, then she snatched his hand up, "But fine. At least come wait by the door so you don't look like a big gay burglar." She dragged him back on up the walk, mane drifting wide, digging a thumb into his palm. Through the dining room window,

Brian could see bodies seated round the table; immobile guests at the party. A frisky breeze nudged them along.

"You didn't say what the occasion was."

"*Yes,* you'll need to meet everybody," Mallory rolled over him, "And it's best if we go one by one so you can really focus, but that means no looking around willy-nilly. *Direct* eye contact until we find It." Once they'd scaled the granite steps to the throng of potted blooms, his hand slid from hers and the lady marched inside.

Brian stayed put. He shimmied out of his backpack, craning his neck to peer in the front hall, alert for puppy or cat. Not a whisker appeared.

"*He's here, everyone!*" Mallory lobbed to the dining room, as she rounded back into view from the lounge, clutching her snakeskin checkbook, "*Crisis nearly over!*" She waggled the book at B, as if to say, *Happy now, fucko?*

"Thanks a lot."

"Don't mention it, *Briii,*" she sang, her gait a little loopy, and she deposited a fountain pen between her teeth so she could wrench its cap off, "You deserve every little cent." Madame Daydrunk strode forward to grasp him by the shoulders, then gave him a smart swivel, balancing the open checkbook on his back.

"*Fifty...just kidding, five...thousand...dollars,*" she ground out, the nib of her pen digging into his wing, scratching right over his spine, "*From yours...truly.*" She ripped the thing out, then handed it to him. In the memo line, she'd drawn a smiley face, its eyes a pair of Xs.

"Tell me again what—*what* am I doing?" said Brian. He folded the check and slid it in his jorts.

"Hide and seek," said Mallory, "Come on, it'll be fun."

He knew the floor plan well enough to know she'd steered him into the dining room and turned him to face the closest wall, perhaps the corner. If he tried to picture it, there was a low buffet there, right? The one with glossy painted cabinets, and an extra wide chair at its side. Mallory's hands shifted, rings nubbling over his cheekbones, his eyelids. Over his own shallow breaths, he could make out the rustling of otherwise silent bodies: jewelry shifting, a throat cleared, the suck of air through clogged nostrils.

"You look exhausted," buzzed Mallory in his ear, "But very thin, so something's working."

"Oh, thanks."

"Are you sleeping?"

"Not really," Brian admitted, for it was the truth, "Couchsurfing. Very glamorous, overstaying one's welcome everywhere. Fucking hair trigger landlords, y'know?"

"I don't, we've always owned," said Mal, "But I swear by sleeping, Bri. I'm a glutton for it. I bundle up between Campbell and my demon, and I'm a happy, little lump of coal."

He shook off the images that immediately crept to mind. Mallory cleared her throat.

"OK, so," said she, easing into hostess mode, "Brian, this is Dr. Paige Fleming."

Her hands lifted. Bri blinked, focusing on the little woman seated before him.

"Hi," he said, politely, if a little awks. He extended a hand, but Dr. Paige Fleming just sat there: silver sapphic bob *à la* chunky bangs, prominent aquiline nose, oversized men's button-down in venture capitalist blue (very North American power lesbian). The shirt covered the dwarf lady's knees, and a bit of capri pant hung out below its hem.

"Oh, and she can't talk," said Mal, "And I'm *mostly* pretty sure she can't hear us."

"K," said Bri, "Why, though?"

In his peripheral, he could just make out another body standing by the window. Reflexively, he angled his head to look, but Mallory grabbed him at once, making impromptu blinders with her hands.

"One at a *time*, I said," she hissed, "Now, look our Dr. Fleming right in the eye."

Brian bit his tongue, but obeyed.

"Do you see anything there?" Mallory pressed, "Something that shouldn't be?"

"*Um*, any—I don't know how to–"

"Does she look how she'd normally look if she were just someone you happened to know, through...I don't know, over-30 kickboxing?"

"Sorry, just—*why* am I the one doing this?"

"Because I'm not *fucking looking at her, Brian!*" Mallory seethed, spittle spraying his earlobe, "I can't, or we'd *all* have been ensnared. And then we'd starve to death here, quite ironically surrounded by a thieves' fortune of scrummy cuisine. And then I'd never have called you, and you wouldn't have a cool five-thou in your pocket. And you're just *not* a stranger to this sort of thing, so it *has* to be you. Campbell's useless, he's taken LSD and fled to the basement."

"But *what* am I –"

"*Bu-bu-but!*" Mallory mocked, squeezing his head, "My guests have been stuck for hours, Bri. Spring luncheon is becoming a Barcelona supper. I had to sequester the caterers, who are running triple overtime, and all they've been able to do is serve *moi* the specialty cocktail (which is a delicious homemade absinthe using wormwood my demon grew specially for the event.) And *someone's* had to drink half the batch! Now, I've generously paid *à l'avance*, so tell me if my guest looks like a little lesbian who has the right to exist or one who doesn't."

"She..." Brian shrugged, gazing down, "...she looks like a real, live lesbian. A l-lesbian who's alive."

"A'right, close your eyes again."

The hands slid back over whether he did or not. Mallory scoonched him down the length of the room like they were in a tango, shifting closer to the windows, her front glued to his back.

"*Aaaand...*" she fizzled, situating him, "Open." The next guest stood by the window had quite the sallow visage under spiritless white-blonde hair brushed all to one side. Oblong head rose to an improbable slant so the man's eyeglasses sat off-kilter astride an alarmingly thin nose. He, like Dr. Fleming before him, remained mute, if amiable, hands crammed in his sweater vest pockets, alternately pursing or fluttering his lemon lips.

"How 'bout this one?" Mallory breathed, leaning her weight on Brian, "So I'm only seeing feet, but this should be Simon Price, Campbell's number two at the university. He doesn't look like someone who should be who he is, and often looks like someone who shouldn't be who he isn't, so you'll have to just ignore all that."

"I still don't–"

"Is he or or is he *not?*"

Brian scoured Simon Price's watery eyes. The sunset out in the Circle smelted down to royal purple.

"He is...*not?*" said Bri, half-believing himself.

"K, next up," said Mal, and again she blocked out the world with her talons.

"*Can we just–*"

"This is Simon's wife, Gwen," she said, and they only did a rocking swivel that time, to face the corner where the windows met the wall again. Mallory revealed the next guest.

"Oh," said Brian, heart leaping to his throat, "I know her. I know you. *Oh.*" A largeish woman in a busy lotus print pantsuit smiled warmly, one arm upon the mantel. An old choir teacher? A high school friend's mom? He couldn't place the dimples, the sweet double chin. Most of all, whoever she was, he had surely never met her with eyes that rolled and rolled and rolled backwards in her head, without end.

"What is it. Talk."

"*Sh-sh-she–*" Brian stammered, and he tried to step back, but Mallory held firm, bucking where his spine bent. Gripping tighter than ever, she squeezed so his cheeks bunched forward, so he could do nothing but gaze at the grotesquerie: that face he knew and also did not. Gwen Price's pupils spun by, never at the same time, slightly too fast to focus upon, replaced again and again by the blur of white, then red veins at the back of her eyeballs. A low, whirring *slck-slck-slck* emanated from the viscera sliding round the sockets.

"Do you see It?"

"I...*I see...*"

"Brian, keep talking," said Mallory, and though he could feel her still at his back, her voice seemed to come from a distance ever increasing, like she'd thrown it ventriloquist-style to the lounge or let it run up to the third floor. Gwen Price raised her arm from the mantel; reached it to Brian, palm out, welcoming. Down behind Bri's navel, an extrasensory fishhook tickled round, ensnaring his innards. He wriggled there on the line.

Every 10th, 40th rotation, Gwen's spinning pupils aligned for a millisecond; burst in that snap of zoetropic gaze to daydreams all-consuming, sandwiched by Mallory's hand-blinders. Brian couldn't blink. His vision teared over, but even through the wash he saw the uncanny slideshow: a blue-hot comet roaring through the null of space; the white curvature of cloud cover above the Earth; a stretch of moonlit path forked by sugar palms; crocodiles ablaze, their tails dancing in the night.

Bri's jaw went slack. He could smell pierced ozone. Singed jasmine.

"...trace a five-pointed star," echoed Mallory's voice, from the other side of the moon, and one of those hand-blinders disappeared from view, "...just the outline, OK? Not like a pentagram..." Dimly, Brian was aware of a pressure at his elbow, and his own hand came into view, into the superimposed kaleidoscope of meteor and Earth and jungle inferno. Limp fingers etched a shape in space, and though its five points were a little wonky, it nevertheless seemed to be the ticket, for the dining room, the purple sunset throbbed back in breathless pulses of his racing heart, his vision oversaturated, bleeding back from searing phantasms. Gwen Price's eyes snapped into place like a winning slot machine. Mallory released Brian at once, and down he went.

A huge, collective sigh of relief preceded the clamor of furious voices:

*"A whole fucking day!"*

*"Goddamn, I think I shit myself."*

*"That was so horrible!"*

*"It was Gwen? Of* course *It was Gwen."*

**"THERE'S NO NEED,"** Mallory boomed to the room, "For hysterics. We've troubleshooted the issue, and a beautiful springtide supper will *now* be served just as soon as everyone's had a chance to freshen up. Welcome back, all."

Bri dry-heaved, aiming at the stacked logs in the firebox, leaning heavily upon its folding screen.

*"There It is, in the rocking chair!"*

"Yes, Simon, there It is," Mallory agreed, "Now don't go losing It again. Yes, Grant. I see you. Go help yourself to a shower and a pair of Campbell's boxers. Brian, *truly:* out or in." And out it was, for there were the pretzels he'd scarfed on the train, blasted all over the back brick.

*"I-I'm sorry,"* Brian gagged, a salty nugget caught behind his uvula, spitting where he could, "I tried–"

*"Do you remember me?"* came a sickly sweet voice he guessed belonged to Gwen Price, along meaty fingers suddenly scrubbing over his back, *"I'm a friend of your mommy's, baby."*

"We'll make a place, Bri," Mallory's voice sliced through, "I'm sure we can whip up a gazpacho and a ginger ale. The chefs are very good."

"I-I can't stay–" Brian hacked, trying to shrug the groping mitts off his back. Steadying himself on the mantelpiece, he shot a baleful glare up at the giant oil painting of the floating girl and her hair doppelgänger, then patted around his front pocket, feeling for the $5,000, for its scratchy corners.

"You'll stay," Mallory ordered, and her voice faded from his side, passing into the kitchen: "Portia, can we do a mint gazpach in 20?"

Brian winced, cramping up again. Still, he pushed through, turning to go.

"I'll just get out of your..."

The gathering round the DAS NEST table gazed on in twisted parody of the Golden Ratio, every line, every face of interest in fitful scale to those closer or further from the mantel so no body buttressed another, and every figure seemed to lurk in plain sight. Brian flinched away from a still-fumbling Gwen Price, scanning round to her spoiled milk husband at the window, to diminutive Dr. Fleming seated at the far wall, then at the guests he'd yet to meet: the oily man in a slick tailored suit half-stood from his chair, clutching at his own ass; the haggard young lady at his side breastfeeding a coveralled toddler, the too-wide crown of the kid pocked and bulbous like a mushroom cap; the hale and hearty fellow down at the end, in sensible khakis and a color-blocked button-down, his hands hirsute, his flesh pure animal from the neck up, with fluffy ears atop a black-and-brown woolly face and a drooping proboscis, its end a pair of sniffing pink nostrils; and finally, the colossal disembodied head lumped in the corner rocking chair, her features human, if decapitated, her dimensions that of a prize pumpkin, easily four to five sizes that of Brian's own cranium, and scowling as though she'd devour him whole were she able to roll across the room unassisted.

But of that very strangest dinner party, only one face caught Brian's attention to the immediate exclusion of all others. He ran the back of a hand over his lips, smearing sick down his chin, ears pinned back.

"Uhh, excuse me," he croaked to the room at large, scooting right down the table and past the jumbo head in the corner to cross the checkerboard tiles in the front hall. A sick suspicion sunk like a stone in Brian's gut, slipping right under the post-vom cramps. He shuffled into the lounge and around the sofa, teeth grit to stop the tears that fell anyway, and dropped to his knees in front of Ursula.

"*Nooo,*" he moaned, "*Come on, man.*"

The taxidermist had done a fine job, capturing in the lift of one ear her pep, in the sweet fold of her paws that demure worldliness. Someone had finally gotten her groomed, hopefully while she'd still been alive, and her apricot curls sat bouncy as back in summer, just waiting to be tousled. The glass eyes, though realistic, were the wrong shade; a golden honey instead of her amber molasses. Nevertheless, they stared ever onward, ever unseeing. Brian choked back cry-snot. He reached out and almost booped her nose, but stopped himself. A brass plaque on the sculpted wood stand read *DIE GUTE MAMA.*

"For your pukey belly," said Mallory, and he looked up to find her standing over him with a tumbler of ice and bubbles.

"*What did you do?*"

"To Urs?" Mallory trilled, "Nothing!"

"Then what the fuck."

"Grief is a very private process, Brian," she tutted, "I'm allowed to mummify my feelings."

He stood to rip the soda from her hand.

"*How did she die, Mallory?*"

"Well, no one really knows," said Mal, and she squatted at the poodle's side, to stroke her stuffed snout with a pinky tip, "We had to go out of town for dueling conferences, and, *well,* you had proven untenable at the time. So we had no one we could call. It was Campbell, really, who said–"

"You just left them here?"

"Like I say, it was really Campbell's idea. He thought our demon was ready. Very much an if-not-now-then-when situation. Punt the baby bird from the nest."

"So you left her."

"For a long weekend, Thursday through Monday night. When we came back, there she was, surrounded by her brood. She'd gotten them all in the guest room and then jammed the door shut somehow with the dresser, if you can believe. Campby had to muscle it open, sweet manling. He pulled his shoulder."

Brian's chest crumpled.

"*Y-you,*" he gasped, "*You–she–*"

"Oh, don't start," said his hostess, "We just made up. Drink your ginger ale." And leaning on the empty pooch, she pushed herself to standing, still a little tipsy-wobbly.

Brian gulped the soda down, its syrup catching thick in his throat.

She assigned him the foot of the table, with a hastily-scribbled place card above the setting. Breadcrumbs towered in his cold soup. Sundown breezes swooped in and out of the open windows, dancing through the flames atop the tapered candles so shadows played over guest, over ceiling. Brian set his drink beside his name and sat heavily, swiping under his eyes. The evening's hostess retreated to her kitchen.

"The last time I saw you," bubbled Gwen Price, leaning past her lemon-headed husband, who sat on Brian's left, "You were *such* a poopsy little people–pleaser. An extra chubby, *extra* flamboyant cutiebutt in the mix with all us ladies getting pedicures. I let you pinch my elbow fat."

"Hi, Mrs. Price," said Brian, "Nice to see you again."

"How's your mother?" she said, chins rolling with fondness, "She's such a great gal."

"I don't know," he admitted, "We don't—we haven't spoken in three years."

"Oh, that's a real shame," said Gwen, "But then again—and I said this to you, Simon—she does avoid talking about you. I said this, did I not, Simon? My friend at the liquor store, remember?"

"The Mid-Atlantic matron with the, *uh,* very symmetrical face and impressive rack?" Simon puckered, out the side of his mouth. Gwen burst into peals of squealing giggles, fanning herself under her collar.

"I don't notice those things!" she cried, face gone red, *"Us girls don't look at each other like that!"*

"Well, that's categorically, sociologically false," Dr. Fleming interjected. She sat beside the woolly-headed man who had a trunk for a nose, one hand round the back of his chair.

"I don't notice my *friends' racks!"* Gwen howled, and she reached down the table for Brian's hand in commiseration, "Can you imagine!?"

"I have and, *uh,* do, yes," cracked Simon Price.

*"Honey!"* Gwen shrieked, and she play-slapped her hubs on his lemon

rind, "But I said to you, didn't I? I said, that gal won't talk about her son because he's a piece of shit, really. And you asked why, and I said, well, he tried to have that nice man fired from the high school, and she won't say it, but you just know he's been to rehab or something terrible. He was so, so chubby and then *so* skinny. And now bald. So everyone always wondered maybe heroin, but I thought club drugs and anonymous sex, which of course makes one grapple with the specter of AIDS."

"None of the above," said Bri, then he reiterated to everyone: "Just a good pair of clippers and disordered eating."

"Oh, I've always wanted to try that," Gwen swooned, and she reached for her fork, to stab the darling birdlet on her plate. Brian dipped spoonfuls of gazpach till cool mint tingled down his throat.

"Brian, I'm Dr. Paige Fleming," said Dr. Fleming, who had clearly been waiting for a lull in the conversation, "Deputy Chair over in Esoterica." She stood to reach past her trunked neighbor, offering the most rigid hand. Brian stared at her, lower jaw crooked, then he stood with a sigh to reach way down the table and shake, practically climbing aboard, little as she was.

"Yes," he said, sitting again, "We've met."

"Well," huffed Dr. Fleming, and she, too, sat, "I believe I was possessed at the time."

"No, *I* was possessed, Paige," Gwen Price checked, pointer wiggling, just endlessly fucking chipper, "You all were enthralled. Not that it's a competition, because I'll win."

"All right, Gwen," Dr. Fleming sneered across the table, "Still, I'm curious, Brian: did you share the same audio-visual delusions we all did? The fallen star, the great inferno in her wake?"

"*Uhh, yeah,*" said Bri, just trying to eat, "I guess."

"Well, he makes six for six," Dr. Fleming mused, sneaking a glance at Simon, "These demons are nothing if not precise. And since we have a moment *without* Mr. McKenzie or our hosts...I'd like to reiterate that I believe publishing should still be on the ta-"

"Well, really, *uh,* five for five," Simon cut in, "I don't think It got Heather." Everyone looked to the gaunt young woman in a baggy frock with one boob out, that mushroom bambino on her lap still suckling for all its worth. Heather didn't look up, lost as she was, lovestruck for her fungus baby.

"Get her," said Gwen to Dr. Fleming, who furiously shook her bob, "Flick her." Then that troublestarter leaned way back in her seat, kicking under the table until she'd found her mark. Heather recoiled with her babe, eyes roving wild. Gwen giggled, caught.

*"Huh?"* Heather rasped, swallowing hard, like she hadn't spoken for weeks, *"Did I say something?"*

"We were just wondering, hon," said Gwen, trying to push herself back up, a little stuck under the table, "Whether you saw all that wacky stuff we did."

"I...I..."

*"You must be very proud,"* said Dr. Fleming, overloud, gesturing to the toadstool tyke in Heather's lap, "Does he sleep through the night?"

"Oh, he's *so* good," Heather raved, seeming to see the place setting in front of her for the first time, "He's so, so good. Mostly I keep him up 'cause I can't stop pushing his button nose. He's gonna save the whole, wide world." Everyone looked to their plate. The thing beside Dr. Fleming with the head of a whatever tented its fingers, resting wooly forehead on knuckles.

"What the hell is that thing," said Brian.

*"Uh,* which?" said Simon Price, reaching for his absinthe.

"Any of them."

"That's Dr. Fleming's–" Simon started.

"You've already met *ours,*" Gwen interrupted, leaning over her hubby again, "That big heffer in the corner." They all turned to the head in the rocking chair. Still she smoldered with silent fury aimed solely at Brian, with much gnashing of her matchbox-sized teeth. Unnerved, B turned back to his gazpach.

"We call It *Kbal,*" said Simon, a sprig of arugula plastered to his front tooth, "It's a live specimen for the Department of Cosmic Phenomena."

"Mostly she's a head," said Gwen, "But sometimes she's a fun, little breeze under your skirt, or a hot worm in your brain. She crash-landed in the Cambodian jungle 10,000 years ago."

"8,600," said Simon, "We drilled into the, *uh,* mandible, carbon dated the bone shavings."

*"God, she hated it!"* Gwen yowled, breaking into those fire alarm titters again. She turned to chuck her cloth napkin across the room so it landed on the head, bunched over a big eye. The demon fumed.

Brian pushed himself away from the table.

"Yeah, sorry," he said, and he couldn't stomach any more, didn't really care, "This is fascinating. Mallory's in the kitchen, yeah? I gotta shoot her a quick, *uh...*" He stood, soda in hand, and wandered off through the kitchen portal.

*"Told you, hon,"* Gwen's voice trailed him, *"Such a piece of shit."*

"Where are the puppies?" Brian asked of Mallory, who stood bosomed in hovering caterers, fielding questions and tasting chocolate sauces. An absinthe bar dominated the kitchen island, the grande glass fountain and its circlet of spouts perched over a ring of glasses topped in grated silver spoons. Between the fountain's legs, an ebony bowl of sugar cubes perched on a built-in shelf.

*"Brian,"* cautioned the lady of the house, "During a soiree, it's impossibly cheeky to enter a hostess' kitchen uninvited. Then again, you are like family now."

"Where are Max and the puppies?"

"I don't keep tabs on Campbell's cat, but I'm sure he's around somewhere," said Mallory, dipping her finger in a proffered bowl of whipped frosting, its shade bruised peach, "I haven't stuffed him yet, if that's what you're thinking." A server passed through with a round of drinks on a tray, stopping to angle around Brian as she did. The same oily guest who'd gone off to clean his ass came bumbling rather sheepishly down the kitchen stairs in shirtsleeves and a crisp pair of plaid boxers, suit pants folded over his arm.

*"Maaal,"* bleated the pantsless guy, "What a showerhead. Thanks, doll." He nudged past the caterer at the fridge to smack a wet peck on Mallory's cheek.

"You can scrub your filthy bottom in my shower anytime, Senator," said Mallory, then she gave a little wave over, "Brian, this is State Senator Grant McKenzie, an ex before Campby."

"Do I spy a fellow Moth? A Moyamensing man?" said the greased fuck, with dripping hand outstretched, "Senator McKenzie."

"State senator," Brian nodded, eyeballing the hand.

"No, Brian's just our housesitter," Mallory frowned, "No affiliation, barely a bachelor's degree. But I highly recommend pissing him off if you have time. He's adorable with steam coming out of his ears."

"You sound like my constituents," said Senator McKenzie, making devil horns behind his head with pointer fingers, nearly dropping his pants in the process, "You haven't caught the woke mind virus, have you?"

"Your fly's open," said B.

McKenzie looked down to confirm. He tried to smooth the fabric back in place.

"They're Campbell's shorts," he said, "So he must have quite the hog on him, huh, Mal?"

"Not really," said Mal and Bri, as one. The bar server came back around with her tray.

"Don't mind if I do," said the state senator, and he flung pant legs over his shoulder to snag a drink on his way back to the party, "Gotta check on Heather." After he'd gone, Brian trailed Mallory round the island.

"I wish you could have met Pieter and Rina, the Fabers," she pouted, consulting a list stuck to the fridge, "They're our no-shows, which is very unlike them. He's over in Speculative Biology at the university, she's big pharma. Very Bert and Ernie, I find them sexually hypnotic. So that means we're down a demon as well, I'm sad to say. And likely the oldest haunt of our little bunch. Theirs is a free-floating bubble of undersea magma Pieter tracked off the coast of Reyka–"

"I want to see the puppies before I go."

"Well, I don't see why not," Mallory shrugged, and she wound over to a spout off the big fountain, "Only one of the caterers took them for a walk, so I suppose you'll just have to wait." She snatched up a sugar cube and dropped it on a silver spoon, then opened the tap. A generous tipple soaked the sugar on its way to the glass below, then one of the chefs swooped in with a lighter; the cube went up in a lick of flame, melting through the spoon slats. Bri and Mal watched the sweet sink in the green.

"Have one," purred Madame Absinthe.

"I'm off booze," said Brian, "And I thought you only drank out of vases."

Mallory squinched, one eye closed.

"Why would you think that?"

"That was all I could ever find," he said, "You guys don't own drinking glasses."

"Cabinet over the microwave, Bri."

"Well, *no–*" he said, looking up at the spot, then he cocked his head, "No, because I've..."

He crossed over to flip the cabinet open: glasses, from wine to water to shot.

"Honestly," Mallory chuckled, between quaffs of liqueur, "You make the most bizarre assumptions about me. I own drinking glasses. I haven't killed my pets." The caterers milled about at a noticeably slower pace, hanging on every word.

"I didn't say that you—*OK, yeah,*" B sighed, "I guess I've been chugging vases all year like an idiot." Mallory pushed off from the island, a whiff of lion tamer in her heel-toe, like if she had a whip, she'd have long since cracked it.

"I'm sure it was all very cloak-and-dagger," she said, hips shifting closer and closer, "And I'm sure you told your cattiest gays, and now your friends think I'm *très* kooky."

"I don't have any friends," said Brian, "But if I did, sure."

"*Mmmbully* for you," Mallory relished, riding a shiver, "Isolation's the first step towards really becoming somebody." The same server angled between them with a plate of something pan-seared and dripping. The smell off the meat milked a burst of saliva under Brian's tongue; turned his gut with its fattiness.

"Tummy settled enough for foie gras in a gorgonzola fig reduction?" the server posed.

"Nope," he breathed, trying not to hurl a second time.

"But I suspect the bigger problem with *youuu, Briii,*" Mallory mused, and she took the plate of liver in his stead, ferrying it to a corner of the counter, shaking out her mane, "Is your fixation with punctilios and their chain reactions. *Did I do it right, Mommy-Daddy? Will I get good spanked or bad?* It shouldn't ever really have to be said aloud, but decency just is not a bloodhound, so absolutely none of us are on the run. We're proton collisions. Allegiance only to the violence in my heart, the sweetness of my bite; never the flesh on my bones. Never my choices. And really, babe, I see such a dazzling, nasty man trapped under the psychic obesity of you."

"Tremendous," said Brian, still swallowing hard.

"Someone who still has all his *haaair,*" she dangled, "That Brian doesn't worry. He still has a copy of our house key. He's up in my office right now, noncorporeal and hard as a rock."

"Can I get his number?" lobbed one of the caterers, and the room broke into giggles (sans Bri).

His hostess raised her fork and brows aloft in merry punctuation, then she dug into her foie gras and absinthe. An orderly construction line formed for a tiered cake by the back window, the chefs queuing along the counters with what looked like puzzle pieces of a whole: mini-architecture, in penile columns and vulval archways. Meanwhile, a familiar feline came loping down the kitchen stairs, scuttling straight for Brian's shins with a happy cry and a hard nuzzle.

"Aw, look who's still alive," chewed Mallory, juices dripping down her chin, "You must be relieved, Bri."

"Hi, mister," said Brian, kneeling down to get a pinch of cheek fluff, a flick of tail.

*Moww,* moaned Maximillius Felinus, and his little chest swole and shrunk, *Mowwwwwww.*

"I know, bud," Brian whispered, and he hefted the blue cat up to his shoulder so they could be face to face, "I miss her, too." Max put a paw to Brian's chin. From the party room burst a bilious round of cackles, with Gwen's siren titters cresting the others in lofty cadenza. Then, on the tail of that cacophony—and from under everyone's feet—rose a blood-curdling shriek which stopped the catering team in their tracks and jolted B's blood pressure sky-high. The cat went rigid in his arms. Mallory's head slumped back, joints slack, having been taken hostage by a humongous eye roll.

"That'll be Campbell," she announced, upon recovering, "What a terrible baby he's been. Famously prick-jealous at parties."

"Has anyone checked on him?" Bri asked, glancing round at the team, who'd snapped back to work.

*"Portia!"* Mal sniped at the lead chef, the young woman's lapels braided navy to the others' whites, "I said *no* huckleberry!"

"Maybe he hurt himself, Mallory."

"He'd deserve it for leaving me to host," she batted back, then she crossed the room in half a breath, to wind up and smack a jam jar from Portia's hands. The glass shattered out of sight behind the island with enough force to send globs of ruddy gore ricocheting up to cabinets and fridge.

*"Sorry, Mrs. Dahlhaus,"* boomed the chefs in unison, and a pair of juniors broke off straightaway to attend to the mess. Poor Portia melted into the cake-making queue. Out the kitchen windows, another server in uniform paced up the drive, laughing to the phone at his ear, running a hand through a James Dean coiffure, the bouquet of leashes in his fist tugging him along in a halting jog. Brian let Max hop down on the island to sniff at a fountain spout, then he went up on tiptoes; he could just make out the tops of poodle heads scampering round the back corner of the house.

"Was that the puppies?" Brian asked of the chefs closest to the cake tower and the windows behind it. The one wearing a black bandana leaned her head around the monolith to peek, then she gave a thumbs up.

"They'd better have poopied," Mallory munched.

"Jason looks like he's on a call," said the chef who'd looked, "He'll prolly be right in."

Brian nodded in relief, then another feral, room-piercing wail ruptured from under the kitchen tiles, pinging off the glass fountain with a splinter so everyone's shoulders jumped to their ears.

"If I were to get my *checkbook*," Mallory ventured in the all-clear, a hunk of liver quivering on her fork, "Could you pretty-pretty please take care of Camby, B-man?" Then, upon seeing his face, she quickly added: "We've *just* confirmed the puppies are safe and sound."

"I don't know what you think I can do," said the B-man, gripping himself by the ribs.

"Campbell likes you," she insisted, "Let him spin out a little. Rub his back. Fifteen thou, or a smallish painting of your choosing."

Everyone looked on. Brian reached for Max, perched on the island corner. Mr. Cattish sniffed his finger.

"I think we're approaching some kind of annual gift limit," said B, after considering, "You might want to talk to your accountant."

"Death and taxes for thee, not me," Mallory pished, then she pointed to the row of premium knives in their wall-mounted block, "Grab one, just in case."

They split to round Ursula and the leather studded chaise, then Mallory handed over her absinthe so she could snap in half to heft the parlor palm from its stand, fishing under terracotta with pincer fingers. A cool blue band ran through the handle of the knife Bri had grabbed, and his pulse throbbed against it.

"My spouse is normally very cute when he dissociates," Mal wheezed, strangled from her forward bend, "We love to bundle in his parents' things, chase each other in the night. And our demon lives for a roleplay."

"Hold up," said Bri, stepping over to the basement door, and he tried its handle, which held fast, "Did he lock himself down there or did you do that?"

A brass tinkle answered his question, for a little key had discharged from the bottom of the pot with a spurt of soil. Upon unfurling, key in hand, a bloody headrush overtook Mallory, leaving her swaying, cheeks and forehead gone scarlet. The lady stumbled forth, swiping for Brian's arm, balling his polo in a fist until the spell passed, her expression near orgasmic. B tried not to spill her drink, but a splash slipped over the edge, drenching his wrist.

"I was meant to be his stepmother," Mallory whispered, as the blood drained from her head, "That was the plan way back when, but then Rainer wouldn't leave Mammy. She was a Campbell, of the Philadelphia Campbells, they owned all the lace mills out this way. Gave birth at 70, real galvanized Scottish steel. By the end, she was just scraps of tartan. And my husband's never recovered from being two surnames smushed together. No room for a man at all, really." Another shriek from below punctuated the point.

"*Sooo* cute," said Bri, as a signal for her to let go. He tugged, but she gripped harder still. He twirled the knife in his other palm.

"Tell him it isn't too late," the Lady Bain-Dahlhaus instructed, chin set, her champagne mane tousled, upended from the bend, "We haven't had cake yet, and Campby would want to know. He's been *edging* for cake. You understand? We're all of us on the brink."

"Heard."

Mallory let his polo go, then like a drunky vampire bat, she swooped in for a ravenous peck. B nearly dodged it, but the smooch landed at the extreme corner of his mouth. In recoil, he swiped over the spot, nearly nicking his shoulder with the tip of his blade. He half-expected the back of his hand to come away green, rotting. Unfazed, his hostess with the mostest dangled that little piece of brass.

"You boys have fun," she chirped, and they traded absinthe for key, then Mal gestured in pantomime to the door under the stairs before retreating some, circling round to perch upon the chaise. Brian turned the key over in his hand. He blew soil from it.

"I won't be taking a painting," said B, meaning *go get that checkbook, sis,* then he unlocked the blue door and palmed the key. A bare bulb on the other side jumped on with a pull of its chain. Brian stepped through.

"Campbell?" he called downstairs, past the pool of light at the bottom, "You down there, man?"

B squatted to his heels. A free-standing pillar partly blocked what seemed to be an ample, unfinished underhall. Paint chips littered the cement floor. Whole swaths of the walls had pocked and crumbled to orange-white dust.

"I can't see," he said to Mallory, who watched from the chaise, "Is there another light?"

"You'll see when you're down there," she nodded, leaning back to set her absinthe on the coffee table. Brian went to his butt.

"Campbell?" he tried again, "You good, bud?" Keeping a hand round the doorframe, he bumped down a step, fingers still gripping inside the lounge. He leaned over his knees and more pillars shifted into view: five or six uneven rows spanning the breadth of *DAS NEST*, all battered, all blocking two-foot-wide slices of the basement. From his angle, some of the pillars lined up to a vanishing point so he just made out half an uncovered lightswitch beyond. A musk like wet clay settled at the back of Brian's throat. Nothing whatever stirred.

"I think, *uhh...*" he whispered, trying to keep the knife out of sight from basement eyes, *"No, yeah,* I changed my mind." And he raised his ass from the top step.

*"Watch your fingies!"* cried Mallory, suddenly on her feet, and Brian just had time to whisk his hand away as she gave the chaise two quick shoves: one to angle the foot against the open door, then another at the head to slam it shut. By the time B reached his feet and tried the knob, he was already trapped.

"Are you fucking kidding me?" he deadpanned. He didn't even bother taking a shoulder to the wood.

"I jammed the chaise under the handle," Mallory's voice rang through the door, "I'm just gonna plop awhile, K, B? And I'll catnap till I'm off the carousel, and when you have my man ready, I'll open her up. Sound fair?"

"No," Brian called back, "This is extremely *un*fair, Mallory."

*"Well,"* she sighed, and nothing else needed to be said.

Brian slid the knife into his waistband for safekeeping and pulled out his phone. Not a single bar of service flickered in the top corner, fucking duh and also obviously. He swiped the flashlight on, then drafted a new text, shaking his head all the while:

> *If you get this, I've been locked in the basement (kidnapped) at the big house in Hemlock Circle in Wynnewood. Please call the police.*

On second thought, he added:

> *But tell them there are friendly dogs and a cat here, so please don't come guns drawn or anything. Thanks very much.*

Upon prompting him to select a contact, Brian scrolled awhile through drinking buds and sex acquaintances. Some names he could barely bring himself to look at. He settled on *Mom,* then sent the screen to sleep with a grimace before he could click *Send.*

"Hey, Campbell?" said B, his voice having shrunk somewhat. He got the knife out again. The light from the bare bulb made a fuzzy pool beyond the bottom step. Brian trudged down and stopped there, pointing his flashlight from wall to wall. The hall under the house stretched off to murkiness, but he could still spy the bare lightswitch, off between crumbling pillars.

"Call out if you can hear me, K?"

Only the scrape of his own feet, the flick-hop of crickets filled the gloom, then:

*Mowwwwwww,* came a low siren growl somewhere beyond those pillars, its undertones distinctly human. Brian whipped his phone around so shadows fled pell-mell. A human-sized tail, sleek and black, twitched around a corner, but when he aimed the light back to check, he could see it was just an extension cord. Muffled party talk crescendoed above in alien octave.

"I think I know how you feel," Brian tried, shying his head around the closest columns, "There was this Vanessa Williams concert at the Mann a while back. I took it very seriously. Sunburn, alcohol poisoning. Edibles beforehand, shrooms at intermission. Very Team Do-Too-Much. There was also a...verbal altercation with a group of breast cancer survivors on a bus tour? I didn't know that at the time, so *not* my fucking intention. But. And I don't even remember 'Save the Best for Last,' which has honestly been a really big blow to my sense of cosmic justice. So Campbell, if you want to just lay your head on my shoulder and cry it out, I totally–"

*"Ich bin nicht Campbell,"* whined the cat-man in the dark, *"Ich bin der Katzenmeister."*

The mewling led Brian down another row. Unmistakably, a papier-mâché ear stuck out from behind a pillar down by the far wall, not far from the lightswitch. Bri changed his grip on the knife; hid it behind his back. Circling round brought Campbell further into view: he wore the same oversized puss head as in the photo of his dog-headed Hedonisticum students. Underneath, the familiar sight of his nude dadbod huddled close to the column so as Brian passed the pillars to its side, he was just a white mass of flesh from shoulder to droopy butt to supinated ankle. Something about not only the man, but the cat head hiding its face gripped Brian in shivers.

"There you *aaare,*" he cooed, trying to project calm, "How ya feelin', champ?"

The head turned some to peek over, even as its body snugged away. Wire hanger whiskers sprouted from the pink nose. One eye drew wide and mean, angled to high condescension.

"Hi!"

*Miaow.*

"Uh-huh," said Brian, and he squatted maybe ten feet away, the blade tucked close to his forearm, "Hey, do you remember where your clothes are?"

The cat-man hissed.

"No prob," Bri brightened, the phone shaking in his hand, "Do you want to come sit with me?" To which *der Katzenmeister* pounced, easily halving the distance between them, landing on the cement with an audible scrape over his very human knees. Bushy moobs and belly bulged, hairy shoulders balanced high on knuckles. The papier-mâché head tottered, but came to rest at a cock. Campbell's scrotum dangled improbably low, testicles swinging.

"*Du bist der Schildknaaapp,*" he moaned, from under his second head, "*Der Naaarr.*"

"Yeah, I took French," Bri shrugged, free hand on the cement floor to steady himself, "And I blocked most of it out, honestly."

"*Ah, französische?*" Cat-Campbell chuckled, "*Dann du bist der <u>damoiseau</u>.*" He flipped round into a magnificent stretch along the floor, white cheeks clenched to dimples where a tail ought to be. The cat head angled up and away, haughty as anything.

"Cool, cool," B muttered, shifting to criss-cross applesauce, and he set the knife down at his tailbone, within reach. Again, his eye caught an outline of interest: a deepish alcove set in a wall which would have been just below the kitchen stairs; no, the powder room? He'd gotten a little turned around. He looked back for the basement stairs, but they were lost somewhere past the jumble of cement columns. Campbell brought a limp paw up to where his cat mouth would be and set to cleaning himself. In that alcove behind, something gleamed; some form magnifique caught the light off Brian's phone.

"I didn't know all this was down here," said Bri, "It's not really on your guys' map in the hall."

"*Es ist das Fundament des alten Hauses meines Vaters,*" der Katzenmeister languished, between licks, "*Rainer...Rudolph...Dahlhaus.*"

"Is that—that's your dad, right?"

"*Ja, mein Papa.*"

"Yeah, Mallory said he was big man at your college," said Brian, and he leaned forward like a teacher at show-and-tell, body language wide open, "You know, when I get too fucked up, I think about my dad, too. All the things I wish I could say. I get it." The words landed like a wet fart on the cement. That big cat head reared back at a snail's pace, like it was gearing up to sneeze, until it just stared up at the unfinished ceiling. Fuzzy shoulders shed felinity. Proud moobs deflated.

"Mine was a long time ago," Bri clarified, digging that hole, "I'm not actively grieving or anything. I mean, I fully hate him, if that's your thing. Mine never did anything wrong. A+ guy by all accounts. My, *um*—Andrew always gets so mad at me when I say that, but he has his own...unresolved dad stuff. But *I* was a kid. Andrew was an adult, basically. Mine was sudden, his was cancer. So you can't really—I just think you can be allowed to hate someone for not being around anymore. My mom doesn't understand that. She refuses. But it can be no one's fault, and it's still completely rational to just be so fucking angry every day you want to die or take LSD and be a shrieking cat in a basement. I'm sure you know this, Campbell, that it never really rights itself, but sometimes the basement can be kinda–"

The cat-man grasped his papier-mâché helmet from behind, sliding fingers round its base, worming his face out beard-first. B winced.

*"Why are you bringing up grief right now?"* Campbell blurted, sweat glistening upon his reddened face, his bramble-bush, "I don't grieve. We don't grieve, ever."

"Oh, I-I just thought maybe we were commiserating," Bri stammered, "Like, Dead Dad Club?"

*"Mein Papa ist tot,"* Campbell realized, his pupils like shining pools of ink, *"Mein Gott, Papa ist tot! Oh fuck!"* And he reared his head back to shriek again, moobies trembling with the surge of rage in his heart.

*"NO, CAMPBELL,"* Brian cried, swinging a hand back to rest upon the knife, *"CAMPBELL. CHILL OUT, BRO."* But all he could do, aside from stab a bitch, was point the phone light steady and true and watch as waves of grief-wrath rocked Campbell again and again. The galoofus shrieked himself to absolute retches so he had to drop to all fours, tongue waggling, long strings of saliva catching in the nest of his beard. The papier-mâché cat head rolled away in disgust.

*"Whyyy,"* Camby moaned, pallid thighs jiggling, *"Whyyy-uhhh did you saaay thaaat-uuhhh."*

"Campbell, I am *so* sorry," said Brian, and the sick thought passed that he ought to have a little popcorn for the show, ought to get comfortable against a column, "Let's breathe. Do you know how to breathe down deep with your diaphragm?"

*"I don't wanna."*

*"OK,"* said Brian, rolling his eyes a little, and he did move to a column, just to rest his back, sliding the knife along the ground as he went, "You want to tell me about your dad?"

*"Yeah,"* Campbell snuffed.

"OK, bud," said Bri, settling in, "You tell me about your dad."

"Well, he was pretty neato," said the beheaded *Meister,* twisting a palm against his eye, "He was born in Brandenburg, in the old Kingdom of Prussia? Picture a red-assed little changeling bastard among sexless, joyless Old Lutherans. Pops was like a Germanic Steve McQueen, or a fox, because he totally *Great Escape*'d their, *um,* God through a hole in the ground. And he really loved classic cars and *Cranberry–Apfelmus.* He came to all my football games. He, *uh–*"

Campbo hiccupped.

"–helped found Moyamensing with the other Savants, which was pretty hip for the time, and then he arranged for me to teach there after I busted my knee in Boston, which was also pretty hip, because I wasn't exactly the most qualified or even interested back then. But I got better, thanks to Mallory and her spells: *das Konversationsdeutsch, die Verhütungsmittel für meine Schüler.* She's why my penis is so impressive."

"Uh-huh," said Bri, "Right."

"I'm the luckiest guy I know," said Campbell, and he, too, scoonched to criss-cross applesauce, uncircumcised pecker snugged to a button atop his ballsack, "Witch wife, hero dad. For my Sweet—*hic!*—16, he took me whaling in the South Pacific, and even though his legs didn't work any-more, he harpooned a pygmy blue all by himself."

"Wow."

"1984, so he would have been...*hic!* 133 years young."

"Oh. That's..."

Campby grinned, his face alight in sudden recall.

"Pops had this cutaneous horn growing out of his eye socket. We'd dress it in tinsel, and Mallory would kiss it three times on New Year's Eve. He called it his living flower - *meine lebendige Blume.* It made a curlicue like this." Campbell twisted a finger out from his eyeball a good four inches, then sighed deep, with his diaphragm. After a last hiccup, his belly relaxed so his junk could barely be seen.

Upstairs, half a dozen chairs scraped back from the table, followed by the muffled blast of some old skool house beatz, thumping back by what might have been the lounge. Dust fell as a parade of feet passed overhead; the ponderous roll of what may have been a giant head tipping end over end. Brian angled the light up to watch the powder fall. He cleared his throat.

"So do you feel a little –"

"Hey, so," Campbell said, and in the split-second Bri swung the light back on him, he'd somehow got to his feet again, made taller, wider by his silhouette's enormity off the little light, "Do you want to see him?"

"Who?"

*"Mein Papa,"* said Campbell, his eyes pure black and white, "C'mon." And he turned and walked off between two columns, flat butt dimpling. Brian kept the light on the spot even after he'd gone.

"Yo," B meeped, "Come back." But he didn't. Brian pushed himself to standing, then bent again for the kitchen knife. At a squat, he shone his phone over by that far alcove, picking up the figure tucked within; the mannequin modeling. A burst of twisting shapes sprung from its head, and he couldn't quite make sense of what he was seeing, not even flicking the light back and forth so the shadows took dimension, metal glinting.

"Found him!" came Campbell's voice, further on, tucked out of sight, "Come see, come see!"

With a heave, Bri complied, clutching his weapon at his side, not even trying to hide it anymore. *Der Meister* waited a few rows down, where several columns were cleaved straight through, in a barbarous line, so one could see to the stacked-stone walls behind them. Professor Flat Ass hunched over the standing paintings stacked there, rifling through. At the party above, someone jacked up the sick-ass beats so they pounded through the floors like a late-nite Berliner rave.

"Are those load-bearing?" Brian asked, meaning the ravaged columns. Campbo shook his head.

"Not since Mal arsoned the manor-house in '99," he said, lifting a big boy from the stack, its frame charred wood, "With Papa's permission, of course."

"Oh, of course."

"He always wanted to go up in smoke, and we had to make room in our married life," Campbell clarified, and he flipped the painting around, "And that old place wasn't demon-friendly. Lookit: the stud himself." In gleaming oils, a young teen Campbell with a full bramble-beard posed between two straightbacked armchairs, one occupied by an imperious pucker-face of a matron in head-to-toe tartan, the other swallowing up the supercentenarian propped in its cushions, that shrunken potato barely passing for human, even idealized in art. Splotches of sweet orange and apple green served as stains on his argyle sweater. Thickets of white ear hair grew wild and free, matching the unruly brow that ran continuously from over his bleary left eye to the keratinized growth which served as its mate, spiraling out from the old man's right socket. Enameled text at the bottom read *R. DAHLHAUS & FAMILIE.*

"Oh jeez," Brian exclaimed, his face screwing up, "Was that thing cancerous?"

"It was a *gift,*" said Campby, beard going still, eyes narrowing, "He metastasized into the loam of the universe, where spirits *hin und her.* The ant farm between planets. That squirming mess." Dilated gaze dropped to the knife in Brian's hand.

"Well, you guys..." Bri lied, buoying frown to smile, "Make *quite* the attractive family."

"What are you gonna do with that?" asked Campbell, dropping the family portrait so it came to leaning on his legs, nubbin dangling o'er the frame, "That's my Garasuki." B's knees locked up.

"It's just protection, Campbell," he said.

"Uh-huh," said Ole' Empty Eyes, beard trembly, and he pointed up to the main house, "Did Grant McKenzie give you that knife? Or did my wife?" The question sent Brian hemming and hawing and snaking right on back through the columns, shoulder scraping round a bend. Campbell trailed at once, letting the painting drop facedown in the dust. A stretch of unbolstered floorboards above their heads sagged in time with the bodies bouncing to synth and bass.

"Have you guys ever done counseling?" Brian offered, "I know straight people really get off on that."

*"Gimme that knife."*

*"Ooh,* what about a ginger ale?" B tried, swiping wide as a warning, just barely missing a slice over Campbell's titties, "Or gazpacho? Your caterers are very good." He went serpentine again behind the next pillar he passed, then kept on ass-backwards into one of the ravaged ones so he nearly fell into the exposed rebar at its center, a rusty stalactite of the stuff hanging overhead. Campbell lunged, and Brian just managed to roll out of the way. The big doof came inches from goring himself, but stopped just in time, the half-column breaking apart under his mitts.

"Campbell, please!" Brian begged, "Someone's gonna get hurt, man." He broke into a clumsy bolt, muscles too cold to run well. The walls splayed out of sight as Brian skittered into the dark, far past what should have been the bounds of *DAS NEST* up above, so he could almost imagine a different sort of house sat atop their heads, one to match the breadth between the old supports; a country castle, wide in stature and great in pride, even by Main Line standards. Burned-out columns numbered too many; became a colonnade to hoist a long-gone ballroom. The light off his phone swung ahead with every pump of Brian's arms, more strobe than torch. Cement underfoot cracked away to loose backfill. His pursuer's bare feet slapped pit-a-pat, two paces behind, then went silent on the soil.

When he couldn't take it anymore, Brian wheeled around, blade bare, but Campbell was nowhere to be seen, unless he'd ensconced himself along the underground arcade; those cement cloisters to all sides, blocking the lost exit. Panting, Bri backed to a more central position so he could see between the darkened rows...under the hundred struts...

"I remember now," taunted Campbo-Bambo, from behind every column, *"Der Homo.* You suckled my plants."

"I got 20 years on you, fucker," Brian warned, and for the first time that long year, he felt capable in his own skin, "If you try me, I will kill you."

*"Fängt an mit B..."* said the hundred Campbuses, and Brian swore he just missed the creep in every flash of light, swore a flick of human–cat tail slipped into every resurgence of shadow...and those columns seemed to creep closer all the while...*"Bradley? Nein, nein: Brent? Nein, nein, nein: Braaandooon."*

*"STOP BEING SUCH A DICK!"* B shrieked, *"I KNOW YOU KNOW IT."* His fingers cramped around the knife handle such that he wasn't sure he could ever let it go. On his next spin around, he spotted what might have been the bottom of the basement stairs off thataway. He pinned his phone light to it so the steps took shape, then flew towards salvation, only for—*ba-whump!* – two bushy, sweaty arms to lock round his waist, driving him to the dirt in a hard shoulder tackle. Bri kept his grip on the knife as they fell, even as all the wind rushed out of his lungs, but landed with arm fully extended. Before he could bend it back, Campbell hefted himself overtop and slammed a heavy palm over that elbow, his ballsack dragging up the small of Bri's back.

*"I didn't get cake!"* grated *der große Meister, "Das ist nicht fair!* She promised! Years ago she promised!"

*"GET THE FUCK OFF ME,"* Brian summoned, bucking all 250-something of sweaty Campbell ass to one side; still, though, Basement Pops kept a deadlock on that arm. Bri's phone spun away in the tussle, landing screendown, its backlight casting a dire glow up and out. He just managed to wriggle a pinned hand out from under himself and wrap a second fist round the knife, then Campbell did the same a second later. The Garasuki tipped to and fro as they grappled for its handle. The guys locked eyes.

*"Let it go,* son," barked the professor in Dr. Dahlhaus, authority bubbling up to float atop the doof's high like pond scum, "We can still work something out—*but only—if you—let go."* And just the paternal tone (OK, plus the wild beard, the lingering slime of dick'n'balls chafing by) undid a knot in Bri's spine. Root chakra opened, and abs unclenched long enough for biceps to weaken, for fingers to go all buttery. The knife slipped through to Dahlhaus advantage. With a wild hog cry, the victor scrambled to rise triumphant, but before Brian could even get eyes on the blade again, Campbell's bare foot promptly slipped out from under him, and rather than fall to his knees, or flat on his face, he went flailing back upon his hip, and—*slllck!* – buried the Garasuki to its hilt in his own forearm, the tip bursting clean on the other side.

"No, don't – *holy shit!"* Brian hacked, rubbing dust from his eyes, his tongue.

*"Ahh,* I've stabbed myself," Campbell proclaimed, "It's all the way through. *Ahh,* a knife in me."

"Oh *God,"* Bri spat, "Of course you fucking did, you fucking oaf." He leapt to standing, then weathered an enormous, incongruous yawn, all that cortisol sloughing off to a wave of fatigue in the absurd lull. B grabbed his phone, then reared back to land a choice kick at Campbell's ribs, only stopping at the last, when the big guy flinched. Brian dropped to a squat to inspect the knife, wrenching his patient closer by the thinning crown of his melon head.

*"I just want cake, OK?"* Campbell sobbed, *"OK? I'll be good now."*

"Don't turn your arm," Bri sneered, and he leaned over to grab under Camby's pits, "Come on. If you hit an artery, you'd be bleeding more." They scooted off for the stairs, Brian doing most of the work, really putting his ass into it, despite his ballooning contempt. Campbell's bottom left a snakey trail in the dust. At the bottom of the basement stairs, they stopped so B could mop his brow.

"I'm scared to go to the party," Campby admitted, "I don't like people in my house. And the catering team is an alumni venture. Faces I'd rather not answer to because of...actions."

"Well, they're already here, and you're being rude," Brian pointed out.

"She expects me to be so *on*. I can be a very charismatic lion, but not when everyone's looking."

"Maybe you should tell her that."

"We avoid kindnesses," Campbell bristled, "Needless obligation *ist ein Erektion–killer.*"

"You're lucky I'm good at context," B noted, "Get up, I'm not carrying you upstairs." If he hadn't waited for Campbell to go first, for the lull in the sniffles as the himbo negotiated stairs on one good hand and two shaky knees, he might not have heard it:

*Euuuywwwh.*

"You hear that?"

*Euuywwh.*

Bri whipped around, checking over both shoulders, off into the dark underhouse, then he brought the light down the length of the basement stairs, catching that void underneath. A shape wriggled there. Bri crept closer, leaning his head to one side.

The creature in the dirt barely resembled a 6-month old puppy, let alone the yippy baboo he'd last seen in winter. Little Äther could barely lift her head, let alone cry for the weakness in her limbs, in her shrunken neck. Patches of chewed-down hair lined the swollen belly distended entirely from the scallopridge of a dozen visible ribs. She squeezed her little eyes against the light. Her tail twitched into something like a wag. The dust around her body showed no sign of movement, of any recent rising up or laying down. Again, she tried to whine, but no sound came out. Her tongue went limp.

Brian uncurled. He puffed up his cheeks, letting his head drop back, too pissed to cry. Campbell neared the top of the stairs, then backslid two steps, cradling his stab wound.

"Owie owie," said the doof, "Do I have to? Can't we stay down here and cuddle till they go?"

"I will cuddle a foot up your ass if you're not upstairs in 2 seconds."

Campbo griped, but hopped to. Bri swiped around on his phone to open the camera app, then took a nauseating pup-shot; then another five or six with the flash on, even though he could tell the light pained her. With a click, he scooted to texts to attach the series, deleting the stupid fucking 'kidnapped' draft along the way. Upon selecting the only appropriate contact, he swallowed his pride so quick, as a matter of course, like he'd never even had a gag reflex for that. Lo and behold, a handy bar of service flickered to half-life. Bri sent off the batch, the plea, then stripped his polo to wrap Äther in it.

"Come on," he gruffed, his heart broke the fuck. Back upstairs in a tick, he stomped over Campbell in the cramped landing and rapped at the door, then pounded so he could be heard through the pounding b-b-b-beatz.

"I don't think she'll let you bring that to the party," Campbell muttered, a little woozy, but he managed to stand all the same, propping his pierced arm on the wall, "And you know, this doesn't feel like much? Well, *ein bisschen* if I bump it. I know LSD isn't an analgesic, so maybe it's just shock." Bri kept pounding until he could feel the chaise scraping out from under the door handle, then he shoved straight on through to a blitz of barking faces, the other poods leaping at the ends of their leashes for the bundle in his arms, all four babes huge, hale, and hearty. The chocolate phantom snarled, his brown eyes rolling. The gingers muscled among themselves, tumbling one over the other, then rising like heads of a fluffy hydra. Mallory anchored, now as stark-nudiefied as Campbell, drink in one hand, doggie lead in the other, her mane unbound, volumized with humidity, with transient static. A strobe at her back flashed green across the entire first floor.

"Welcome back, boys!" she cried, with a boobulous shimmy, *"Tanzparty!"*

Campbell stumbled through the snapping dogs, knife arm flung high.

"I got stabbed all the way *throoough* down there!" he crowed to Mallory, to their party carrying on in the front hall upon checkerboard dance floor: *ohh,* nudiebutts all, from lanky Senator McKenzie hip-bumping on down to a groovy Dr. Fleming, twisting her short-statured behind. With lusty cheers, the gang hailed Campbell's stabbing. The wooly-headed animal-man waved his trunk high, broad chest covered in gorgeous, downy black fur. Gwen and Simon Price rolled their giant head between them like she was a big beach ball. Even poor, dusty Heather McKenzie sat au naturel on a sharp-backed chair pulled in from the dining room, foot tapping the tile, that baby-shroom still at the suck in her arms.

"Big, brave puss," Mallory fawned, and she let her absinthe drop to the rug so to launch two dozen kisses round her hubby's stab wound. Again and again her leash arm tugged toward the basement door, fastened still to snapping pups by the loop in the lead.

"Get them, please," yipped Bri, fully trapped on the landing by the onslaught of pup.

"I thought I missed cake," Campbus sniveled, helping himself to love handles, drawing sulky circles round his wife's bumpy areolas, "I was very, very scared I'd never taste again."

"I couldn't do that to you, darling," Mal moaned at his ear, and the Garasuki's bloody tip snagged in her mane as she drew him tighter still, "Unless I *really, really* wanted to."

"Guys," snapped Bri, but the Dahlhauses could only gasp between smooches, his wienus inflating, her flesh goosedappled, and somehow their fronts had already got sticky. They tongued crazy hard. Mallory dropped the leash lead, and suddenly untethered, all four poodlets leapt for Brian and Äther. A flash of fangs nipped upon polo and elbow and silken ear. One of the apricots mounted the chocolate phantom.

"*Bri!*" Mallory gasped, for Campbell had begun biting her neck, "I never knew you had it in you. Well, maybe I suspected. Stabbing's so very forceful, though, and you're, *well.* Why do you still have bottoms on?"

"Get your dogs," said Brian, trying to fend them all off.

"You're not bringing that thing up here, are you?" said Mallory, noticing for the first time the tiny face in the shirt bundle, and she broke off to chomp Campbell back, for he'd bit down to blood, "I *forbid it.* I threw it down there for a reason."

"She needs water, Mallory," said B, "A vet."

"Absolutely not. You bring it up here—*ohh, fuck* – I'll wring its neck." Campbell had worked a few fingers in, and Mallory rode him, one leg mounted in the crook of his unstabbéd arm. Out on the dance floor, Gwen did a dirty dance between Grant McKenzie and the wooly-headed beast-man. Simon Price and Dr. Fleming mirrored a disco hustle, line-dancing away, then at one another, bare toes gripping the tiles. The mondo head rested backwards and upsy-daisy by the front door, thick locks falling away from the base of Its skull.

Wasser, the chocolate pup, leapt again, nabbing Äther on an exposed paw; her brow furrowed, but she could not even summon the stuff to yelp. Brian lifted her almost to his chin. He kneed the chocolate away, but the others swarmed in its place, sending him almost reeling back down to the basement. He careened, but got a hand on the wall.

"Fine, *if you're not gonna fucking–*" B burst, giving up, then he snarled rabidly at the aggressors, kneeing them off again in their shock at his animism. Bri practically dumped the shirt bundle behind, leaving it on the landing under the swinging bulb, then he slammed the basement door and braced himself for another barrage of leaping bites, but the bullies went right for the door. They tried to scratch through to their sister, to no avail. Pissy, the apricot bubs mobbed Brian again half-heartedly, but he shoved them off. Wasser stretched his neck out to give B's foot a sniff, then the grouch–baby snuffed and followed his mates off through the lounge.

"Come boogie–woogie!" Gwen Price called from the hall, shaking tatas all up on the state senator, "We're letting our chakras breathe!"

"Join us, B," Mallory heaved over her husband's shoulders, and Campbell's dimply ass clenched and released, again and again, "It's DJ Musik-Schlampe all night long! The 12" original: *one night only in an abandoned rubber factory, summer of '97*. This was playing when my demon found me on the dance floor."

B took a bracing breath. Those house beats stretched their muscles, really flexed to fill the space. Bass stalked the ground floor; shrieking synth pounced up the lounge stairs, only to tear back through from the kitchen; bells flit in ostinato, the same five notes writhing without end, twisting above their heads like petals in a breeze.

"*Could I get a drink?*" Brian requested, raising his voice over the rave.

"Really!?" Mal erupted, and her nails slid pink through the tufts down Campbell's back.

"Really-really," said Bri, and he had to mean it, and he *so* did, "Headfirst off the wagon, just for you."

"*Fuck, I might cum,*" Mallory shuddered. She gave her weight over to Campby, who faltered, but kept thrusting.

"K, just," Brian ventured, and he saw the opening, the skin he'd have to wear, "I don't think they'll do one for me like they did for you, with the flame and the sugar? OK, maybe they're supposed to, and I'll ask, but I feel like they're already super annoyed with me?"

"Smaller circles," his hostess growled at her mate, then came the delayed eye roll, and she crowed over the music: "You have to put on big boy balls. Or in this case, Bri, just whip 'em out."

"I can't go in there naked," he wilted, "Your chefs are mean. *Please?* I'll loosen up, I swear."

Mallory survived another catastrophic eye roll, then she unstuck herself from Campbell.

"Edge, puss, edge," she said, soothing the big bramble-butt, and she ran two hands through her mane, retreating kitchenwards, "And watch him with that fucking door, I *don't* want that dog up here." Bri over-acquiesced, making a show of restoring the chaise to a blockade, then he perched on it. Still, Campby came over to check the basement knob.

"Where's the key?" said the knifed doof.

Brian shrugged, even as he could feel it in his back pocket.

"Dare you to try it," Campbo warned, then he tweaked B on the nip and gave in to hump-stepping, his hips leading him to the dance floor, good arm pumping, *"Musik-Schlampe! Musik-Schlampe! Musik-Schlampe!"*

Bri whipped out his phone.

After a few rounds of flame-sugared green, after shedding jorts and sneaks and socks, and letting Simon Price shake a surprisingly thicc booty all down and dirty on the tiles, Brian approached Heather McKenzie where she hunched upon the lounge stairs, bouncing her shroomy tot on bony knees. He willed himself not to glance at the blue basement door.

"Hey girly," he tried, neon from absinthe, shivering in boxer briefs, "I'm the sitter. You want a lil' break?"

"Oh, I *really really* can't," Heather shied away, *"We don't allow—"*

"That's what they all say, mom," he ran right over her, "But I bet a big butt you haven't eaten, and I might've seen a plate over there with your name on it."

"He's not good with strangers, though, so..."

"Lady, neither am I," Bri lied, double-timing his knees to the ever-bouncing beat, "So I could just hold him like he's a really expensive purse while you shove dinner in your face."

Heather seemed dubious, then she winced, doubling over. A belch more croak than burp clawed its way up her throat, then expired on the tip of her tongue. The stench of her empty belly hit B in the sinuses.

"Plus there's cake," he rallied, breathing through his mouth, "And you work so hard, mama." He bestowed upon her a sympathetic pout. Heather salivated. She swiped at the drool rushing forth.

"OK, but just for a minute," she relented, twisting out of the belly cramp. With a wrenching groan, she lifted her fungus tot in the air to gaze longingly upon Its almost face; the shallow divots that made eyes and flapping mouth. Heather panted, face crumpling.

"Duh, babe!" Bri chirped, "We'll be right here." He set his drink and phone down to grab the demon round Its tubby middle, and Its milky cap flopped right back with all the gracelessness of a toddler. Jaw grit, B wrapped another hand round the baby's back, to support Its head. Heather tore herself away inch by inch, reaching for It still, then she turned tail to scurry off, tearing through the hall with arms glued to her sides, ignoring her husband as he reached for her across the dance floor.

The senator leered back at Brian. B made a show of rocking the baby.

After a while, with no Heather in sight, they settled back on the stairs again, watching the dancers give it their all. The shroom kid gurgled, blowing bubbles. Though metaphysically sick, Brian couldn't deny It was a cute little stinker. They swayed to the music. The baby chortled at the sight of the poodles nipping at the Prices' giant head. Bri checked his phone again for texts. At the next crescendo and release of the house mix—at least one mad reveler climaxing in tandem with synthesized glockenspiel—Dr. Fleming tapped out, ambling over to join the wallflowers in the lounge. Face red, body glistening, she shook out her ashen bob and climbed to sit a step above, so she'd be eye to eye with Bri. The doc cleared her throat.

"I see you've met young Master Lyophyllaceae," she said, nodding at the baby.

"Is tha'his lil' demon name?" B slurred, "He looks like a lil' Lyo-phyll...*yup*."

"*Lyo-phylla-ceae*. Its family taxonomy, far as we can tell," said Dr. Fleming, "Of the Agaricales order, the gilled mushrooms."

*"Ooh,"* said B, "Yummy yummy with a lil' garlic."

"Well, yes, It is edible. Your Mallory sautéed a slice of Its heel in '08, very much against protocol. Which seems to be her M.O."

Bri play-pretended chomping the demon's white button toes.

"Chicken sometimes," he said, and the room spun two seconds after he swung his head around to her.

*"What?"* Dr. Fleming cupped an ear to strain over the laser sound effects.

*"They taste like chicken sometimes!"* he hollered.

*"This one is apparently quite nutty,"* Dr. Fleming called back, and she leaned her lips to his ear, "It also saps one's ability to love, just so you know. The longer you hold It, the less affection and trust you can feel or express for other lifeforms that aren't the demon. We believe It's commanded trillions of eukaryotes, from bacteria to animalia. Entire armies of termites, monitor lizards. And It has no problem latching onto humans."

"Sooo," said Bri, squeezing the bebe close, leaning in to the doc, "You're saying It already loves me?"

"That's not what I'm saying," the doc shook her head, "The McKenzies sent their girls to boarding school. *Heather couldn't* – if you keep holding It, your dopamine pathways will erode. Even a few minutes–"

"He's such a good dancer," Bri interjected, pointing out Dr. Fleming's beast-man, who was doing The Saxophone with his trunk for a horn, "Is he single?" That ambient, brain-shaking bass thumped a little lower for a molten jazz fusion solo, atop those incessant bell-chimes. The humans on the dance floor got *lowww.*

"He is not," said Dr. Fleming, "He's a 408 year-old mountain tapir humanoid, and he's — It's — I'm really so very..." She tapered off, watching her demon work that sax.

"I bet *you're* gonna be a dancer," Bri said, bouncing the portobello bub on his knee, "Yes, you will. *Yes, you will!*" His darling trilled its mycelial lips.

"I should take him," husked Dr. Fleming, and B could have sworn the doc brushed a knuckle up her cheekbone, but the world moved four frames a second, and his stomach lapped in green waves, "Give me the demon now, Brian." And he didn't really think she'd steal It away, but what if she had designs on his charge? What if she skittered into the night, the tyke shrieking for Its daddy, baby-snatcher cackling on broomstick high? A reflexive panic took hold, and B squeezed the thing much too hard, wild with drink; if It had been a real baby, he'd have snapped Its neck. The demon just giggled, head bulging within the chokehold, spongy body wriggling with glee.

*"He's not going anywhere with you!"* Bri barked.

"You already forgot," said Dr. F, and before he could tear upstairs with his child, she laid a thumb over his temple, like a mother checking for fever, "If you don't help that dog, no one else here will." The words didn't exactly inspire Brian to sobriety, but he did, for a piercing moment, recall the basement pup he'd found, the one he'd named himself...the one a friend loved. He felt around for his phone.

"I don't, *um,*" Bri's lips worked, and a stone sunk fast in his gut, "I-I wish I–"

"I know," said the doc, and she took the demon away, gentle as could be, "I'll hold him now, all right? You go, while they're not looking." And indeed, when B swung his head back around to the hall, no one was. A low roar, a distant cymbal played on through the house, charging up for another profundo rise. The party people made a loose dance circle, arms entwined, resting heads on neighbors' shoulders. Saggy butts swayed, no one quite on beat. Bri stood from the stairs, phone in hand.

"OK," he said, and the low roar may have been in his own ears, for the longer he was on his feet, the more it receded, "I'll go." And he almost turned back to thank her, but Dr. Fleming put a hand to his rear and shoved; not hard, but enough for a start. B's knees popped with the sudden jog. He beelined for the basement door, shoving phone down his undies so he could lift the chaise on its tall end and drive a hip under its wooden whorl. The light from the bare bulb shone through as he cracked the door. Squinting, Bri bent to pull the polo bundle close and get a hand underneath. The little heap nearly toppled, unwieldy, but he slid it through before it could fall apart. In his haste, he pushed the door shut but did not wait to feel it click; could not replace the chaise. Lifting the puppy close to his bare chest, he doubled back around the banister, squeezing past Dr. Fleming on the steps.

"The mountain tapir says, *whee-whee-whee,*" she cooed to the tot on her lap, *"'Yo soy El Rey Nube.'* That's what that mountain tapir says."

Up and around the bend to the second floor Brian climbed, and though he willed every bit of boozy warmth to leave his body and enter the puppy's, he could not feel Äther move. She had grown so much colder in the folds of his shirt. He picked his way down the hall, feet sinking in the runner underfoot, the purple landscapes melting past their frames. The door at the far end stood open a crack, and Bri moved to it, easing it open so he could tiptoe to the landing and peek over the side to the cut of light upon the kitchen stairs. There were no mounted speakers in the stairwell, so when someone hacked a coughing fit outside, Bri whipped his head to the quarter arc windows, where the catering van waited down in the *porte-cochère*. He could see a few of the chefs smoked just beyond the stone pillars.

The phone in B's undies buzzed. He fished it out, almost butterfingering it over the railing as he did.

*Here*

Read the text, so B hopped to, creeping downstairs. The bundle in his arms twitched. They hunched way over upon nearing ground floor, checking to see who remained in the kitchen. A single chef counted blades in a knife roll by the sink, booty-popping while she worked, hairnet bouncing to the house beats. Bri crept into the room, sweeping past the marble island and its fountain, keeping an eye on chef all the while. The hairnet spun round as they neared the back door, dancer's eyes squeezed shut with end-of-shift joy, then she spun away again. Brian and the puppy slipped out of the house. Once they hit fresh air, they hoofed it down the walk and around the back corner of the kitchen, right past the catering van, where poor Portia marked inventory on the hood, globs of huckleberry still splotched on her head chef's whites, her clipboard.

"I hope you liked your gazpacho, sir," she perked up, as Bri scooted through, "Have a lovely evening."

"You're better than this, Portia," he threw back over a shoulder, and the minivan waited ahead, purring down where the cul-de-sac began, almost out by the main road, "You know it, and I know it."

Jess rolled her window halfway down as he cut across the circle, the asphalt cool on his soles. He held Äther tight as he could without crushing her. Nerves tried to quicken his breath, shorten his stride, but the booze swept right in, ever the hero, crushing all resistance. A fat, happy moon hung impossibly low.

"Where are your clothes?" she called, as he drew closer to the car, her face all a-frown.

"Hi, Jess," he said, "Nice to see you. How're Alan and the kids?"

"Fuck you, Brian, you're a piece of shit," said Jess, but without too-too much rancor, and she sucked at a metal straw in a travel mug reading *Breathe, Boo* in teal lettering, "You look very thin, by the way."

"Oh, hey, thanks," he said, "How's Andrew? Where is he? Is he here?"

"My brother's in the back," she said, adjusting her rearview, "And he doesn't have to talk to you."

"Heard," said Bri, "That's totally fair."

"I know it's fair," said Andrew, from the depths of the van, and B had to lean close to Jess' side mirror, so he could see past her seat, to the rows behind, "We don't need you to tell us it's fair. You're not the one who decides what's fair." He sat in the way back, past the empty car seat, the light off the single streetlamp slicing half his face out of the shadows.

"I want to say it's *absolutely* not fair of you to make him come back here, Brian," said Jess, dropping her mug in its cup holder, "Why couldn't you have met us literally anywhere else?"

"*Yeahhh*," said Bri, sucking his teeth, sobering some, "I'm sorry about that. It's just I'm pretty drunk–"

"Of course you are," Andrew cut in, from van's rear.

"And I didn't think I could make it to a second location. I'm on the lam from the...party. Plus I'm in my underwear, and it's residential around here, and I don't have a car. And I didn't want the puppy to get hurt, and there aren't any sidewalks or streetlamps past the–"

"OK, OK," Jess waved him off, then she pointed at the bundle in his arms, "That's not her, is it?"

"Yeah."

"Six-month standard poodle?"

"She's not doing good, Jess," said B, and gingerly as he could, he hefted Äther up through the driver-side half-window, to Jess' waiting arms, "Watch her legs."

"*Oh my god,*" she whispered, upon lifting the polo sleeve from Äther's face, "I'm calling the vet." Jess grabbed her phone from the center console.

From the back, Andrew scaled the middle row of seats, nearly tumbling headfirst in his rush to dive forward and see. He'd kept a close trim since the demon shaved him down to oozing scalp; fuzzy wifts now cradled his head like a cub reborn. Brian huddled close to the van, suddenly chill in the night air. Äther twisted tighter in Jess' lap, cracked nose sliding under the polo sleeve again.

"It's after hours," said Andrew, pulling himself into the front passenger seat, "Don't call your vet. I'll look up the emergency clinic."

"Nice," said Bri, knees knocking, "Your brow grew back. I-I was worried it might not've." Jess hung up. She turned some in her seat, away from the man at her window, popping the collar of her jean jacket.

"Yeah, my eyebrow grew back," said Andrew, and he looked up from his phone, but not towards Brian; not towards *DAS NEST,* nor its shapes writhing within, "And I had a great plastic surgeon for my earlobe. People can hardly tell."

"I can't at all," said Bri, "Yeah, it looks great. So does your hair. *So fresh.*"

"Wayne Pet Hospital," said Andrew, to Jess, and he turned his phone to her, for the number, "Tell them we're 10 minutes away."

"It's prolly more like 20?" said Bri, teeth chattering, nips like ice cutters on Jess's window, "But if you hop on Montgomery, you can cut right down–"

"I don't really want you to ever know what it was like for me," Andrew interrupted, "And I *really* want to tell you everything. Isn't that so cruel? I wanted to tell you while it was happening, Brian. I kept thinking I should text you. *The nurse hummed Ariana while he checked my butthole for contraband. Brian would love that.* Nightmares. Throwing myself out of bed so I'm on my feet before I know I'm awake. *Brian should be the one who has to get me back to sleep.*"

"Yeah," B agreed.

*"On this plastic fucking hospital mattress.* I had to pack away pictures of my—family photos, because I can't look at—him. Anymore."

Jess's phone had dropped to her lap next to the pile of puppy. She hung on her brother's every word. Andrew noticed. He waggled his screen at her.

"Call, *please,*" he begged of her.

"Sorry, sorry," Jess muttered, but she keyed the numbers at a snail's pace, unable to split her attention.

"Andrew," Bri tried, "I want to say—please, I *have* to say it."

"No," said Andrew, and he did look at Brian then, finally, "You think you do, but I don't deserve to have to hear it. All you ever need to know is none of this stopped me. I'm still moving to San Fran in May."

"Yes, you are," Jess slipped in there.

"I performed the *night* I got out of Pathways. Spent more than 36 hours there, too, thanks to you, so maybe don't pity-brag about that anymore. And just so we're clear, I *didn't* try to kill myself, Brian. I remember *everything.* You served me up."

"We don't need to relive this," his sis reminded him.

Bri clutched at Jess' window, where it stopped halfway down, practically dangling there.

"I know you didn't do that, Andrew," said Brian, "And I did serve you up. *I want* – you deserve to get to say all this to me. I want it." B nodded encouragement again and again, readying himself, gritting his teeth in anticipation. And Andrew very nearly barrelled on, all that righteousness kindling deep in his chest, sparking in every hiss of his teeth, but then that acid glare floated puppyward. Jess reached out to clutch her brother's hand, the number on her screen only halfway keyed. Brian panted at the window, a fish on dry land.

"It would just be for you," Andrew decided, shaking his head, "And I'm not helping you anymore. We came for Baby Spice. Jess, *please* make the fucking call."

"Who are we calling?" chirped Mallory, at Andrew's window, tits smushed upon the glass like Bri's, mane blown out in the spring breeze. The Yoons yelped in shock, Andrew slamming back in the passenger seat, gripping his heart.

*"Noo,"* Brian moaned, and the driver's side window strained to breaking as he tensed upon it, as he nearly clambered inside, *"Please,* no, Mallory. They're leaving."

"The caterers are just pulling out, you *guuuys,"* warbled the lady bare through the glass, and she motioned for Andrew to roll his side down, "Why don't you pull through to the back, and we'll get you greased up and wriggling?"

"Jess, *leave!"* cried Brian, even as he pushed off her window, to slide around the front of the van, to be quicker to the other side, "Don't look at her, just go!" Without hesitation, Jess readied the paddle shift on her steering wheel, but Andrew already had his finger on the trigger, the glass beside him sliding down Mallory's front, her greedy, drunken grin unleashed before him. Brian stumbled around the minivan's hood.

"...you did to this dog," B could hear Andrew say, as he moved back into earshot on the passenger side. He approached with one arm out, almost sliding it between Mallory and his friend but for not wanting to cop a booby feel. Jess, for her part, had a fistful of her brother's sleeve, and she spun the wheel with the hand still clutching her phone as the minivan lurched to a halting start around the cul-de-sac, avoiding the parked cars.

"Gosh, you smell so familiar," Mal snuffed round Andrew's window, and she side-stepped into Brian so they both had to march on at van's side, "Eau de shining armor. Did B-man host you at my home over the holidays? Did you two try on my biggest shoes?" Up the *DAS NEST* drive, the catering van rolled out from under the *porte-cochère* to tip down toward the street. Jess sped up to pass before it emerged. Andrew tried to muscle his sister's hand away, to no avail. He leaned as far as he could out the window, teeth bared.

*"I know what you are, Miss Mallory,"* Andrew ground out, "And I know what you have in that house."

Mallory faked Bri out, juking around him so he nearly fell trying to catch her, then bounding ahead.

"So you should pop in, come say *hiii,*" she whinnied, almost at a jog, "We're moments from unveiling a Black Forest cake doused in a rhubarb-aphelion liqueur. Come pig out, chickies!"

*"You honestly–"* Andrew fumed, then his head disappeared from view. Jess squealed a second later, then the minivan swerved before jolting to a halt, having made it nearly three-quarters round Hemlock Circle. The catering van rolled on by, Portia double-fisting the wheel.

"Did you just *bite* me!?" Jess cried, but her brother ignored her, popping his door to step out just as Brian caught up to Mallory near the streetlamp. Bri grabbed Ms. Nudiema'am round her middle but she bucked wild, flailing. His mouth flooded with champagne mane, with the grapefruit sulphur of her. He tried to spit the stuff out but more slipped inside, sliding between his fucked-up teeth.

"You people think that thing in there is a demon," Andrew lobbed at them both, and he shot a glance up at the house, at its green strobe through the windows, "Or a child or a pet or whatever the fuck you think."

"Umami," Mal added, foaming at the mouth, "Inmate. The dark star that goes with everything."

"I promise you it isn't," said Andrew, and he came just as close as he could, beyond Mallory's swiping claws, those kicking hooves. Brian ate the blows, wrestling her with all his might to a virtual standstill.

*"Andrew–"* B tried.

"It's a *reflection*," Andrew avowed, "Of everything we're not. You'll never find anything real there."

*"Ohh,* sweets," Mallory beamed, reaching, writhing, "We're the reflection. We bounce all the light back, absorbing nothing. Blameless. *Bloodthirsty."*

Jess laid on the horn for a good beat while her bro gazed at the strange flesh before him; woman and man locked in desperate struggle to harm, to save...unstoppable she, unmoveable he. Andrew backed away.

"I have the hospital," his sis called, out the open passenger door, "You have to talk to them, Andrew." Brian couldn't see the poodle lump in her lap, but he hoped it stirred more and more; hoped Äther found solace there.

*"Go!"* B choked out, as Mal elbowed him in the ribs, "Andrew, *please* fuck off." He could see his former friend had reservoirs yet to drain, more than Bri himself could ever hold back, but somehow Andrew bore the weight long enough to let it all melt to pity. Distaste. He left everything unsaid in the cul-de-sac like a pup unwanted, then made for his sister's van. Before closing his door, he looked out to the street one last time.

"As someone who really used to love you," Andrew said to Brian, chin set, *"Please don't go back in that house."* Bri tried to drink him in, to summon the words, but all he could really do was try to hold on over a bucking shoulder, squint through shaking tresses.

"Can you take her?" Jess was saying, as the passenger door closed, and the silver van started up again, "I can't hold the wheel and my phone and my cup and–" And then they were off, rounding the Circle, banking onto Hemlock Way, accelerating down the hill, breaking Bri's orbit, and the Yoons had gone for good. An afterimage of brake lights burned in their wake.

Mallory fought like hell till the van was out of sight, then she settled finally against B's chest, a marionette snipped. Their panting slowed to tandem sighs. She clutched his two hands, pinning them high on her belly, and they bent over together so he leaned on her for a few good breaths, spent, exhaling hair.

"I could really go fuck up that cake," Mallory whispered, turning her face to his, draped over her shoulder, "You want to go fuck up that cake?"

B looked at her.

"...uh-huh," he said, then he peeled himself off, disentangling from her grip, "We should scoot before the neighbors see."

"What neighbors, baby boy?" buzzed the party queen, and she shook her hands out as she walked back up toward her home, cheeks dimpling, the soles of her feet ghostly white beyond the glow of the streetlamp. Brian crossed his arms to give himself a squeeze, and to spin slowly round to see for the first time that, beyond the Circle's pool of lamplight, the other houses stood unlit that spring eve, despite the usual cars parked in every driveway, the front doors open wide to the elements. Lightless windows stared, hollow-eyed, from all sides.

And that chubby moon above seemed to wink; to say, *gotcha, bitch.*

Bri shuffled back around to face *DAS NEST* and the silhouette of his hostess against the party lights, trudging up the front walk. Up on the second floor, a darkling window hiked up, and Andrew leaned out, his smooth shoulders glinting in the moonlight, hair tucked behind both ears to keep it from his face. He waved to Mallory below.

"Hi, *youuu*," she called up to It, "Come down for dessert, why don't you."

*Das Gegenteil* ducked back inside.

Brian tried to think out there, the streetlamp not much company, that moon awfully full of herself, and before long, without a plan or much of a care, he made his way back up to the house.

Where once roamed a barbarous, polyphonic DJ set now hissed through every house speaker the world's longest drum roll, with only the lightest overlay of electronica to keep the mood, to keep one from losing one's mind in a night gone liquid. Someone had shut off the green strobe. Bri bowed at the ankles crossing the front stoop, diverting the attention of those huddled upon the tiles in cagey pairs and trios, human and demon alike breaking off from hushed tones to scowl at the gate crasher. Of their hostess, naught could be seen, for she'd already gone further into the house, upstairs or down, left to the lounge or maybe opposite, to the dining room, the kitchen. Brian didn't get a chance to investigate.

"Come to gloat?" goaded Grant McKenzie, as B shut the iron-and-oak door.

"Sorry?" said Bri.

"You should have left," Dr. Fleming sourpussed, shaking her bob, and the tapir-man rubbed her shoulders with his shaggy human hands. The poor doc's cheek had rent open in a trio of scratches drawing from under her ear almost to her nose, the lacerations raw but mostly unbloodied.

"What happened to you?" Bri asked.

"The, *ah*, McKenzies...got their demon back," said Dr. F. Indeed, Heather McKenzie cradled her mushroom beeb with renewed passion, the thing's pocked cap tucked under her chin, her free hand held to eagle's claw, nails at the ready. Brian nodded and tried not to make any sudden moves mama's way. The Prices, for their part, stood somewhat as a buffer between teams McKenzie *und* Fleming, their big head reclining at their feet on the base of her skull. Gwen and Simon had long locks of Its hair in their hands, and they stroked the silky ends in tandem, positively morose.

"I didn't mean to kill the vibe," Brian offered the group, and he did a half-hearted shimmy in the unwelcome silence, "Are we not dancing anymore?"

But to this, they all of them gathered that night could only split themselves down the middle to gaze to the back of the space, down the front hall that Brian had never known to be—*never held* as so large, down the tiles that rolled underfoot, black and white tremendous, checkerboard tomorrow...where oak-paneled walls dimmed to shadow, then to starstuff in a void, and a round table had been set out among the constellations for cake. B stepped toward this splendor, past the other guests and the internal bounds of the *DAS NEST* design, the incessant drumroll pounding at his back. *And that spread!* Champagne buckets stood sentry on a table celestial beside dear blood-braided china and matching flutes, on baby pink tablecloth before a towering construction of ganache and cherry and heavy whipping cream, the gooey chocolate tiers reflecting hungry nebulas, bedecked from the base of the cake stand on up in architecture venereal, edible: a *DAS NEST* arcade of womb–like rooms and priapic halls (what shapes tucked within, what manner of cardstock beast!) and dueling sets of stairs twined upon by braids of black licorice which cascaded to a fleshy fondant dais for toppers: hand-drawn replicas of the Moyamensing gang and their host & hostess, and above these, floating cherubic from a wire arbor of blackberries and mandrake stars, a his-and-his of twin Brians, bald and grinning in none-too-flattering birthday suits.

B's head swam. Stars spun so they stretched to neon streaks all around.

Beneath the buffet, a broken cake dish under his belly, lay the top half of a Campbell Dahlhaus in sodden pool staining the chessroad red, his bottom half out of sight behind the curve of the table, arm steadily leaking where it lay upon the puddle-dropped fabric, the Garasuki lodged there still.

"*Gib mir...d-den...Pussy K-K...Kuchen,*" Campby managed to choke out, through lips gone blue, and the mask of his face was colorless above his beard. He gripped a fistful of pink linen, trying to raise himself up, but only managed to lift his head and thump it back down, right in his own fluids.

"There he *iiis*!" trilled familiar vocal frizz, and like the next slide in a deck, the mundane world cracked back into place, for Mallory had flipped Brian round to face the party, the front door, whence she grabbed his phone and then pantsed him, "You don't need armor anymore, *B-for-Baldy.*" Bri's undies hit the deck. The other guests took their eyeful, reaching a consensus of appraisal, none concealed. And since it had already happened and he couldn't reach for them through his wooziness, he stepped out of the legholes and nudged them away.

"You didn't — *you never said I'm the centerpiece,*" he sputtered. He spat phlegm on the tile.

"Well, because you're not," Mal laughed, and she slipped his phone behind her back, only to reveal empty hands again, the witch. Paige Fleming tossed gaseous pity B's way, her disappointment palpable.

"So this is it?" asked Senator McKenzie, squeezing his wife all the tighter; the babe in her arms.

"Entropic dessert," muttered Simon Price, biting a thumbnail.

"*Das Gegenteil* is all settled downstairs," Mallory clapped, and Brian saw the fear jolt across everyone's face. Even the mushroom fussed.

"We have a few last–" Dr. F started.

"It's ravenous," Mal interrupted, then she prowled over to the tapir-man, taking his wooly hand from the doc's shoulder, turning it over in hers, "Should we not proceed, It would come up here and rightfully take us all."

*"We as a group have objections,"* the doc chewed out.

"Do we?" asked Mallory of the group. Sheepish nods spread. The tapir-man opened Its snout but only a squeaking sort of wheeze sounded from his mottled throat. Brian noticed Gwen Price staring at his dick; caught, she snarled back. Bri turned some, toward that unreal periphery, where floaters swam and nonform snatched at the margins of wall and tile.

"Well, Pieter and Rina aren't here, for one," said Grant McKenz.

"Very good point," Simon agreed, pinning his tongue to his bottom lip, hands backwards on hipbones, framing white-blonde pubes, "I have to believe, *uhh,* Pieter would share our trepidation."

"Of course he would," said Dr. Fleming, and she pulled her demon back from Mallory's grasp, "And I gather that's why he isn't here tonight—the Fabers *or* their demon. *She's* made sure of that." Brian eye-balled Mallory, but she remained, as ever, ineffably abreast of all proceedings. Her mane swelled, extension of her lungs. Between the Prices, the big head demon's eyes whirred forever back in her big fucking head. B tried to ground himself in the tile underfoot, in the hiss of the neverending drum-synth, but the floor seemed to treadmill under his sole, even as he stood perfectly still.

"Well, I know what my dear, departed father-in-law would say," said their hostess, sneaking a peek over her shoulder at the singularity in the heart of *DAS NEST*, where her doof lay bleeding out, "Rainer would encourage *dialog.* Call and response; out of you, into me."

"But you don't work for the school, honey," said Gwen Price, and she shriveled some as Mallory's gaze fell upon her, *"Just devil's advocate."*

"You don't work, period, Gwen, darling," Mal ate, "And we all know I am not supplemental to our curriculum this good season. Our fabulous night. I am syllabus and final exam and every time any one of you asked permission to piss. None of this would have, *could have* happened without me or my demon or Rainer before us. *Well,* or Campbell, but we all know that's lip service." Nobody disagreed. A few checked with outsized frowns to see if he'd died yet.

"No one's suggesting—" Simon tried, palms out.

"It seems you all are," Mallory grinned, a croc, a she-wolf, "So make your point, fermions."

None dared speak; then:

"You have a most peculiar, predatory relationship with your husband and your demon and it spills over into everything you touch," said Paige Fleming, unabashed at last, "You've slithered into our institution, usurped great minds, a founding family of the Professoriat, turning educated men to your own advantage, and that of your demon. None of us earned our degrees in the countries of our demons, nor have we romantic partners or loved ones descending from those countries. You are inexorably linked to Germany through schooling, through marriage, though admittedly you are not German yourself. I did my homework. And I don't envy you your...girlhood, Mallory. But you've suggested we play this *game* of your own concoction by which we were all meant to compete — for lack of a better word — by worthy deed, by unworthy servant, and yet at every turn, you and yours come out ahead, almost by design. You've likely murdered two of our friends, and done who knows what with their demon. At no point has this so-called tournament been equitable or scientific or bent itself towards sportsmanship."

"I mean, Mal," laughed the humorless state senator, and McKenzie ticked off the assembled demons one by one, "Cambodia...Zambia...Peru...and yet *somehow* the winning demon just so happens to hail from the world's third largest GDP?"

"Prevailing, one might add," said Simon Price, "Here in a state with the, *uhh,* very largest population of German-Americans."

"10 little miles from Germantown!" Gwen tossed in.

"And let us not forget our Pennsylvania Dutch," Simon hopscotched, "They who speak High German, who live, *uhh,* a short drive away, and who really are, i-if we're being real here, *uh,* living descendants."

"Perhaps it's all serendipity, Mallory," Dr. Fleming concluded, and her chin drew high, and she wrapped her tapir-man's arms about her, hugging herself in Its embrace, "But I suspect it's just you."

The Lady Bain-Dahlhaus nodded, taking it all in. She glanced at her B, who breathed in time with her.

"I haven't conscripted the Amish," said she, resplendent in the light from the sconce by the front door, from the quasars and supergiants playing over her rear end, "Though now that I'm picturing it, that does seem really funny. Here's my counterpoint: you ungrateful cunts knew what you were doing, and at no point did you ever actually believe your demon would best mine." The collective gulp made a dissonant chord.

Bri couldn't help but smirk. He dropped his head so they wouldn't see.

"*Hey,* Mal—" Grant's voice broke.

"Time falls over you now," said Mallory, and she drew arms behind her, wings at rest, before heels followed, sliding back into the shade of the lounge, belly full, "Say your goodbyes."

With his back to the wood paneling, knees in armpits, Brian sat where the house ebbed away at the edge of the starwindow. Not that he'd ever studied his own place in the universe, but no body seemed local out there, no filament familiar. The view revolved and capered, sending a hash of prisms over the tiles extended in space, over Campbell's body where he lay at rest. Red sundogs glanced off the ganache. The longer Bri took it all in, the less neurotic he felt. The less anything.

The McKenzies went first into the lounge. The senator steeled himself, taking his wife by the arms from behind to steer her in. It was all Heather could do not to scream, but since she held her baby, she rode the terror like a beast to the slaughterhouse. Still, the frantic mom tried to catch Dr. F's eye.

"Take him, Paige," she begged of the doc, even as her husband took her by a fistful of hair, "Please, my baby!" The mushroom kid shrieked with glee while Grant dragged her forth. Brian heard their panic rise, then bottom out in the lounge. And someone must have scooted the chaise back to its original spot, for the basement door creaked all the way wide, then those fungal giggles went flying out of earshot, down the stairwell to a sudden finito. Two spheres smashed together over the cake table on the chessroad, an ice giant obliterating a protoplanet. *DAS NEST* trembled to its burned-out roots.

The McKenzies shuffled back in, side by side, unable to touch or look at one another. Heather's arms would not lower, like she held her demon still.

"Next!" came Mallory's bark from the other room.

The Prices took one last dunk of their demon's hair, pressing their faces to great armfuls, rubbing it over eyelids, over lips. While they got their fill, out from the dining room stepped Maxcat, and he stopped by the demon head for a nice yawn and a rump stretch, slinking past Its big ear. The Prices drifted back to reality. Max joined Brian by the wall, to sit at his side, nearer the house than the stars within. He lay his blue chin on B's foot.

"Here we go, hon," Gwen sighed, and she and her hubs bent low, getting two hands each under their demon's cranium, rolling her end over end. Its wide eyes never opened again to Brian's sight, though as It disappeared into the lounge, It looked more at peace than it had for some hours. That time, a ponderous roll marked the demon's passage from the world, deafening some on the lounge rug, then picking up speed on the hardwood before the basement door, and finally careening down the stairs in a huge clatter that never resounded. Brian's vision blurred with tears, though he truly felt nothing at all. Starward, meteor showers rushed from scintillation to sparks. *DAS NEST* shuddered and swayed.

Maxcat swallowed, jaw rising and falling on B's toes. Gwen and Simon passed the tapir-man on their shuffle back in, who was trying his demonly best to gently disengage from Dr. Fleming.

"Oh, no, *no!*" the doc freely wept, "I don't know who I *am* without you." He brought her hands to his snout and licked them sweet, then reared high in a lovely whinny, the underside of Its trunk bisected and pink. Dr. Fleming lay a hand to heaving throat, receiving the baptism. Stark acceptance enveloped her sorrow, and she had to let her demon go. Once more, the lounge received a visitor.

"So long!" came Mallory's offstage cheer, then after a tick, the basement door slammed shut. Everyone in the hall braced themselves, Dr. F holding her sobs as best she could. As their hostess reappeared in the lounge portal, the whole of *DAS NEST* gave over to quaking and groaning, plaster dusting heads, and the light of creation appeared suddenly over the chessroad in space, shedding nuclear blaze over all, streaming white-hot into the hall so Brian had to look away, had to grab the cat to keep him from running off. Aftershocks rolled in quick succession until the view dimmed again, with only one star to be seen in the expanse: an immobile blue gas giant. One could look right at it without squinting. Flame roiled out from its navel, an omphalos alight. The guests pressed forward, drawn like moths.

"They're here," whispered Mallory, in rhapsody, "They're in us now. Everyone line up for cake." And where there had been grief, new hope arose; where there had been fear, greedy smiles bloomed. Heather McKenzie looped her arms round Grant's waist.

"He's back!" she reveled, bouncing for joy, almost lifting her man, "I see him! I *feel* him again." She tore ahead, racing down the tile road to dance beneath the star, leaping for it, grasping at its light. Grant detoured to Mallory first, taking her by the shoulders and dipping her to passionate smackeroo.

"You fucking savage," he growled, as Mal belly-laughed, "You really really did it."

"Thanks, senator," she said, tugging her mane to one side after he righted her again, *"Go get your gal."* The Prices trailed the skipping state senator, arm in arm, Simon's lemon head held to princely height, Gwen an alien empress. Dr. Fleming approached with a touch more trepidation.

"I...I want to say," Paige faltered, "Well, I *am* sorry, Mallory. Theory of course can't compare to experience. And I feel It here, closer than he ever was before." She thumped a fist between her breasts, then she and Mal grasped hands in commiseration.

"Oh, Paige," Mallory clucked, "I was never worried, not even for a teeny, tiny, eenie-meanie-miney moment." She chucked the doc under the chin and sent her packing with a boot to the butt. Dr. F turned back to Bri as she jogged ahead, that silver bob bouncing.

"I wish you could feel it," she called back from the beyond, "I think you would understand."

Then it was just Mallory and Brian and the cat left in the hall part of the hall. B stood. Max rolled over to stare upside down into the starry aperture.

"Well?" said Mal, and she came to stand in front of him so there was no distance between them.

"Yeah," said Bri, "This is everything. Kudos, I guess."

"Aw," she melted, "It did take decades of work, and I am pretty sensational."

"I'd still like to visit with the puppies," he decided, "I don't really know where my clothes are, but I'd like to see the puppies one last time before I go." Mallory's jaw had dropped in happy incredulity.

"The puppies!" she gasped, "You lifesaver! I almost forgot! *And you're not going anywhere!"* And with that merry threat, she barreled off toward the kitchen, flinging herself round the corner of the dining room.

Brian brought his two hands before his face and revolved them, inspecting the pale for irregularities, for new lines. Was B still B, or had cosmic change sprouted in him, too? On the tile, Max flipped again to all fours. He lifted a paw to smack past the edge of the starwindow, and the whole view refracted, shimmering out from his kittyness. Before his lady returned, Bri bent to scoop the cat up, and they crept for the front door.

"Wait for me, OK?" he whispered, then he cracked the oak-and-iron to send Max through. By the time he'd crossed back, Mallory was just wheeling a large crate in, with Ursula's remaining puppies all cowering inside, bunched upon themselves in whimpers barely audible over the endless hiss leaking from the house speakers. Atop the grating lay a pile of familiar parchment scrolls held by blackwood finials; Brian recognized them from winter, from the video Andrew had shown him of Mallory's Mass Extinction setup. He took a step into her path, hand raised.

*"Heya!"* he tried to trill, voice cracking, "Hey, poodles! So they seem a little less...riled up."

"Oh, they're terrified," said Mal, untouched, "Move aside."

"Ooh, what are these," said B, waggling fingers over the scrolls, taking up the one on top. He slid a bare foot before the crate's wheel so she had to pause while he unrolled a column of names scrawled within: *Amber Bowen, Daniel Valdez, Joseph Griffin, Abby Snow (and baby Ann)...*

"Lambs," she said, snatching the list back, "Hecatombs, so we don't get peckish or bored. *Move.*"

*"Just*—just hang on," said B, "What are you gonna do?" But Mal pressed on anyway, rolling the crate right over his littlest toe. Brian crunched reflexively, reaching for the piggy. When he could think again, he limped after her, beneath the spinning cork floating at the end of a liquid flight of prosecco, bubbles twisting round themselves. Tableside, Simon and Gwen took turns scooping flutes through the air and dishing them out.

*"Mwana Ubowa,"* Grant and Heather clinked, then they included the doc, who took her own glass and raised it in return.

"My Cloud King," said Dr. Fleming.

"To *Kbal,*" added the Prices.

"*Oh*, and to Tracy!" said Heather before anyone could sip, "Aw, poor Trace. Remember, Grant?"

"She crawled under the house like an animal," the senator shared with the group, "Buried herself up to the thighs. I was so relieved she had the spare key, we thought she'd lost it."

"I had a much too sweet Isobel," said Dr. F.

"Our very industrious Robert," Simon threw in.

"Robert was an asexual," Gwen said, palming hips and belly in circles, "He never pounced, and I made myself very available."

"Are these all your Brians?" Mallory asked, pulling up to the table, and she nabbed her own flute to arc it overhead, catching herself a hefty pour, "Let me do one, let me do one: *to B, the least worthy and very most consequential, he who stitched my colors to his heart.*" The gang turned to raise bubblies on high to the hindmost arrival; Bri stopped short, incisors bared. In their crate, the dogs crawled under one another so whoever was on top had to wiggle-worm to the bottom again, ad nauseam.

"I don't want any," B gruffed.

"Nobody offered," snorted Mal, and the party turned to help themselves to the stack of rosy napkin folds, stepping over Campbell as needed, turning hungry eyes upon the cake now, the whole works at a slow melt from the ambient heat of the new star above. Edible architecture writhed. B reached out and got fingers round a corner slat of the dog crate, to ease it a few inches back. Simon undid his fold first to reveal a personal butcher knife, gleaming in starlight. The others followed suit until they were all of them bladed up. Mallory pulled her own napkin free of its prize to swipe along her brow, catching the sweat that had nestled there, then she tossed it off the road so it billowed out into the beyond, free of gravity.

Gwen stared up at cake's peak, jaw slack.

"*Can we*...start anywhere?" she ventured, licking her chops.

"Open season," Mal fried. Like rats, the craving guests surrounded that chocolate and cherry tower, only their hostess refraining from the initial gasp-and-plunge of Price and McKenzie and Fleming stabbing, thrusting elbow deep, carving great hocks of real estate out from within. Grant hewed a slope for himself in no time at all, then once commandeered, he beheld with wonder the jackpot before smashing his face to the icing again and again. Heather gave up on her knife early, gripping its handle between her teeth so she could scale the cake as high as she could, reaching still for that star above; though upon tumbling down an avalanche and noticing her man, she grabbed the back of his head, to help him smash faster. Dr. F annexed the bottom, gooiest tier along a major arc, where a mons split in black and white marzipan tile, cresting to clitoral chandelier. She eased her acquisition back to topple it off table's edge, then belly-flopped right on down. The summit of the beast surged from their collective decimation, warping inwards so its top tier and cardstock people went revolving, then spinning into the crater, never to be seen again. Only a sweetmeat staircase remained aloft.

By subtle degrees, those sparkling midair bubbles slowed, then began spinning counter to how they'd spun, floating fizz wisping off like whitecaps, frothing directly up to the thirsty star, to that new blue and its suck of atmosphere. A breeze licked by, tickling Brian's bare back, sweeping in from the house. The crate in his hand rolled a little left and right. Wasser, the chocolate pup, reared up to lick B's fingers through the slats.

*"Mine!"* yawped Gwen Price, to no one in particular, *"Every last bite!"* She'd made of herself almost a fresh layer cake, having scooped a landslide her way. Half the time, she missed her own face from the ill-timed fistfuls she kept raining overhead. Her better half was buried in the same landslide by his twig of a knife arm, so it wasn't clear if the lemonhead could move or no. Simon had stuffed so much cake in his cheeks that he could only suck for thin air through that pinch of nose, dripping with crème chantilly tears.

Mallory radiated delight at the chaos, clutching her knife to her chest, and were it not for that whip of wind picking up, she might have doubled over with laughter. As it was, she and Bri both had to lean backwards, pitching themselves more and more against the draft. Even so, both took several bracing steps down the tile just to stay erect. The ginger puppies joined their chocolate brother on hind legs, only none had kisses but rather whines, pawing up at B's anchoring hand, and they'd soon nudged Wasser aside. In its fright, a ginge took a nip of knuckle.

Paige Fleming rose from the cake angels she'd sculpted, and had soon clambered back up the table linens, eyes set on another big chunk. Seeing her coming, Gwen bounded forth on all fours, spraying mashed cherry and fondant, intent on fending off the wee doc. Knives sparked.

"There!" came Mallory's joyful cry, and she tried to turn back for Brian, but the rush of starsuck had her stumbling forward instead, hair flying about, "He's finally crowning!" B followed her gaze to Campbell's limp body, now totally exhumed from the undertable, a collateral lump of cake smushed into his beard from the carnage above. At first, Bri thought it might just be the windshear or a trick of cosmic light, but then it happened again: the corpse gave another involuntary jump. Inert neck rolled, bending to one side, so as the body wriggled out into view, the head gave way to grislier and grislier angle. A shape swole suddenly against the side of Camby's gut, then it ricocheted, bulging up to his throat and right back down, pressing out from within, over by where his spleen should be. Mallory let herself be blown to the table, almost somersaulting over top. She steadied herself on its edge and shouted to her compatriots, who were trying to keep the cake they'd seized, even as it took flight all around, rising to that hungry mouth above.

*"Gather now!"* Mal managed over the gale, *"To me, my cambions!"*

But they could not. Indeed, the same phenomenon that lurched Campbell's body along the tiles ignited within the others. A lump like a wing unfolding tumefied from the senator's low back, then subsided. Heather's right leg swole, her skin a pair of too-tight leggings. Mid-lunge, Gwen slipped on a handful of ganache, cracking her chin on the table, leaving Dr. F the chance to raise up for a fatal stab, but the thing beneath her skin chose that very moment to extend most violently from her armpit, sending the doc whizzing off, arcing then dropping into the cake crater like a shuttlecock over a badminton net. Before Gwen could find her balance again, she, too, stretched as no human flesh should stretch, a second, bigger head waxing under her own face, desperate to tear itself free. Her Simon writhed from the same boiling bumps, trapped still by his buried arm. Contortions of pain and pleasure rocked the glazed faces.

The next time the dog crate rolled a half-moon, Brian tugged it clean to one side so he could get a grip round another corner. Once steadied, he dropped his butt to a squat, using his body weight to keep heels on the tile, wheels on the ground. The pups hunkered as well, one of the gingeys snap-snapping at the wind.

*"BRIAN!"* bayed Mallory, for none other had answered her call, *"Get over here!"* She dove on Campbo's body, to keep it from bouncing away, though when she and B locked eyes through the crate, he shook his head resolutely. Grit gathered round Bri's heels; he chanced a peek to see one of the potted plants from the lounge come tumbling by, drawn in from

the house, spraying soil, followed shortly thereafter by coats from the hall closet and discarded nudiebutt attire and taxidermied Ursula and the map that hung in the front hall, the *DAS NEST* cross-section, which all went spinning along the checkerboard road to the cake table, where all heavier things gathered, clattering together, not quite ready to ascend.

The protrusions in Campbell's corpse reached a fever pitch, vexed to emerge. Mal straddled one of those hamhock thighs, sweeping hair from her face, then she raised her own butcher knife high. Brian watched to see where her blade took root, but the crate shuddered, slats vibrating across his view; when she withdrew to stab again, her stainless steel was already red.

*"They're hatchlings!"* she howled, bathed in claret spray, *"We have to break their shells!"*

Down and down gored Mallory's knife. And if Bri missed the show, if he couldn't see the action, the fiends atop the table more than made up for it with their own fabulous puppetry, the squatters in their meat capering madly, joints doubling, limbs lifting to grotesque arabesque. Mid-pirouette, a hillock shifting twixt shoulder blades, Heather McKenzie rediscovered the knife she'd tucked between her own teeth, and she drew it out to meet the back of her husband's neck, now smashing into bare table where a slab of cake had once been. Back and forth Grant's head bounced, even as the muscle of his neck rent asunder from his wife's cutting edge. His own knifing arm returned the favor, perhaps on reflex, ramming his wife low in the gut, eviscerating her in jagged slices up to her breastplate. Spindly paws split Heather's fat and dermis to reach forth from within. Having lost track of Paige Fleming, Gwen Price lay savage eyes upon her husband. Simon shrieked as she descended, arm still stuck. Her first jab went deep in his left eye.

Brian tried to back toward the house, but the wheels of the puppy crate bounced, lifted. His own heels threatened the same, but he squatted deeper, ass almost to the tiles. The poodles could not open their eyes. The items from the house lifted off from their scatter by the table, disappearing up, up, up by weight into the blue flames. In that hurricane rush, violence became a love language, every poke and prod a smooch, every cleave and rupture a canoodle. Blood and chocolate made aphrodisiacal warpaint. Like lady Lazarus reborn, Paige Fleming roused from the chocolate crater, launching herself bodily through the tempest to land on Gwen's shoulders, driving her mess of a knife into the jiggling tissue of her quarry's neck.

Bri began to slide, and the crate in his hands to slip. He willed himself to hold on, for the dogs if not himself, but he could feel them slipping away. The metal cage twisted mid-air, wrenching his fingers to and fro. Every gasp seemed to be B's last, for he surely could not snatch the wind that raced by, could not inhale to replace what was lost. Yet even as the whole world—galaxy, universe—tightened to a tunnel, as the strength in his grip eroded, he could not possibly miss the forms rising from Price and McKenzie; from Dr. Fleming as Simon freed himself at last and Gwen took a break from ripping her man apart so the pair could descend as one on the doc. Wispy critters streamed from their gaping wounds, creatures more condensed vapor or undiluted humor than actual biostuff. A diaphanous mushroom cap crammed itself through Heather's belly, the impling fanged, its moldy knees and elbows tapered to needlepoints. Great noxious plumes of puke green spores seeped from the back of Grant's skull. Simon and Gwen each had Paige by an arm, whereupon they visited relentless skewering upon her little body, even as tendrils poured from their own traumas, even as gaseous feathering rose from their victim to swirl and coalesce, Dr. F's coming to resemble something like a tapir, but meaner, famished. And of that first specimen, Brian could barely catch a glimpse, for Campbell's interloper took shape mostly blocked by his wife, who by then surely must have opened his body a hundred times or more. Strips of flesh on her blade, braided in her mane waggled in the squall. Still, B leaned his head far as he could (or maybe he was passing out), so he could just make out a Rorschach-like blot beyond Mal, its configuration split down the middle so each portly half rolled inwards, perfectly symmetrical, making of its face an ever-shifting reflection, sometimes Campbell-like, sometimes with eyelets dropping below the muzzle or to either side of the pig snout or vanishing entirely, that no-face worst of all.

Everything, everybody, every star gave up their last resistance, supped inside that sphere of influence, the voracious blue maw. Bodies dropped like empty waterskins, shed of unearthly viscera. Tiles peeled off the impossible road. The crate flew from Brian's hands, and he went careening after it, bracing for impact, reaching for Mallory as he winged by. Meeting unbearable heat and pressure, the last impression he had was of being flicked like a bug by the finger of God, then came nothing but the void.

B blinked.

A quadruple vision of twin palladian windows pulsed and merged, one of them lopped off at a slant where the front of the lounge opened to the sky. He lay upsy-daisy over the back of the sofa, the small of his back draped over the underside. A constant pissing stream fell upwards in his vision, and he drew his gaze down to the upper stories of *DAS NEST*, to the splintered teeth that used to be flooring, and the broken pipe up in the third floor bath raining over the gaping facade. He tried to move and was relieved to ache all over, so he knew he still had a body. A hand flopped up to paw around for bumps or lesions; he could feel a slice to the scalp, but nothing wildly deep. The wound was already half dry. When he tried to flip or crunch to sitting, vertigo proved too much, and he guessed he'd been concussed. With a gulp, B braced himself by an elbow and lowered to the parquet headfirst, managing to get his hips down pretty quick and take the pressure off his neck. He knelt a while, grunting.

The waterfall from the third floor made a pond amidst detritus. Bri crawled over so he could rinse soot off his hands, splash a palm's worth over his face. Upon standing, trickles ran black down his belly and legs. One of the wall-mounted speakers went bust with a shower of silver sparks. Brian retreated from the puddles, plenty conductive already.

A shift in debris drew his attention to the mound that used to be the front hall, the rest of the floor partly obstructed beyond. Flat fronds of plaster from the remains of the ceiling slid off the wreckage to reveal the puppy crate packed on its side, door in the air. Bri moved to it, stepping over the coffee table in his path, the bricks from the hearth. The eruption from the nexus point had blasted all furniture to both ends of the first floor, piling it high against the lounge stairs, the far wall. Neither the blue basement door nor the dining room hearth could be seen through the mess. Out the open front wall, moonlight streamed down upon the front door, which lay horizontal, surrounded by shingles and brick in the yard.

*"Motherfuck,"* Bri muttered, and he gasped for pain trying to lift him-

self overtop the pup crate, white-hot shooting out from his lower ribs. With shaking hands, he reached up to undo the latch, then lifted the door high. No cries could be heard within. He pulled the cage down to more of an angle, but could not free it from the larger pile. He went on tiptoes to peer inside. The four dogs sat sphinx-like at the bottom, ears pulled back, eyes trauma-wide. Another brickslide fell, then burst apart on the dining room side of the rubble, and a changeling flew forth, oblivious to B, almost too speedy to make out, were its shape not so indelible: a spectral double-head, stacked one on the other, lemon oblong upon mulberry squat. B followed the geist's flight out into the Circle, where its silhouette joined other likely shapes up in the sky, cavorting above the trees, that coven reassembling.

Bri looked around for something to stand on. The chaise lay cracked in two. He could see highback chairs in the dining room smashed to pieces. Another disturbance, closer than the last, signalled more of the house falling apart, and a flood of plants dropped through a hole up in Campbell's office floor, terra cotta shattering upon impact. Aftershocks unearthed a familiar mane from the rubble, champagne locks strewn about like naked roots, the antique desk crushing her legs. B thought she was dead until he drew near.

"Oh, good," she said, voice cut to monotone, "I was worried I'd have to tough it out."

"*Are you*—does anything hurt?" Brian asked.

She shook her head slightly.

"I can't feel my body." Pink bubbles of phlegm fluttered at her nostrils.

"Well, you're still human," said Bri, "You still look human."

Mal rolled her eyes.

"*Great,*" she drolled.

"The puppies," he said, turning back with a grimace, and he went to point out the cage, then realized he was past her cone of vision, "Their crate is stuck."

"I need you—*ahh,*" Mallory gasped, blood bubbling, "To see if there's cake left. Just a lil' lick of icing."

"There's nothing left," said Bri, edging closer so she could see him, "Your house exploded, Mallory."

"Yes, I see," she said, gazing up in awe at the great swirls of dust, the missing front wall, "It happened here. My cambions. My demon."

He loomed over her till her eyes focused again. She smiled, teeth red.

"I couldn't have done it without you."

"Maybe you shouldn't talk," said Brian, and he dropped beside her, on a clump of wet hair, "Maybe you should choose your words. *Is there anyone you want* – I don't know what you did with my phone. You took my phone."

"You had to be truly spineless. And hairless."

"I can carry you," he said, ignoring the dig, "But I don't know if we should move you. If you can't feel anything–"

"My lovely mollusk. Exceptional slug."

Maybe it was the dust, but B couldn't help but to weep. She gazed at him with such pride.

*"Was Andrew right?"* he sobbed, more to the house than his mistress, "It was all the German stuff, right? And you guys really are Nazis? I didn't mean to do a Nazi thing."

*"Shh, shh,"* Mallory soothed, and if he closed his eyes, he could almost pretend she was his mother, "Don't be absurd. Rainer hated the Führer. The Kaiser, too, for that matter."

"You promise?"

"Fascists make terrible hedonists," said Mal, "Too many rules. No, all you did was squeeze our lube."

"OK, but what about all the—your map, the sign outside...*Spandau Ballet.*"

"Just Spandau," she reminded him, "It's a borough of Berlin."

"No, I remember."

"You're so provincial, B. A fetish for one's father-in-law doesn't make one Eva Braun 2.0."

"Sorry, I don't mean to be insensitive," he snuffed, "It's just it's kind of creepy, big picture. That's probably my own biases. But you also put a, *um,* conversational spell on Campbell."

*"Brian, Brian,"* she lamented, as if he'd drained the life from her, as if his mother really had taken her place, "I put *so* many spells on Campbell. Be honest: did you ever hear my demon speak a word of *Deutsch*?"

He thought about it and had to shake his head.

"So It went out of Its way to accommodate a Yankee know-nothing," said she, "Which is probably the most Germanic thing It's done in years."

Brian sat with that. *DAS NEST* swayed side to side. For long moments, he thought they might be buried together.

"We have to go," he said, "Or call someone."

*"Not yet,"* Mal rasped and cattish eyes teared over, now wide and frantic, "Find checkybooky, I write you numbers. I don't care how big—*bigger, better.* Just sniff me out a cake."

"The cake is *gone,* Mallory," he said, definitively, "Your guests ate it up. They're flying."

Wracks of pain rumbled over her features, twined her cervine neck. She took several gulping breaths.

"I need it, Bri," she said, gripping to reality, *"We* need cake, or the spell won't...won't work."

"Tell me," he said, and he took her limp hand in his, "I-I don't understand."

"Yes, you do," she said, eyes fluttering, "The absinthe...they're already in us. But we need cake to...*to...*" Her eyes glazed over, so Bri shook her by the cheeks, none too gently. Meanwhile, more stuff rained down from the second floor, disturbing the piles all around, jarring the dog crate horizontal. The wide corner post of a heavy, raised bed fell through and lodged in one of the breaches, preventing further spills from above. Brian realized he'd never actually braved the master bedroom before, and now he never would.

"Mallory," he said, leaning closer, willing her his lucidity, *"Lady.* Stay with me."

"Take my knee-length lynx," she heaved, seeing him again, *"Become me.* I know you want to."

"I'm—*never* – thanks but no." B tried to pull his hand from hers and found he could not, her talons had sunk so into his palm, "I don't need anything else from you."

Mal moaned. Convulsions took her. For the first and last time, terror reigned behind her eyes.

"Then it was all for shit," she croaked, choking on her own blood, for it rose, filling her mouth, lapping inside with every futile jerk of her tongue.

"Absolutely not," said Brian, and he wiped tears and dust on his inner arm, "You made all this happen. You grabbed light in your fist and squeezed it *to—to* organic honey. You swallow dead air and poop Fabergé eggs. You're living magic. Whatever you want you get because I say so. You say so. *We say so, together.* That's the spell. No cake. If you want to change, *you fucking change."* For a time, nothing but dying happened. They never broke eye contact, did mistress and man, even as the shell emptied out and her consciousness receded past his waking perception. Still, he sat with her. One by one, pups braved their way from their crate, jumping down from the open door that had fallen to an easier angle. Either Erde or Luft or Feuer had sustained an injury to a hind leg, and it was this last ginger that took the longest to limp over and surround Mallory where she lay, to encircle her in death.

A near imperceptible shift marked the moment she was really gone; then, just as sneakily, that same stir came to reverse, radiating in again. Bri had let his eyelids drift, but somehow he knew to look at her body.

Up through a mouthful of still blood worked tenfold squirming worms, digits which stretched her jaw, her cheeks to the point of rending, then well beyond. Pink flesh split to reveal gossamer inside, that pure realization of spirit B had somehow always known was there. Mal's late doof had become an ink blot manifest, in putrid symmetry, but she was, naturally, an off-beat; syncopation of magic and anima. As the old form ruptured from throat to groin, the wraith reborn rolled inward and outward, neither side ever matching, but bursting in inspiration from what was, so It graced this third dimension as naked causality. An everpresent aura of white gold suffused out from within; in from without. Brian and the dogs followed her ascension...tailfeather come stamen come sphincter come tentacle come tusk come teat, ad infinitum. Swirling eddies of cinders and grime moved through her, joined to expand her essence. Mismatched peepers regarded the blown-out house, then settled upon canine and human.

*"B, B, B,"*         *"Oh, Bri,"*

said the divergent halves,
one right after the other,

*"You've unleashed me."*     *"Don't you want to come fly?"*

Wasser's chocolate snoot twitched and sneezed. The Mallory brew aimed Its blissed-out malevolence pupward.

"I might hold onto mine a while," said Brian, diverting Its attention, "But yeah, I'm glad I could help."

The shade of his lady drew Itself wide. Something like a mane shook out.

*"I'm letting you go,"*        *"Gosh, you love to tempt fate,"*

she bade sweet farewell,
forever soused in that warm rancor,

*"Kissy, xo, xo."*        *"Maybe your imp'll be straight."*

No horsepower, no visible thrust sent her off to the sky, but rather the effortless glide of a follow spot over painted backdrop or sunbeam shifting from hardwood to carpet. Out from the hollow of *DAS NEST* It rose, to the horde cutting mercurial capers against the witching hour, a diva moon at full height above the fray. As Mallory joined her mates, the bacchanal gave over to feral whoops, to loop-the-loops and shrieking double helices. The implings cleared a path victorious for their aviatrix to sail amidst their ranks and take her rightful position at the head of the hunt. Huntress passed from sight first, then the others followed in haphazard diffusion, taking off both port and starboard, shooting low over the Wynnewood treeline or arcing high so they turned to black dots against the night sky.

Regrets most foul bubbled down Bri's spine, and he stood to shake them down his legs, then away, away. Whichever pood had the bum leg limped close to lean hard against his shin, her brown eyes heavy; he bent to scoop the gingette up in his arms. The others followed as he wended his way out from the husk of the house, collecting along the way his jorts which had snagged on a big splinter of the oak-and-iron frame, now broken beyond repair. B tried to step into them on the veranda, but found he could not hold the pup and bend over with the ache in his ribs. Upon flinging the shorts for safekeeping over his shoulder, another brick-roll sounded from the house. Looking back, Brian and the dogs marked well the bulging distention of flotsam blocking the blue basement door as the last being inside worked to bust from Its cocoon.

Housesitter and pups made it halfway down the walk before drawing to a halt, arrested by the demon at their backs. Brian lowered the hurt pup to the grass with a grimace.

"Hi," he said, pivoting round to take in the whole, cursed picture of demolition and fiend. Even having seen Its armor in the Dahlhaus family photo, even having clocked the plates and great-helm lurking in the basement alcove (though he hadn't, of course, made the connection at the time), nothing could truly prepare him for the splendour, the dread of Its twisting horns nor Its spiked gauntlets, greaves like logs, the double-wide visor which shielded the form within so It could look like anyone, anything under there, or, B supposed, nothing at all.

*Das Gegenteil* lumbered down the walk.

"They just left," said Bri, and he fought the urge to run, knowing whatever spell had kept them safe in orbit had long since worn off, "I'm really glad you're just a demon and not a Nazi, *um*...demon. Not that I assumed—and you look fab, by the way. This gig really suits you."

It stopped a pace away. In the moonlight, the rose pink of Its plate mail took on heliotropic hues.

"I saw your...star. So that's probably your best look. Yeah, no, just stunning."

The armor moved not an inch. It made no concession to a state of mind, if It had one at all.

"I guess you're a force of — or really two places at once. Is it better down here or out there?"

The dogs' teeth chattered. They skulked behind Brian, wet noses upon the backs of his knees.

"I hope you got enough to eat. The, *um*...those other ones. Dr. Fleming—I think they all steeped their demons especially for you. Not on purpose, of course, but Mallory made sure it went your way. She really cares about you."

The demon lowered Itself to the poleyn over Its knee. Right gauntlet lifted, extending to the poodles, palm up.

"We can't go with you."

The hand did not descend.

"It's enough already."

Its hand would not descend. The damascened codpiece at Its groin throbbed like a heartbeat.

"*Fucking greedy*," Brian snapped, and the attack was two-pronged, in and out, "You don't know your limits. I'm saying no. I'm saying *leave*."

*Das Gegenteil's* other gauntlet rose, vambraces wide and waiting. The dogs barked alarm.

"Here," said Bri, and he ripped his jorts off his shoulder to dig around in the pockets, "She wrote me another check." And producing the slip with its embossed gold borders, he ripped it in two, then again and again so he could rain the five–thou down like petals upon the walk.

The armor watched the fall, great-helm following the drift.

"I spent the rest. That bong broke when I got evicted. Fucking dropped it down the—*doesn't matter.* I drank a few hundred, ate a couple grand. I can't give you the piss, the shit. I don't know where my phone – *you want my shorts?* Take them, they're all I have. And they actually used to be jeans, I didn't buy them like this."

He spiked the jorts with all his might, though his ribs lit up in pain.

"I get it," he panted, including the moon, the dogs, "You can only hurt a friend so much. The scary part of 'come watch this German demon' is demon. Someone offers you 10 times more than you're worth, *run.*"

*Das Gegenteil* did not take up the jorts, nor did It scoop the scraps of check. The poodles cried.

"Let them live," said Brian, "That's all. Please, dude." He licked ash from his lips, then swiped over the mismatched teeth down front, the ones he'd been molding for months. Where once he could trip his tongue over a jagged corner came the smoothed-out nub of orthodontic progress.

The full moon held her breath, giddy with delight.

"Or *here,* have my teeth," said B, pulling his lip to his chin, "These four. Mallory paid for them. They're yours. If you let us leave."

The great-helm tilted back an inch so Its visor gazed up at the offer. Could It consider such a trade? Left gauntlet lowered so the right could raise, fingers fanned to shake. Wasser whined, and B nudged him to shush.

"Yeah? *Deal,*" said Brian, hesitating not a half-breath before taking It by the hand, fingies barely cresting three of Its fat knuckles. *Lovers' first touch.* Prickling heat or stinging cold veined up B's arm: he could not tell the difference past the pins and needles. *And the strength of It!* He expected his hand to come away crushed, but it was just numb. Even shaking it out did no good.

*Das Gegenteil* arose from bended knee, joints creaking.

Again Bri drew forth his lower lip. Bracing himself, he wondered if he should have specified the cat's welfare as well, but a quick scan betrayed no Max to be seen in the yard. Before he could voice this last reservation, the demon moved forward, clearing the distance between them to cradle the back of Brian's head, reclining him as dance partner, as wife, then It reached in his mouth and wrenched in one swoop the whole crooked row of lower incisors. The pain nearly blinded. Were it not for the support at his neck, B'd have collapsed for sure.

*Das Gegenteil* stood him erect. In Its steel palm lay the four bloody prizes, longer than one would have guessed, and finally free of their crowding. Demon curled a fist to crush Its claim in articulated fingers so a white sprinkling fell upon the grass. Bri sucked for air over gaping sockets, the oxygen alone sheer agony. He tipped forward to let loose an ooze of spit-mash blood.

"*Square*," B sputtered, gesturing between himself and the demon, and he squatted to reach past Its considerable boot for his jorts, then to step into them at last. The sweetlings panted, their panic breaking. Brian buttoned his fly. Nothing left to say, he shot the armor a limpish salute.

Was the debt paid? He willed it so. Maybe he believed.

But even as they broke for the Circle and cleared the stonework at the end of the drive, he could sense the change in the puppies. They each fell from heel so he found himself advancing alone to the asphalt.

He didn't want to turn back, and almost kept on, but the whimpers. The screams.

The drips from his mouth drew a red arc in the cul-de-sac as he looked back.

Where the humans had burst forth in ephemera, free-floating and fine, the dogs remained of matter. The gore was minimal compared to the others, for their smaller bodies held so much less of the stuff to go around, and the lamb curls soaked up so much of the wet. The biggest shock was that what was born from within, what clawed from ginger belly and shook free from skull was not bio but metal; plating which shone with moonbeams as the blood rolled free, repelled by a ghastly sheen. Cruel barbs lined their collars. Pronged tails arced like scorpions. The Hound that had been Wasser had one of his hazel eyeballs hanging from the steel fang...no, the tusk astride its jaw. *Das Gegenteil* moved through their mess, collecting them at Its side.

Brian kept tracing that red line in the pavement until he'd turned right around again. Still he pinched his bottom lip to its lower extremity, his hand soaked to the wrist. A streamlet coursed to his elbow and he could feel the drop hanging there. He pressed on.

The rear of the new hunt passed directly overhead so Bri felt the whiff of breeze before they moved into eyesight, taking their time, the demon

Itself bounding in slow-motion strides that cleared half the Circle a go, the Dreadhounds at the same creeping airborne gallop, as alive as they'd ever be, as fate would ever allow. *Das Gegenteil* dipped between two oak trees and disappeared in the shadows there. Bri couldn't bear to watch the puppies go, too, and it was a good thing he didn't, because he chanced to see, by one of the rain gutters, a phone of his own make and model. He shifted course to swing by and pick it up.

"*Lucky me*," he burbled, for the familiar background wasn't too badly cracked. It didn't recognize button inputs so well, but he tried the front camera for the face lock, and it admitted him at once, missing teeth and all. He had no missed calls. No texts. He clicked over to his favorited numbers with a shaking thumb and clicked *Mom,* despite the late hour.

It rang twice before she picked up.

"Hey," he grunted, no longer terrified, "Sorry, did I wake you?"

Brian adjusted his lip to speak more clearly. The streetlamp out by the main road made a handy beacon, and he struck out for its light, eyes closing now and again, not with sleep but relief, for he'd done his awful part and could begin at last to make sense of it. No cars passed by, no late-nite pedestrians braved the twisting hills. He looked only ahead as he turned onto Hemlock Way, leaning back somewhat to counter the downgrade.

"No, I'm fine," his gurgle faded into the night, "That's just my voice. Hey, could I swing by and grab some old clothes?" Moonlight lit the broken Circle, moved especially bright over the empty spaces: blacktop and driveway, mailbox and yard. Brick and broken door. Carcass and big house. Only a blue cat with yellow eyes darted finally through that place of death, slinking out from behind an elderberry tree to run along the inside of the cul-de-sac, then out toward the man on the main road, for nothing's better than a little company on a long, lonely night.

ENDE

# ACKNOWLEDGEMENTS

T HIS BOOK WOULD not have been possible without the help of the folks who lent me their time, opinions, voices, houses, humor, and friendship. *HAUSSITTER's* cover and internal art were illustrated by the incredibly talented, attentive Adrian DKC, with expert typesetting by the scrupulous Phillip Gessert—many thanks to them for their brilliant work. *Danke shoen an* Günther Grosser of the English Theatre Berlin, who generously gave his time to correct and elevate my many fumbles in German translation.

Many dogs and cats have touched my life, and all of them are in this book. My late poodle sister, Buffy. My late poodle niece, Hermione. My late labradoodle niece, Winnie; her doodle brothers, Seamus and Tony; and their cat-bro, Hagrid. Jake and Sophie. Dusty, Spenser, Theo, Hannah, Bonnie Rose, and Willow. Mackie, Piggy, Hobbes, and Calvin. Puttochino. Slater. Honorable mentions to my childhood bunny, Harrison Ford, and my childhood goldfish, Michelle Pfeiffer. And of course, big love to my son and heir, my beautiful void cat, Oberon Orpheus Norton.

Thanks to friends who alpha & beta-read and raised funds, like Angela, Rob, Johanna, Jeremy, Matty, Joy, & Han. Thanks always to my family: my late father, Fergus; my mother, Pat; my sisters, Emily and Megan; my brother-in-law, Mark; my nephew, Teddy; and my nieces, Lucy, Patty, Mary, and Maggie.

Thanks to me.
And thanks to you.

BRENDAN NORTON IS an actor, writer, and editor. He has written several plays, as well as years of solo performances and stand-up comedy. *HAUSSITTER* is his first novel. Born and raised on the Main Line, outside Philadelphia, to a family of New Yorkers. Fordham College at Lincoln Center alum and proud member of Actors' Equity Association.

www.ingramcontent.com/pod-product-compliance
Lightning Source LLC
Chambersburg PA
CBHW050447110726
47899CB00003B/839